LIFE AND LOVE ON MOUSE ISLAND

1 WOMAN, 1 DOG, 1 HOUSE: FINDING HOME

a novel by

ANDRÉE JANNETTE

This is a work of fiction. Names, characters, and incidents are the product of the author's imagination or are used fictitiously. Any resemblance to actual persons living or dead, events, or incidents is purely coincidental.

All rights reserved. No part of this publication may be reproduced or transmitted in any form or by any means, electronic or mechanical, including photocopy, recording, or any information storage and retrieval system, without permission in writing from the publisher.

Printed in the United States.

Copyright © 2025 by Andrée Jannette

ISBN 979-8-9863742-2-2 (paperback)
ISBN 979-8-9863742-3-9 (Ebook)

*To Jeanne, my partner in everything.
To my extended family: Cathy, Mike, Mary, Sharon
and all my nieces and nephews, thank you for
welcoming me so warmly into your lives.*

*Many thanks to the stalwart individuals who agreed
to read this book in its various iterations, especially
Jeanne Cook, Catherine Roseman Smith, Dana
Ewing and Sue Swords.*

*Thanks to my editors Anna Bierhaus and Lisa Seed
for their valuable suggestions and my designer Asya
Blue for her wonderful cover and interior designs.*

*Thanks also to my 3-legged rescue dog Frankie
who served as a role model for the dog Sadie who is
featured in this story.*

CHAPTER 1

"AUGH!" A blast of frigid air hit Isabel square in the face as the charter boat rounded the peninsula and headed into the wintry waters of the Atlantic Ocean. Gasping for breath, she staggered backwards and pulled her scarf up over her nose and mouth. Tears streamed down her cheeks.

The boat's pilot, Captain Charlotte, looked back at her, "Are you all right, Ms. Flynn? We have a way to go."

"How far do you think?" Isabel shivered.

"About an hour."

"Damn," Isabel thought. At sixty-one years old she was about to embark on a new adventure and here she was freezing to death because she hadn't checked the weather report and didn't have the proper clothes. She was wearing a lightweight leather jacket, jeans, sweater, and Ugg boots. What she needed was an igloo.

"Unfortunately, there is no real place for you to get out of the elements," the Captain said. "The main cabin downstairs is filled with fumes from a leaky gas engine which I guarantee will make you nauseous and give you a mind-blowing headache at the same time. Though you are certainly welcome to go down there if you want…" she cursed as a larger wave than the rest came crashing down on the foredeck. Her long blonde braid flying in the wind, her brilliant green eyes squinted against the wind, Charlotte spun the wheel and kicked up the power to head more directly into the waves.

Isabel grabbed hold of the gunwale railing as the boat dropped into a trough and heeled over sharply. She was frightened by the rolling of the boat and worried that the forty-five foot boat wasn't big enough to handle the rough waters ahead.

"Have you made this trip before," she asked nervously.

"Many times. I grew up on Mouse Island." Captain Charlotte glanced at Isabel. "Is this your first time on the island?"

"Yes."

"It's a beautiful place. Of course, I'm biased. I've lived here all my life. But this is kind of an unusual time for a visit. Have you ever been to Maine in March?"

"No."

"Well, this is mud season in Maine and it can be difficult to get around." Charlotte looked at her curiously. "You know there aren't many places to stay on the island right now. The tourist season hasn't officially started and a lot of places aren't open yet."

"Yes, I know."

"Not much for sharing are you?"

"No," Isabel said. She had moved to New York City in her twenties after growing up in West Chester, a vibrant college town outside Philadelphia. Living in New York she had learned to be cautious with what personal information she shared. Especially with strangers.

She was curious about one thing though, "Why is it called Mouse Island?"

"One of the founders, many generations ago, had a daughter who had a pet mouse she adored. That's how the island got its name. Those of us who make a living through tourism would prefer a sexier name like Moose Island or Bear Island. But it is what it is."

Charlotte turned her attention back to guiding the boat through the demanding ocean waters. Isabel watched her handle the vessel with complete confidence. The Captain came across as adventurous and ready to take on whatever life threw at her. She was someone you would definitely want in your corner when the going got tough.

Isabel sighed and wished she had that bold quality. She was 5'2" (and shrinking), 150 lbs. (and gaining), with brown curly hair flecked with gray that on humid days resembled an out of control chia pet. She was perpetually out of shape due to her passion for Häagen-Dazs's vanilla ice cream. She figured Charlotte was probably in her fifties, about 5'7" and looked like she ran a marathon every weekend. Her skin was lightly tanned and glowed with health.

Isabel hesitated and then asked, "Do you know the Evers House?"

"Yes, of course. It's a local landmark," Startled, she turned toward Isabel, "Is that where you're staying? That house is a wreck. The old lady didn't keep it up, not even the most basic of repairs."

Isabel was taken aback at this news. "Her lawyer told me it was in decent shape. He's the one who arranged this whole trip for me."

Three months previously, a lawyer representing the Evers estate had contacted her unexpectedly to say that she had inherited a house from a recently deceased relative, Catherine Evers. Both her parents had passed away years earlier so she couldn't ask them about this unknown connection. Tired of city living, especially during the pandemic and subsequent lockdown, she decided to take an uncharacteristic leap of faith and retired from her position as a grant writer at a non-profit. She sold everything she owned and headed north to her newly acquired property on an island fifteen miles off the coast of Maine.

"Have you ever been to the house?"

"No."

"Did you know Ms. Evers?"

"No, I never met her."

Suddenly a monstrous wave slammed into the boat pushing the bow skyward at a sharp angle.

"Hold on," Charlotte wrestled the boat back under control as water sluiced down the deck. Isabel grabbed onto the railing again and held on for dear life, the rushing water nearly knocking her off her feet. The cold had her shivering.

"I'm heading to the leeward side of the island. The water will be calmer there." Charlotte added, "There is a blanket in the life jacket bin there."

Isabel found the wool blanket and gratefully wrapped it around her, relishing its warmth. "Is it always this rough?"

Charlotte shrugged. "Navigating the Atlantic Ocean in winter has never been easy. It's definitely tougher now with climate change."

"Wonderful," muttered Isabel, thinking, "What have I got myself into?"

"You know, you can see the house from the water. Would you like me to take the boat by there?"

"That would be great," Isabel brightened up at the thought. "Thank you."

Charlotte turned the boat into a protected inlet and motored closer to the land. The waves dramatically lessened in size. Isabel was able to let go of her white-knuckled grip on the gunwale and stand comfortably. She peered at the shoreline trying to catch that first glimpse of her new home.

Charlotte slowed the boat down, moved in closer to the shore and nodded at a clump of downed trees half in, half out of the water. "You'll see it in about a minute. Those trees are kind of blocking it but I think we should still be able to catch a glimpse."

Isabel could feel how excited she was getting her own home, a real house, after a lifetime of renting shoebox-sized apartments. She had assumed she would never have enough money to buy a home of her own but now this remarkable gift, had fallen into her lap. She could feel her anticipation growing. Clasping her hands tightly together, Isabel tried to remember to breathe.

"There it is!" Charlotte pointed.

At first Isabel couldn't see anything but downed trees and overgrown shrubbery. Then as the boat shifted slightly, the house came into view.

It was a classic two story New England style house: steeply pitched roof, wide wrap-around porch, and a multitude of tall windows. There was a stone pathway that led from the front door of the house all the way down to the water where a half-submerged dock bobbed up and down.

Isabel felt her stomach clench a bit as she looked at the house again. At this second glance, she could see the paved walkway had gaps in the flagstones. There were a number of large decorative pots scattered around the yard, many of them empty and broken.

The house itself was a lifeless grey with black shutters. It definitely needed refreshing. As Isabel stared at it all she could think about was how little she knew about owning and taking care of a house. Especially an older house of this size. She thought back to the movie "The Money Pit" and wondered if this house was going to be her own personal "Money Pit." She tried to shake off her worries.

"How far is the house from the town proper?" she asked.

"A couple of miles."

"Do you have Ubers or taxis here?"

Charlotte chuckled, "No, nothing like that. Most people either use a golf cart, an ATV, or a bicycle to get around the island. But no worries. We'll find you a ride with somebody."

"Okay," Isabel felt a wave of anxiety pulse through her as she thought about the realities of life on an island.

They motored into a small marina where Charlotte maneuvered close to the dock. A man, long and lean in blue jeans and a well-worn flannel shirt, caught Charlotte's rope toss and tied the boat off. His salt and pepper hair curled out from under a Mouse Island Marina baseball cap that was pulled down low over his blue eyes.

"This is Sam, the marina manager," Charlotte said.

He smiled at Isabel and two dimples winked into view. He leaned over the boat railing and reached out an oil-grimed, calloused hand to help her onto the dock. "Welcome to Mouse Island."

She looked at his hand and hesitated. She saw something in his face change. The warmth drained out of his eyes, his smile dimmed and a cold formality set in. He carefully wiped his hands on a work rag and reached out again. Isabel grabbed his hand this time and muttered an embarrassed apology as she stepped off the boat and onto the dock. Charlotte handed Isabel's things to Sam. He piled her luggage around a nearby bench, then disappeared into the marina office before she could thank him.

Charlotte turned to Isabel, "Look this is a small community. It can be difficult if people get the wrong impression about you."

Isabel stammered, "I-I didn't mean to offend him. It's just in New York…"

"Yeah, a word of advice, I wouldn't go around comparing Mouse Island to Manhattan if I were you. At least not out loud."

Isabel nodded.

"Wait here," Charlotte told her. "I'll find you a ride."

CHAPTER 2

Isabel looked around at her at the people in the town square. How did they make a living on the island… if they made a living at all? Was there even a doctor here… what if she got sick? She started to panic. Feeling light-headed she tried to calm herself by taking deep breaths, in and out slowly to a count of four. She sat down on the bench and cradled her head in her hands. She continued to breathe slowly and deeply, eventually beginning to feel a little less anxious.

"Hello there." A male voice behind her startled her. Isabel twisted around. The voice belonged to a slender young man in his twenties dressed in overalls with an eye-catching graphic, Island Solutions, embroidered on his jacket. He had thick curly black hair which swept down over his deep brown eyes. His eyes sparkled as he watched her give him the once over.

She stammered, "Did Captain Charlotte send you?"

"Yep, she told me you need a ride to the Evers House. I'm Jason Smith by the way."

"Hi, I'm Isabel Flynn and yes, I'd appreciate a ride."

"Sure, no problem. Let me get my truck. I'll be right back."

He quickly returned in a brand new, bright red Ford pickup. Isabel noticed the truck was decorated with the same graphic, Island Solutions, along with Jason's name and contact info.

He grabbed her suitcases, "Is this all your stuff?"

"Yes, it's all mine." Isabel winced as Jason casually tossed her luggage in the back of his truck. He helped Isabel climb up into the passenger seat, then slid into the driver's side as Isabel strapped on her seat belt. He started the truck and headed out of the town down a scenic, tree lined street.

"Are you familiar with the Evers house?" Isabel asked.

"Yes, I used to deliver groceries to the woman who lived there. I also did some minor repairs on the house."

"How bad a shape is the house in? I wasn't aware that there were any problems but it sounds like from Captain Charlotte there are some issues with the upkeep."

"Well unfortunately the woman who lived there didn't spend money on much of anything other than groceries and her cats. She had a lot of cats."

Isabel sighed, "Of course she did." Seeing that the street now ran parallel to the beach she turned and gazed out the window. She caught her breath...

The ocean shimmered in the bright sunshine as waves crested and broke on the sand. Sea foam surged up a gentle slope towards a tidal line of seashells and driftwood. Sea gulls darted here and there looking for food. Piping plovers raced across the sand, moving so fast their delicate legs accelerated into a blur.

"Wow," Isabel breathed, truly taking in, for the first time, the spectacular beauty of her surroundings. She leaned her head against the window, gazing at the view and felt the sun warming her face. The chill she had experienced on the boat faded away as she let go and relaxed.

CHAPTER 3

"Here we are." Jason turned onto a long, tree-shaded driveway.

Isabel saw a mailbox tilted way over, the numbers indecipherable. That was a priority, getting a new mailbox with visible numbers so that emergency vehicles could find her house. She took out a pad and pen and started writing.

Jason looked over and caught her eye. "Making a to do list?"

She nodded and said somewhat primly, "There are two types of people in the world. Those who make lists and those who don't."

He tapped his chest pocket and pulled out a small notebook. He grinned at her.

She couldn't help laughing.

Jason drove around a small grove of trees and there was the house.

Isabel saw the house definitely needed a paint job, the porch was missing a number of planks and some of the shutters were seriously askew. In spite of that, she could feel her excitement building.

She dug in her purse for the house key and said excitedly "Let's go!"

"Wait a minute," Jason called out as he started to get the luggage from the back of the pickup truck. "I don't know what kind of condition those steps are in. Let me just check them..."

"I'll be careful" said Isabel as she scrambled out of the truck. She was anxious to see the house... her house.

"Wait!"

Isabel put her foot on the first step. It was fine. The second and third steps were also in decent shape. She stepped onto the fourth and it disintegrated under her feet. She let out a squeak as she fell through the steps and hit the ground underneath.

At first, she thought something might be broken. Both her ankles hurt like hell and she couldn't climb out of the broken step. Jason came over on the run and carefully reached in and pulled her out. She looked down and saw her lower legs were badly scraped and bloody.

Jason said, "I'm going to take you to the clinic to get checked out, some of those cuts may need stitches." He helped her limp back to the pickup truck, lifting her into the seat and securing her seat belt.

Isabel could really feel the pain now. This was not how she had envisioned her grand arrival at her new home. She felt like crying.

Jason drove as quickly as possible to the clinic, eventually pulling into a pleasant shopping mall that bordered the ocean. The mall included a veterinary office, outdoor café, beauty salon, and medical office building.

"Here we are," Jason slid out of the truck. "Just wait here for a moment, I'll go get him." Isabel sat back in the seat and closed her eyes. She felt drained and downhearted as she considered the realities of her new home.

She heard someone say "hello" and she looked into the warm brown eyes of a man in his sixties as he peered in the open window. He had somewhat of an aging hippie vibe, with a kind face, shoulder-length grey hair tied back in a ponytail and tie-dyed scrubs.

He smiled at her, "Hi, I'm Dr. Mike Wagner. I hear you've had a traumatic introduction to our island. Let me take a look at your legs." She opened the door and carefully eased her legs out of the truck. "Well, it's not great, but it's not terrible either. I don't see any lacerations that need stitches. Jason will take you inside. One of the nurses will get you cleaned up. Unless you've had one in the last year, you'll need a tetanus shot. Nice meeting you." He shook her hand and started to walk back inside. He turned back and said, "Oh, by the way, welcome to Mouse Island."

She murmured, "Thank you."

Jason helped her climb down from the truck. Once she got inside she was surprised at how crowded it was. From the outside everything appeared quiet but inside there were all kinds of patients in different rooms waiting for tests, to see the doctor, to be discharged. The nurse took diligent care of Isabel, cleaned up her scrapes and cuts, gave her a tetanus shot and a lollipop and then sent her on her way.

Jason walked her out to the truck, and helped her into the passenger seat, "Here we go again."

She sighed, "Maybe we will actually make it inside this time."

He laughed, "Fingers crossed."

When they got to the house Isabel let Jason go in first, watching from the passenger seat as he tested the steps and porch. She had learned her lesson well. He gave her the all clear, helping her down from the truck and then escorted her carefully up the steps and into the house.

"Do you know if the electricity has been turned on? The house has stood empty for about a year now," he said.

"The executor of the will said that they would make sure the electricity was on."

"Hmmm, I can check that for you."

"Thanks, I would appreciate that since I have no idea how to deal with fuses or electrical systems or anything like that. I'll pay you of course for helping me."

"That would certainly be helpful. I am saving up for graduate school."

She looked at him surprised. She had assumed from his work track and work clothes that he was a local handyperson.

He said mildly, "Never judge a book by its cover."

Embarrassed, she realized that was exactly what she had done.

"I'm sorry," she murmured. "What about $20 an hour to go through the house and just make sure that all the utilities are on and working, the water, the electricity, and whatever else needs to be turned on. If you could just check out all that stuff."

"Sure thing," he said tilting his face towards the sun as a breeze ruffled his hair.

"God, he looks like a model," Isabel mused. Thinking back to Captain Charlotte and Sam the marina manager she wondered if maybe there was an attractiveness prerequisite to live on the island. Everyone she had met so far looked like they had stepped off the pages of an L.L. Bean catalog.

Well, she certainly wasn't going to meet that criterion if that was the case. She glanced down at her arms and legs now covered by pink antiseptic gel and Sesame Street bandages. Dr. Mike's nurse had quite a sense of humor. Isabel smiled ruefully to herself. She started to laugh. Jason glanced at her, looking a little concerned. He came up beside her offering his arm for stability.

She smiled at him, "Let's go inside."

CHAPTER 4

"All the utilities are in good shape," Jason confirmed an hour later. "There are definitely some minor repairs that need to be made, some windows replaced, screens repaired and it looks like all the rooms need painting. I don't know about the roof. I'd like to come back tomorrow and fix that front step. What I can do is see what needs to be repaired and give you an estimate."

She said, "That would be great. That way I can decide what I can afford to do and what I can put off."

"In terms of where you can sleep tonight, there is a primary bedroom. I don't know what condition the sheets are in or the mattress for that matter. I can flip it for you and make the bed so you can just relax. If you have any Advil, I'd take some and let it do its thing."

Isabel said, "Thanks. You have been tremendously helpful, Jason."

He headed upstairs while she sat on the couch and looked around the living room. There was dust everywhere. The room definitely needed a good cleaning. She also noted a couple of huge spider webs in the corners of the room. She shivered, wondering how big a spider would have to be to make a web that size. She remembered the line from the movie Annie Hall about spider the size of a Buick. The thought of that line made her laugh but at the same time she wondered if she should look for a broom in case she needed to defend herself.

Feeling a little shaky, Isabel realized she was exhausted. Using her coat as a pillow she lay down on the couch, closed her eyes and rested. The sounds from overhead – loud bumps, muted crashes, mild cursing – were comforting. She smiled listening to them and then drifted off.

"Isabel, Isabel!"

"What….what is it?" She asked groggily, not quite sure where she was or who the young man was peering intently a few inches from her face. "What time is it?"

"It's about 4 p.m. I finished checking everything out."

"Oh, thanks," she started to get up off the coach.

"You feel all right?"

"Fine, fine," she answered, somewhat embarrassed. She was stiff from lying down. As she struggled to get up, Jason helped her to her feet.

He gave her a quick tour of the house, none of which she absorbed as she limped slowly in his wake. Finally, he helped her upstairs to her bedroom. Here she stopped in shock at the doorway. Jason had found clean sheets and made the bed. He had even cracked the windows open slightly so a fresh breeze swept through the room. The house faced southwest and sat high enough on a hill that the windows offered a stunning view of the sun setting over the ocean.

"Oh, thank you." Isabel felt a little emotional as she gazed around the room.

"I'll lock up the house when I leave," he said. "I'll be back tomorrow to make some of the repairs I mentioned. Good night."

After he left, an exhausted and achy Isabel got into her pajamas and quickly fell asleep again. Around 3 a.m., she was suddenly wide awake. She sat bolt upright. "This is my house," she said to herself with a certain amount of disbelief. Then she said it again, out loud this time.

"This is my house!" Then she yelled it, "THIS IS MY HOUSE!" She laughed and got out of bed wincing at the painful cuts and bruises on her legs. "I am going to walk around MY HOUSE."

First she ventured into the primary bathroom which was dominated by a huge clawfoot tub. It faced a bank of windows but it was too dark to see the view. Isabel turned the faucets on and off and was pleasantly surprised to see clear water flowing from the taps. She would have to get the water checked but hoped that the bathroom had been modernized to a degree and wouldn't require immediate upgrades. She grabbed her bathrobe and headed out into the rest of the house.

The second floor consisted of two unused bedrooms in addition to the primary suite. They were in desperate need of cleaning and updating. Then there was a room which at first Isabel couldn't get into. Finally, she body slammed the door and got it to creak open enough for her to see that the room was a hoarder's fantasy filled floor to ceiling with furniture and odds and ends.

"Yikes," she said out loud. "That's a job for a rainy day...or month."

She walked down the stairs to the first floor and peered into the kitchen. She switched on all the lights and groaned as she looked around. Clearly the toaster oven had been the primary cooking appliance as it held pride of place on the counter. It was covered in grease and crumbs and was totally disgusting. Isabel looked for a garbage bin and pitched the whole thing in without a moment's hesitation. She looked for cleaning supplies under the sink and came across the mummified remains of a mouse caught in a trap.

"Welcome to Mouse Island," said Isabel, "Sorry, mouse," as that too went in the garbage bin. As far as she could see there were no cleaning supplies.

She hesitated, finally screwing up her courage to open the fridge. She was pleasantly surprised to see that it was empty. She was also happy to see an electric stove since gas stoves scared her. She had no idea what a pilot light was or where it could be found. There were piles of decrepit plates and glassware, many of them promotional items, emblazoned with company logos. All of those went in the trash too. She had a momentary thought of "what if one of these is a relic of some sort and worth money," but as she looked over the items she thought, "there is no way." So, into the bin it all went. Isabel was exhausted thinking about all she needed to buy just to set up the house in the most basic way. So, she did what she always did, started a list. Food, water, soda, cleaning supplies, household items, and of course, Häagen-Dazs vanilla ice cream.

"Money, money, money," Isabel muttered. Clearly that was going to be her mantra from now on. She walked through the dining room which had been cleared out so that nothing remained. She wondered where all the furniture that had been there had gone. She asked the empty room, "Did someone sell it? And where did that money go?"

She noticed almost all the windows were covered with heavy drapes which looked like they weighed a ton. She carefully tried to tug them open. Decades of dust rained down on her, causing her to sneeze violently.

"Priority on my shopping list is a hazmat suit," she muttered. Shaking the dust from her clothes, Isabel walked into the living room which contained two elderly couches, some easy chairs and end tables, a rolltop desk, a scratched up coffee table and some lamps with dented shades. Remembering what Jason said about cats she looked at the couches, gingerly took a sniff and immediately recoiled. They had to go. The executors of the Evers had described the house as furnished. Technically that was true. But as to whether you would want to sit or actually touch any of the furniture was another thing entirely. She couldn't believe she had actually laid down on one of the couches.

Isabel had basically sold everything she owned when she left New York. She had wanted a nest egg to help fund her fresh start on the island. Now she was afraid it wouldn't be enough. Especially if she had to replace all the furniture. A wave of exhaustion swept over her and she decided to go back to bed.

CHAPTER 5

Isabel woke up to birdsong and the distant sound of ocean waves breaking on the shore. She had a moment of confusion – unsure of where she was, what she was doing here. Then she remembered all of it.

The quiet would take some getting used to. She was accustomed to sirens, trash trucks, ambulances, and all kinds of strident noises that come with city living. She walked downstairs in her bare feet into the kitchen and realized she didn't have anything to eat or drink other than a bottle of water she had brought with her. She opened it and thirsty drank half of it right down.

She stood and looked out the window and was delighted that she could see the ocean in the distance. She decided to take a morning walk around her property. The thought that she was now a land owner sent a thrill through her. Shrugging on her leather coat against the chill in the air, and wrapping a bulky scarf around her throat, Isabel walked carefully down the path to the water. There were a number of flagstones missing and others were tipsy. Isabel took out her pad and added to her repair/replace list.

She walked down to the water and started looking around for the floating dock. She couldn't see it anywhere and wondered whether it had simply floated away. She decided to go back to the house and wait for Jason. She started up the steps when she heard a dog bark.

Anxiously she looked around. She was nervous around dogs that were off leash after being attacked by a large dog years ago. The owner had apologized and pulled the dog off her but still had not put the dog on leash. Later she had seen the same dog go after and seriously injure a much smaller dog that was on leash. It had been an upsetting experience.

Again, came a loud bark. She looked but couldn't spot a dog anywhere. She shivered and decided to head back to the house.

"Morning, Isabel!" called Jason as he started down the path toward her.

She let out a shaky breath and waved to him. With Jason on hand, she felt safer and her anxiety began to slowly lessen.

"Hi Jason." She took a few steps and then froze at another bark. This time it was followed by a desperate sounding howl. Jason hurried down the last few steps and arrived by Isabel's side.

"What the hell is that?" Jason spun in a circle looking for the source of the noise.

"I think it came from over there," Isabel pointed at some downed trees drifting in the water.

Jason joined her and they began looking through the branches. "Shit," he swore. A yellow Labrador puppy was lying half in, half out of the water. It was covered by mud and one paw was crushed by a foothold steel trap.

"Oh no," said Isabel, horrified at the sight, "I thought those damn things were outlawed."

"There are loopholes, always loopholes," murmured Jason as he waded into the water and cautiously approached the dog.

"What can I do to help?" Even though she was scared of the dog, she was so upset at its plight she was literally wringing her hands.

"I'm going to open the trap," he said, "it's the only way to get the dog out of the water. It will die otherwise."

He gingerly reached out to the dog. The exhausted animal was in so much pain it growled at him. Isabel, who had been cautiously entering the water after Jason, leaped back in fright. She clumsily splashed about trying to regain her balance. Jason reached out to steady her and calm her down. Her out of control movements were upsetting the dog, causing it to struggle and sink deeper into the water.

He took off his jacket, shivering in the morning chill, and gently wrapped it around the dog's muzzle to prevent a bite. The dog made an odd moaning sound, then fell silent.

"If you could hold the injured leg steady," said Jason. Isabel was scared but she supported the leg as Jason struggled to find the release lever. Suddenly the trap snapped open. The dog squealed in pain as its shattered leg was released. Jason quickly picked the dog up and cradled it so it wouldn't try to run away and do more damage to its leg. Shivering, he pulled the makeshift muzzle off the dog and put his jacket back on. "Let's get this dog to the vet."

"Is there one nearby?" asked Isabel.

"Dr. Debbie is our vet. Her office is right by Dr. Mike's clinic." He trotted up the hill. Isabel followed behind him. He fumbled for the keys to his truck. He pulled them out of his pocket and tossed them to Isabel. "You'll have to drive."

She hesitated.

"You do have a driver's license?"

"Yes, but I haven't driven in a long time."

"Well, no time for a refresher course. I've got to hold the dog."

Isabel reluctantly nodded and helped Jason climb into the truck and get settled with the dog on his lap. Isabel hoisted herself into the driver's seat and cranked the key. The engine started with a powerful roar making her jump at the sound. Taking a deep breath, she released the hand brake and put the truck in drive. She cautiously pushed down on the gas and said a little prayer under her breath. The truck lurched forward and she slammed her foot down on the brake.

She turned to Jason, "I can't do this…"

He looked at her with exasperation, "You have to. Just suck it up."

Irritated, she started to respond and he cut her off. "I know you are capable of doing this. We have got to get this poor thing to the vet. It's in a lot of pain."

Isabel glanced at the dog. It looked up at her and whimpered.

"I'll tell you what," she said, "I'll hold the dog and you drive. As long as you can assure me it won't bite."

"I don't know this dog. I can't guarantee it won't bite you. But I have a blanket in the back seat that we can wrap around it and that will make it feel more secure and less likely to act out. Plus, it's a Labrador, one of the easiest going dog breeds there is."

"OK, let's do it."

Jason got out of the truck, waited till Isabel settled herself in the passenger seat, and put the dog in her lap. She awkwardly clutched the dog to her. She could feel its rapid heartbeat and body warmth pressing against her chest. She murmured into its ear trying to calm it.

Jason started the truck and headed back into town.

"All right," she said. "No guts, no glory."

Under his breath Jason muttered, "That should be your motto from now on."

When they got to the vet office, Jason carried the dog inside while Isabel trailed behind.

A woman in medical scrubs was at the front desk talking with a client when they entered. She took one look and immediately told Jason to take the dog to the ICU. She followed them into the room and after introducing herself as Dr. Debbie, quickly checked for a chip.

"Nope, no chip, and no collar." The vet said as she gently examined the dog's paw and leg. Jason held the dog steady during the checkup. The animal was panting with pain and stress. Isabel tentatively touched its head, surprised at how silky the fur felt. The dog turned and looked at her with soft brown eyes. She was struck by the directness of its gaze. She continued to gently stroke its head as the dog closed its eyes.

"Good," reinforced Dr. Debbie, "you are calming her down."

"It's a female?" asked Isabel.

"Yes. It's a female Lab, probably about 6 months old." Dr Debbie explained, "I'm giving her a pain killer and an antibiotic to make her more comfortable." She shaved one of the dog's legs, carefully irrigated the wound and swiftly inserted an IV. She set the dog up to get an X ray. "She is probably going to lose that leg. I will know better once I see the X ray but it looks crushed to me. I think we would have a lot of difficulties trying to rebuild it. I don't know how she got into that trap but she certainly tried her damnedest to get out of it."

Isabel was shocked at the prospect of the dog ending up with only three legs. She asked Dr. Debbie, "But will she be able to run and play and be like a regular dog?"

"Google dogs with three legs on the Internet. You'll see that they get along just fine. They run, they play, they swim. In a case like this when the paw and leg have been severely crushed there are much less issues with taking the leg off rather than trying to rebuild the leg over several operations. Let's see what the X ray says."

A short while later, Doctor Debbie held up the X rays and rendered her verdict. "As I thought, her leg is so shattered it's essentially gone. We just have to remove it." She stroked the dog's head.

"She's malnourished and weak. We'll get her stronger and then remove the leg. Then she can go home. Wherever that is. We need to do a search and see if we can find the owner. In the meantime, we need a foster home for her."

"Well, I hope you find her owner," Isabel said.

The vet looked at Isabel for a long moment, "Would you consider fostering her?"

"Oh no," said Isabel. She took an involuntary step towards the door. "The thing is I've never had a dog before. In fact, I'm afraid of dogs."

Dr. Debbie patted her shoulder, "I have to say that if you have never had a dog before a Lab is an excellent choice. Loving, friendly, easy going, and very trainable."

"I'm sorry. I can't do it. I only just moved here." Isabel felt a little irritated that the vet was pushing this dog on her. After all, having a dog was a huge responsibility. "There must be someone else..."

Debbie sighed, stroked the dog's head, and said "She can always stay in one of our kennels. At least for a while."

There was a long moment of silence. Isabel was quietly watching the dog.

"Thank you, Dr. Debbie for helping us, helping her," said Jason.

"Yes, thank you," echoed Isabel. As she turned to leave she took one last look at the dog, now woozy from pain meds. The young Lab lifted her head, looked directly at Isabel, and softly wagged her tail. Then she let out a heavy sigh and closed her eyes and drifted into a peaceful sleep.

Isabel took a step towards her, then changed her mind and walked out the door.

CHAPTER 6

Jason trotted out to his truck and found Isabel leaning against it. She pulled out her pad and asked, "Can we do some food shopping? I have absolutely nothing in the house. I'll pay you for taking me."

"Of course. I'm sorry I didn't think of that sooner."

They stopped by the main supermarket in town. In addition to carrying name-brand basics, the market also had plenty of handcrafted items from local artists. Isabel filled her shopping cart with necessities then picked up handmade mugs and plates. She added some candles that had a soft natural scent that reminded her of the cleansing freshness of an ocean breeze. She rationalized the expense that if the lights ever went out at the house she would need a light source.

After loading up the truck, Isabel told Jason she wanted to stop at a nearby hardware store. As she entered, a man behind the counter, in his seventies with a bright shock of white hair, broke off a discussion he was having with a uniformed police officer and greeted her. The police officer tipped his hat to her and left.

She said to the shopkeeper, "I want to buy some tools."

"What type of tools?"

"That's the problem. I don't really know what I need. I was hoping you might be able to point me in the direction of a starter tool kit."

He smiled at that, picked up a hammer and put it on the counter. "Start with this. It will take care of 97% of your needs. Something doesn't work, whack it with this hammer and it will most likely go back into place."

Laughing, she said, "I'll keep that in mind. Do you happen to have a book on basic home repair?"

He turned around behind him, "I have just the thing for you." He handed her a paperback book which was well used with a lot of dog-eared corners. Isabel looked at the title, it was called "Tom's Home Repair Guide."

She turned it over and saw a picture on the back that bore a vague resemblance to the man in front of her. "Is this you?"

He nodded. "Yep, many moons ago. I'm Tom, the owner of this store for 40 years now. All the basics of home repair are in there plus how to use a hammer properly."

"This is perfect," she said, "how much do I owe you?"

"Nothing. Consider it a house-warming gift. "

"But you don't know who I am."

"Absolutely I know who you are. You just moved into the Evers house."

She looked at him in astonishment. "How did you know that?"

He smiled, "Word gets around fast on an island. I even know about the dog you saved this morning."

"My God," she said, "That just happened."

"My next door neighbor's daughter works at the vet clinic." He carefully placed Isabel's purchases in a brown paper bag. "By the way, a Lab is the best dog there is. Harry come out here and say hello." An ancient yellow lab walked stiffly from behind the counter where he had been sleeping on a dog bed. Isabel stepped back a few paces as the big dog walked up to her. He sat and politely offered his paw to her. She wasn't sure what to do.

Seeing her reaction, Tom said, "I guess you're not all that comfortable around dogs. He just wants to say "hi." Tom reached down and gently shook the dog's paw. At that the elderly Lab turned around and went back to bed.

"He's getting pretty old so he just sleeps a lot nowadays but he's great company still."

Feeling embarrassed, Isabel cleared her throat. "Well thank you for your help." She turned to leave.

"Wait," said Tom. "Do you have boots for mud season?"

"Mud season?"

He came around from behind the counter and walked over to a display of boots. "March is mud season in Maine and believe me it is mud like you have never seen before. Everywhere you go there's gonna be mud and it's usually terrifically gooey and sticky and hard to walk through. You definitely need a good pair of wellies to get you through it." He sorted through the boots, "I think you're probably size 7 or 8?"

"7 ½"

"Well, these don't come in between sizes but I think you'll do in an eight. You can always wear an extra pair of socks if they are a little too loose."

He handed her a pair of tall green rubber boots.

"Really?" She looked at him askance for a moment and wondered if he was pulling her leg.

He gave her friendly smile, "Ask anyone." He indicated a couple of customers who were browsing through the store while actually covertly watching the whole interaction.

Isabel looked around and asked the store at large, "Do I really need these?"

An elderly woman in her eighties modestly pulled up her mid-length patchwork skirt displaying her well-worn Wellies. "Yes, absolutely. Plus, Tom here would never steer you wrong."

"Okay, Tom. How much do I owe you for the boots," asked Isabel.

"$50."

As she handed her credit card to Tom she heard a snort from behind the counter. Tom laughed. "Harry thinks I should just give you the boots."

"That's all right, Harry," said Isabel.

Tom smiled at her, "With the hammer and the wellies you're all set for a Maine spring."

She thanked him, picked up her bag and left the store.

She spotted Jason peering at the car engine of a woman who was leaning under the hood with him. Isabel walked over. He introduced her to Mrs. Canty, a retired grade schoolteacher, whose car was in desperate need of his ministrations.

"Mrs. Canty was my favorite teacher," said Jason. "Actually, I think she was everyone's favorite teacher."

The woman laughed and said, "Hi, Isabel, welcome to the island."

"You might be just the person to talk to about the history of this place."

"I'd be glad to. Anytime."

Isabel started to turn away then had a thought and turned back. "Did you know Catherine Evers by any chance?"

"I didn't know her well but I did run into her occasionally walking on the beach. She pretty much kept to herself."

"I'm trying to find out more information about her."

"I can't really help you with that. You might try the historical society."

"That's a good idea, thank you."

As they headed back to the house, Isabel turned to Jason. "Is there anything you can tell me about Catherine Evers? I am trying to figure out why she left me the house."

"It's an awesome gift, that is for sure."

"You are not kidding. I just wish I knew why."

"We didn't have much really in-depth interaction. She would give me a list of things she needed at the store, I would get them and drop them off and that was pretty much it."

"OK, thanks."

Isabel looked out the truck window, "I really need to find a way to get around the island on my own."

"There is a public transit bus that runs every half-hour, from 6am to 6pm."

'That sounds a little limited. I'd like to be able to run into town whenever I need to."

"I have a neighbor with a small SUV in fairly decent shape that he's wanting to sell. It might be a perfect fit for you."

"Do you think we could take a look at it?"

"Let me call him and see if that's okay with him."

"Excellent," Isabel eased back against the seat and closed her eyes. It had been an exhausting day so far.

"I have a job scheduled for tomorrow, but why don't I see if we can meet with him later this week," Jason said.

"That sounds good."

Jason dropped Isabel and her purchases off at the house. She stood on the porch, surrounded by a multitude of shopping bags of varied sizes and shapes, and waved goodbye to him.

Feeling a huge sense of relief, she unlocked the front door. As helpful as Jason was, she felt that she needed some alone time to settle into the house properly.

She put away her groceries and decided to have a nice cup of tea before starting cleaning. She sat on the porch steps sipping it and taking in the sights and sounds of the island as a brilliant sunset painted the sky a glittering rosy hue streaked with gold.

Isabel thought back over the remarkable changes that had happened in her life in such a brief period of time. She raised her mug in a toast to Catherine Evers, "I don't know who you are or why you left me this incredible gift. But this is the beginning of a brand new chapter in my life. I only hope that I prove myself to be worthy of it." She took a last sip of her tea and headed inside. On her to do list she had taped to the kitchen wall she added, "Find out who Catherine Evers is."

She realized she was too tired to do any housework. She decided to take a shower and then head to bed. The shower was a revelation: there was fantastic water pressure and the hot water was really hot. She stood for a long time under the stream of water, until she realized she was actually dozing off. Wrapping herself in an oversized terry cloth towel she dried off and got into bed, falling fast asleep seconds after she hit the sheets.

CHAPTER 7

The next morning Isabel decided to start with the kitchen after a quick breakfast of tea and toast. She was thrilled with the size of the room, to actually have enough space rather than cramming everything into one tiny cabinet. In her old apartment every time she wanted to get the mixer out she had to move about half a dozen other appliances to get to it. She sighed when she thought about that mixer. She'd gotten rid of all that stuff to make the move. But now she was going to have to replace much of it anyway.

She stood in the center of the kitchen and slowly turned in a circle, taking in the entire look of the room. The bigger appliances looked like they were left over from the seventies. Isabel wondered if she could paint over their avocado color scheme. She would have to ask the hardware store owner. "What was his name again... Tom, that was it." The linoleum floor was peeling up at the edges. She was curious about what was underneath it. She tugged on it and nearly fell backwards as it came up easily in her hands. Underneath seemed to be some sort of wood. She pushed the linoleum down flush against the floor so she wouldn't trip over it. Then, she got to work, scrubbing the countertops and the drawers, making sure everything was sanitized, spraying every surface with Lysol over and over again. It took most of the day but eventually the kitchen was sparkling clean. She felt a real sense of accomplishment.

There was a big window right over the sink which would give her a marvelous view down to the water once the bushes in front of it were cleared out. She added that to Jason's to-do list. Thinking about it she realized that list was getting pretty long and costly. She was going to have to cut back on some of the tasks or learn how to do them herself.

After getting the kitchen in decent shape, Isabel put a mask on and went around the first floor pulling down the ancient drapes. She dragged them outside and made a big pile in the middle of the yard. For one brief moment she was tempted to just light a match. Instead, she got a few big garbage bags and stuffed everything inside them. She dragged the bags to the driveway and left them there for Jason to get rid of them. She glanced down at her hands and was horrified at how filthy they were from handling the drapes. She went inside and scrubbed her hands till they were bright pink.

The next few days were devoted to cleaning. She had Jason haul away bags of trash, broken furniture and malodorous couches and chairs. After everything was carted away there was little left and Isabel found herself rattling around empty rooms. She decided to see if there was anything she could use in what she thought of as the hoarder's closet, the room upstairs that was jammed full of stuff.

Using the body slam technique that she had used previously, she managed to get the door open enough so she could squeeze inside the room. At first glance it didn't seem very hopeful. There were a few dining room chairs that were mismatched, scratched up and missing a leg or two or three.

A couple of paintings of stern looking New England types glared down at her from the walls. They freaked her out until she took them down and put them in a pile for Jason to take to the landfill. She hoped they were not distant relatives because they looked like the sort who would hang around and haunt a place.

Disheartened she almost gave up. Then she decided to start pulling furniture into the hallway so she could get further into the room. She discovered a few pieces that were actually quite promising. There was a rocking chair that needed cleaning, that she felt would look nice in the living room. A wooden bench would go well in the front hallway along with a matching coatrack. She came across two end tables, plus a couple of dining room table chairs that had all their legs. She found a small table that she could use for dining. She thought she probably didn't really need a larger table because most likely it would just be her dining solo.

She found a couple of dressers with drawers stuffed full of papers. She hoped they might lead her to more information about Catherine Evers. She started to glance through them but then realized how tired she was and decided to wait until another day to take that job on.

In the meantime, she had a lot more cleaning to do. The primary bedroom and the two additional bedrooms all need to be cleaned. She also had to make some decisions about what pieces of furniture to keep and what to toss. For example, the furniture in the primary bedroom was elderly and uncomfortable with sharp edges and zero cushioning. Of all the rooms this is the one she wanted to be the coziest. She was definitely going to start looking into yard sales. But first she was going to do some painting. Though she had no idea how to begin or what colors to choose.

Together she and Jason went to the hardware store to pick out paint. With Tom's help, she chose a translucent blue for the bedrooms, a soft watercolor green for the bathrooms, a warm sand color for the living room and dining room and all the ceilings. The kitchen was destined to be a dazzling white. This time Isabel said hello to Harry properly, patting his head and shaking his paw when he offered it to her. "He's a sweet boy," she said to Tom. He nodded, "I love him very much. He's been my best buddy for a long time."

As they drove back from town with their paint purchases, Jason nudged Isabel and pointed out a yard sale sign.

"Let's check it out," he said, "there's still some things you need to make that house more of a home."

"Good idea," said Isabel. "Do you know this family?"

"Not very well," he said. "They are a well off couple from Boston who decided to start a B&B. I think they saw too many episodes of Newhart." Isabel laughed.

"Anyway, they weren't able to make a go of it so they're selling everything off at fire sale prices."

Isabel commented, "I guess shipping stuff like this back across to the mainland would be pretty prohibitive."

"Yes." He said, "Yes, it is."

They wandered around the yard looking for economical pieces that would add to Isabel's new home. They picked up a couch, some comfy easy chairs, a couple of end tables, and some lamps. To Isabel's delight there was a queen size bed for sale at an extremely low price. It was a beautiful piece, hand carved with woodland creatures climbing all over it. In the kitchen, Isabel excitedly picked up a mixer and food processor and other kitchen staples to replace the ones she had sold before leaving New York City. She was delighted with her purchases and couldn't wait to see her new furniture in place.

Jason called Isabel a couple of days later, "I talked to my neighbor with the SUV this morning and he said come on over. He's always home."

"Oh," Isabel said, "a real social butterfly just like me."

"I think you have been getting around pretty well since you've been here. You've gotten to know quite a few people already."

Isabel said, "Yeah I guess that's true, although an inordinate amount of them seem to be in the medical field." Jason snorted with laughter.

Jason arrived and helped Isabel into the truck, "Let's go see a man about a SUV."

Turning onto a tree-shaded driveway about a mile from Isabel's house, Jason carefully maneuvered through a set of large half open iron gates. It was a tight squeeze. Once through, they followed a long curved driveway to the house proper.

"Prepare for an extraordinary treat," Jason helped Isabel climb down from the truck.

"Wow!" Awestruck, Isabel admired a bronze sculpture of a little girl kneeling in the grass playing with a puppy. "Are these his?"

"Everything you see here he created."

"This is magical. That is the only word that fits," exclaimed Isabel. "I love how he combines nature and art."

"Daniel uses his property as an immersive art gallery, placing sculptures in totally unexpected places. Look around and see what you can spot. Like the squirrel family up in that oak tree. Or the duck mom with babies peering out from under that bush."

Isabel said, "How about that beautiful fox pausing at the water's edge?"

"Actually, that is a real fox."

Isabel spun around and saw that the fox had vanished.

"He's known for feeding the fox in the area. They trust him and whenever they have a new litter they bring them to meet him."

"He's brilliant," murmured Isabel as she placed her hand on the statue of a sleeping child in its mother's lap. "Has he always lived here?"

"No. He was very well-known on the mainland. Then he lost his wife to cancer and he just kind of retreated to the island and pulled up the drawbridge so to speak. When he needs money he sells one of these pieces. "

Isabel winced, "That must be like selling one of your children."

"Not quite," said a deep male voice behind them. Isabel turned around and was transfixed by the emerald green eyes of the artist. He was dressed casually in jeans and sweatshirt, with a Mouse Island Marina cap pushed back on his head. There was something about him, a kind of casual masculinity that was very attractive. Isabel found herself at a loss for words.

"Hi, I'm Daniel Forsythe."

"Isabel Flynn. I have to say I'm awestruck by your sculptures."

"Thank you. If you'd ever want a tour I'd be glad to show you my work."

"I'd like that," said Isabel, conscious that her cheeks were turning red.

Jason cleared his throat.

Daniel said, "I understand you're interested in purchasing my SUV."

Isabel nodded.

"Well, it's definitely a multi-season vehicle. Ideal for island living."

"That sounds exactly what I need" she said.

"Good let's go take a look at it. Jason can show you how to run it and I'm sure he'll take care of it for you."

Isabel immediately fell in love with the vehicle. She especially loved the fact that it was a cheery lipstick red.

Jason turned to Isabel, "And there's plenty of room for the dog if you want to foster her."

Isabel looked at him exasperated. "You know I'm not ready for that at this point."

Daniel asked, "What dog? What are you talking about?"

Jason explained, "Isabel found a Labrador puppy in the water a few days ago, half-drowned, with a foothold trap crushing its paw."

Daniel's face looked like a thunder cloud. "God damn those things. I lost one of the foxes to a trap like that about a month ago."

He angrily thrust his right hand through his thick white hair. "How is the dog doing?"

"She's at Dr. Debbie's," answered Jason. "She will probably lose that leg but I think she's OK other than that. We'll have to wait and see but they don't know who she belongs to or where she came from so they're talking about trying to find a foster for her."

Daniel looked at Isabel, "Are you considering fostering her?"

"No. I don't know anything about dogs and I'm actually afraid of them. Plus, I just moved here, I'm not comfortable taking that on right now."

"I can understand that," said Daniel. "A dog is a big commitment. I'll tell you what, don't worry about the money right now. Just take the SUV, go home with it, try it out for a couple of days. If you like it we can figure out a reasonable price."

"Seriously?" she asked.

Daniel held out his hand, "Jason vouches for you and that is enough for me."

Isabel shook it. She felt the rough calluses on his hand and realized it must be from creating his artwork.

"Okay," said Jason, "Let's head for home." He got in his truck.

"Thanks again," Isabel said to Daniel. She hesitated. "I'd like to talk to you about your artwork sometime. If you would ever be up for that."

"Yes," said Daniel, "that would be fine. Just text me when you would like a tour."

"Great. I'll do that."

Isabel settled herself in the SUV. After familiarizing herself with the instrument panel, she slowly followed Jason down the road to her driveway.

A few days later, Jason arrived early at the house and immediately went to work fixing window frames and replacing broken window glass.

Dozing comfortably, Isabel heard him hammering away at something. She stretched lazily feeling a comfortable heaviness in her arms and legs having spent the past couple of days working on repairs around the house. She found that she really enjoyed the sense of accomplishment that came from doing physical labor and actually fixing something. It was different than she was used to, and it gave her a feeling of being able to take care of herself that she found both reassuring and satisfying.

The next few hours found both Isabel and Jason working hard pulling up the smelly carpet in the living room and celebrating when they found solid wood floors underneath.

"Why would anyone cover this up?" Isabel sat back on her heels and took a long drink of water.

Jason shrugged and asked if she was hungry.

"Starved," she said.

"Ever had a lobster roll?" asked Jason.

"No, I'm not even sure what that is."

"Well, there are two versions — the Maine and the Connecticut. The Maine, which of course is what we make here, has chunks of lobster served cold on a toasted bun with a dab of mayo. The best lobster rolls on the island are down at the fishing pier. But just so you know, it's pretty casual."

Isabel laughed, "As long as they don't lob it at me like some fish markets."

Jason grinned, "They only do that for off-islanders."

They bought a couple of sandwiches and homemade iced tea and settled on a picnic bench overlooking the water. It was peaceful and they ate in companiable silence. After a while Isabel became aware of a continuous sound in the background. She listened for a while but couldn't quite place it.

She turned to Jason, "What is that sound?"

Jason pointed to a nearby sandbar just offshore. "See the seals on the sandbar there? They are singing. Least I call it singing."

Isabel asked, "Singing?"

Jason looked a little embarrassed. "My mom told me they were singing to entice fishermen to come join them in the water."

"Oh, I get it, like sirens."

"When I was really young it didn't mean much to me. But then when I was a little bit older my father went out one day and never came back . He was on a fishing boat that ran into a bad storm and went down with everybody on it."

Isabel felt sick to her stomach, "I'm so sorry Jason."

"That's the downside of living on an island where so many people fish for a living. Sometimes people don't come back."

He began gathering up all the debris from their impromptu picnic.

"Let's go," his voice a little gruff.

"Homeward bound," said Isabel. She stopped, surprised that she had used that expression. She had never felt at home anywhere, moving from apartment to apartment, not really feeling connected to a place or a group of people.

"Jason?"

"Hmmm?"

"Can we stop by Dr. Debbie's and see how the dog is doing?"

He glanced over at her, "Sure."

They rode in silence for a while.

"Aren't you going to make a comment?" asked Isabel.

"Nope."

He pulled up in front of the vet's office.

Jason said "Why don't you go in and I'll pick you up in half an hour or so. I have to run a couple of errands."

Isabel looked at him searchingly "You really have to run a couple of errands?"

He smiled, "Yep."

"Okay."

She got out of the truck. Jason waved to her and then drove off.

She opened the door to the office and was startled as someone yelled, "Stop that pig!"

She looked down and saw a tiny piglet streaking towards her squealing loudly as it ran.

She crouched down and grabbed the tiny creature as it tried to scoot by her. It was squirming so much; she was barely able to hang on to it. Doctor Debbie appeared in the doorway with a red face and looking frustrated.

"Thank you so much," she said, "that would have been a disaster if he'd gotten out to the parking lot." She took the piglet from Isabel.

"I didn't know you took care of farm animals," said Isabel.

Dr. Debbie started laughing. "He's not a farm animal, he's a house pig. His name is Snowflake and he is an expert escape artist." She handed the piglet to one of her technicians. "What's up?"

"I wanted to find out how the Lab puppy is doing."

"Very well. Do you want to see her?"

Isabel hesitated and then said, "Yes."

"She's in the ICU room on your right. Just go in and say "hi."

Isabel felt embarrassed to ask but she needed reassurance, "Will she bite?"

"No," said the vet. "She's the sweetest dog. I'll go in with you if that will make you feel more comfortable."

"Thanks," said Isabel.

When the puppy saw Isabel she started whining and wagging her tail. Surprised by the dog's reaction, but also secretly pleased, Isabel asked the vet, "Does she do that for everyone?"

Dr Debbie smiled at her, "No, not for everyone, just for people she feels connected to."

"But…" Isabel turned to her and found Dr Debbie had quietly slipped out of the room. She turned back to the puppy and saw the one leg was heavily bandaged. "You poor thing," she reached into the crate and gently stroked the dog's head. The dog closed her eyes and made a soft rumbling sound. Isabel stopped petting her, not knowing if she was bothering the dog or not. But the Lab opened her eyes and looked at her and then nudged her hand. Isabel laughed. "Okay, I get the message." She started petting the dog again, scratching gently behind her ears. The dog leaned against her and gazed into her eyes. Isabel murmured "You are a sweet girl."

CHAPTER 8

A couple of days later, Isabel was painting her front door, sitting cross-legged on her porch. She tilted her head to better feel the warmth of the sun on her face. Following Jason's explicit instruction since she had never painted before, she dipped her brush into the paint, then squeezed out the excess paint and carefully applied steady strokes of paint one at a time. She hummed happily to herself.

For the door, she had picked a vibrant blue color that matched the sky. She had spent too much of her life surrounded by bland neutrals and now she wanted vibrant colors in her life. When spring came, she intended to plant sunflowers all around her property. It was her favorite flower and she'd never before had the space or sun to grow it. She thought they would be beautiful against the house. She was considering a New England barn red for the house –soft, warm, and welcoming.

Jason was inside painting the primary bedroom. She heard his phone go off and smiled. He had a new ringtone, a Taylor Swift song.

Suddenly, he strode out onto the porch startling Isabel into dropping her brush. "There is an emergency at the vet's office. Let's go." Isabel grabbed her bag, shutting and locking the door and raced to the truck. Jason already had it fired up and ready to go.

She climbed in and secured her seat belt. Jason floored it, the truck's wheels spraying dirt and gravel as the truck careened onto the main road Isabel braced her feet against the floorboards.

"What's going on, Jason?"

"There is this guy on the island, Pete, and he's a brute. He was abusive to his wife until she left him and he's known for being cruel to his animals. Anyway, he's at Dr. Debbie's right now claiming the Lab puppy is his dog and trying to take her. Dr. Debbie is on an emergency call out of the office and it is just two young vet techs there trying to hold down the fort."

"If she is his dog," asked Isabel. "I'm not sure we have any right to keep his dog from him."

"We'll see," muttered Jason his jaw tight with anger.

They roared into the parking lot and hurried into the vet's office. There was no-one at the front desk but there was a lot of shouting going on in the back where the ICU was located.

They rushed into the back and saw that Pete had grabbed the puppy out of her crate and was starting to drag her toward the door. She was squealing in terror, trying to squat as low to the floor as she could get. Her injured leg was bright red with blood oozing out from underneath the bandage. Her extreme fear had her peeing all over the floor. Pete raised his hand to hit her.

Isabel quickly stepped up and got right in front of his face. "You touch this dog and I swear to God I'll have you up on so many charges your head will spin."

"Who the fuck are you?" Pete snarled. He stepped towards her but Jason got there first scooping up the dog who was shaking like a leaf. He handed the puppy to a vet tech and then moved to get between Pete and Isabel.

"Give her to me." Pete pushed Jason aside and stepped menacingly towards Isabel.

Isabel said "No! We are all witnesses that you were about to hit this dog. You dragged her out of a recovery unit for God's sake. There are laws against animal abuse…" She was so angry her voice was shaking. She hated that the quiver in her voice made her sound weak.

"That's enough," a deep male voice boomed, startling them all.

A huge police officer stood in the doorway. Dr. Debbie was behind him trying to peer around his massive bulk. "Pete, you come with me. Dr. Debbie you take care of this poor dog." Dr. Debbie gently took the visibly shaking dog. She murmured softly, trying to calm the puppy.

The officer had a firm grip on Pete's arm and led him out of the room. They could hear him loudly protesting that the dog was his all the way down the hallway. The front door slammed shut and there was a deafening silence. The tension in the room dropped dramatically.

Isabel asked Dr. Debbie worriedly, "Will they give the dog to him?"

Dr. Debbie glanced at her as she rewrapped the puppy's blood soaked bandage. "I have evidence that this dog is seriously underweight and that she has been beaten. There are a number of old bruises and scars all over her body. We have an exceptionally good animal welfare officer on the island and Officer Burrows, who you just met loves animals of all kinds. He won't let anything happen to this puppy." She injected the dog with a painkiller. "You are quite the warrior, you know." She put the puppy in a recovery crate and laid a warming blanket over her to further calm her down. "The vet techs called to tell me what was going on. I called Jason and Officer Burrows and then tried to get here as fast as I could. But you looked like you had it pretty much under control."

"Well, I…"

Jason interrupted, "She was amazing."

Isabel realized this was a watershed moment for her. She had always been afraid of repercussions if she stood up for herself or for anybody else. From an early age, she'd tried to be invisible, never causing a fuss, just letting things go. But now something was changing inside her. She didn't know what or why but she wasn't going to question it. The only thing she knew for sure was she was going to fight for this dog.

Dr. Debbie nodded. "They are taking him to the police station so I'll call them and make sure they understand that this dog was abused." Dr. Debbie had her hand on the dog evaluating how stressed she was. "It would be helpful if you could keep her company for a while, help her calm down."

Jason said to Isabel, "If you want to stay here I'll come back and pick you up in about an hour."

"Thanks Jason, that sounds good. I'd like to spend some time with her."

She pulled a chair over next to the crate and sat gently stroking the dog. The dog whimpered once or twice.

"You are safe now, I promise," Isabel whispered. The dog twitched an ear. As she looked at the dog, she felt a growing sense of connection. "You're afraid too, aren't you girl. Well, I'm going to take care of you from now on. You are going to come and live with me. Though I have to tell you I don't really know much about dogs, so I might make some mistakes here and there. I hope that's OK with you." The dog gazed intently at Isabel, then closed its eyes, and exhausted, dozed off.

As Isabel sat quietly with her hand resting lightly on the puppy, Dr. Debbie came back into the room to check on the dog.

She smiled when she saw the dog sleeping peacefully.

"That's good," she said, "clearly she feels safe with you."

Isabel looked at the vet, "I want to adopt her. Not just foster her."

"Are you sure?"

"Yes."

"Well, unfortunately a number of her stitches have been ripped open. I'm going to have to do some repair work. But maybe in a couple of days you could take her home."

"That's good that'll give me time to prepare."

Isabel was out painting her front door again when she heard a vehicle pull into the driveway. She quickly stood up and walked to the steps to see who it was. Ever since her run in with Pete at the vet's office a week earlier she had been feeling skittish and on edge. Living alone with the nearest neighbor a mile away, she felt vulnerable. She had called Officer Burrows to see if he would assess the security of her home. Now she saw that he had pulled in at the same time as Jason.

"Hi, I had some free time so I thought I'd stop by and do that security check."

"That would be great!"

Officer Burrows walked up the steps. "I hear your dog is doing well. I talked with Dr. Debbie and sounds like she should be able to come home in the next day or so."

"I can't wait to have her here with me. I've never had a dog before."

Jason turned to the police officer,

"You should see the amount of stuff for the dog Isabel has already ordered from Amazon. This will definitely be one pampered pooch."

The officer said to Isabel, "Well, certainly having a dog will be very helpful to you in terms of keeping you aware of what's going on, if there are any strangers about."

Isabel felt anxious at the thought. "Do you think that is a concern, Officer Burrows? Is Pete a danger to me?"

He looked at her seriously, "No, I don't believe he is. I've known him since he was a kid, we went to school together and he's a bully for sure. But he is also a realist. The dog is no longer his, if it ever was, and he understands that. He has no bill of sale, the dog was never vaccinated for anything, it was never chipped, so he has no proof that he ever really owned the dog legally. He wanted it solely for breeding purposes to make money. To avoid jail time, he's given up all rights to the dog and we have his statement in writing and notarized. He won't risk going to jail."

"I hope not," said Isabel "Thank you for that reassurance. As a single woman living in New York City, I guess I've gotten a little paranoid over the years."

"A little paranoia is not necessary a bad thing, it can be a very effective survival technique as long as you don't get obsessive about it."

He smiled at her, "She is legally your dog now. Just get her chipped and get a license for her in your name." He added, "By the way, you can call me Dave."

"Thanks, Dave.

"Do you have a name for her yet?"

"Yes, I was thinking of names last night and I thought of the Beatles song, "Sexy Sadie. I like that name. Sadie."

"Nice name," agreed Jason.

The men walked up the steps and into the house. Burrows let out a long whistle. "Wow!" He turned in slow circles taking it all in.

Jason said, "Isabel has literally transformed this house. It used to be dark, dank, and dusty, now look at it." He and Isabel exchanged high fives.

The living room, dining room and kitchen had all been freshly painted a very soft pale sand color. The old drapes had all been taken down and new fabric shades of soft taupe put up. The ancient (and smelly carpet) had been pulled up revealing a solid wood floor that Isabel polished until it gleamed. The couch and easy chairs she had purchased at the B&B yard sale were situated in the living room. Jason had cut back the overgrown bushes in front of the windows so now there were sweeping views all the way down to the water.

Burrows exclaimed, "This is amazing!"

Unused to compliments, Isabel found herself blushing. "Jason did most of it." She decided to change the subject. "What do you think I can do to increase security?"

An hour later she waved goodbye to Burrows. She took a deep breath and looked at the comprehensive list of items she needed to get to secure her home. She sighed, thought about how much this was going to cost her and decided to go into town.

"Jason, can you help me find these things on the list?"

"Sure."

"This is beginning to feel like a scavenger hunt," she muttered as she climbed into his truck. After visiting the general store in town, Isabel stopped in a craft shop and picked up some watercolor paints and brushes and a how to watercolor book. It was geared toward 5-12 year olds which Isabel figured was about her speed. She made her way back to Jason's truck. He was sitting on the tailgate reading a book and eating an apple. He looked totally at ease.

She asked him "What are you reading?"

"Stephen Hawking."

"Wow, that's heavy reading."

"Yeah but it's fascinating."

"You know you are totally unexpected."

"I find expectations can be so limiting. Did you get everything you wanted?"

"Yes, thanks."

A few days later, Isabel walked outside with her morning cup of tea and took deep breath, savoring the clean ocean breeze. She glanced around and was startled to see a large package leaning against the wall next to the front door. Curious she walked closer and saw her name on it. She looked around and nobody was in sight. Feeling like Christmas had come early, she ripped open the brown paper wrapping.

"Oh my God," she said stunned. It was a portrait of her.

In the painting she had a cape swirling around her and had her hands on her hips in a powerful stance. There were dogs sitting by her feet and birds on her shoulders. She wore a helmet with gilded wings, curls peeping out from under it and a warm smile on her face. Inscribed on the cape were the words "Warrior Woman." It was signed by Daniel. She looked around to see if she could spot the artist. But there was no sign of him.

"Oh, I love this," she whispered. She felt a rush of warm feelings that someone would do this for her. She wondered if he was potentially interested in her. Even more thought provoking was the surprising feeling that she might be interested in him. It had been ages since she felt that way.

She carefully picked up the painting and carried it inside. She knew exactly where she wanted to place it. On the wall over the fireplace mantle. It would have a place of honor there.

CHAPTER 9

Jason was off island visiting friends and Isabel decided to drive into town and do some shopping. She had spotted a bookstore on a previous trip and had put it on her list to visit. Humming to herself she opened the door and walked into a child's fantasy land. The store was packed with small children and their parents. They were raptly listening to a storyteller dressed in a sparkly pink princess gown and elaborate headdress. Isabel stood quietly near the front door, caught up in the dynamic voice of the storyteller as she captured all the nuances of the different characters. She looked around and realized she wasn't the only adult who was totally into the fairy tale. She couldn't believe how quickly she became engrossed in the story. Within a few minutes the story came to a very satisfying conclusion. Evil was vanquished, good triumphed and everyone lived happily ever after.

Isabel wound her way through the happily talkative crowd to the storyteller.

"Excuse me," she said.

The storyteller turned around. She was in her sixties, like Isabel, and had a warm welcoming smile.

"That was wonderful," said Isabel. "I came in here for travel books and instead got to feel like a kid again. You are terrific."

"Thank you," the storyteller took off her princess headdress and shook out a mass of curly red hair . "My name is Mary. Can I help you?"

"Hi, I'm Isabel. I'm looking for a book about the island…"

"Wait, are you the woman who just moved into Evers House?"

"Yes."

"I have the perfect book for you. A history of the island."

Isabel ended up buying that book along with a few others. As she was paying for the book she asked Mary if she had known Catherine Evers.

"Not really. She was a quiet, very private person. Occasionally I'd see her out for a walk but even then she'd just wave and keep on going."

Isabel was frustrated by the lack of information on Catherine Evers. Maybe that dresser that had all the papers stuffed into it would give her some clues as to why her benefactor left her the house.

As she was walking down the island's main street she spotted a small coffee shop and decided impulsively to go in and have lunch. She settled in sipping her English Breakfast tea, enjoying a turkey sandwich, and reading the New York Times, a lifelong habit that she hadn't indulged since she arrived on the island. As she read the articles, especially the lifestyle, entertainment, and real estate sections, she realized she felt totally removed from that life.

She put the paper aside and gazed out the window, half-listening to the ebb and flow of conversations around her. She smiled as a group of young girls danced by on the sidewalk, carrying baseball gloves, laughing, and chattering.

The small bell over the door tinkled and Captain Charlotte walked in. As she strode toward the counter, Isabel was impressed by how warmly she was greeted by people throughout the restaurant. She was clearly well thought of.

Charlotte picked up her takeout order and started to head back out when she spotted Isabel. She veered over toward her.

"Please join me," said Isabel.

"Just for a few minutes," replied Charlotte. She settled into a chair opposite Isabel. "How are you liking life on an island?"

"I think I'm settling in pretty nicely. I'm getting used to the isolation, the being cut off from the rest of the world."

Charlotte snorted with laughter. She pointed at the New York Times on the table. "I'd say you are still pretty connected."

Isabel smiled ruefully, "Yeah I guess that's true. It's hard to break old habits. By the way, I want to thank you so much for Jason - he's fantastic."

"I'm glad he's been helping. He's a great kid though I guess he is not really a kid anymore. I'm really hoping he goes through with medical school. I think he'd be a fantastic doctor. I know Dr. Mike wants him to join his practice."

"He wants to be a doctor?"

"Yes, hasn't he told you?"

"Only that he wanted to go to graduate school. Not what the graduate school was for."

"He has been fascinated by medicine since he was a small boy. He helped out at Dr. Mike's practice whenever he could. But when his mom got sick he made the choice to get a steady job here on the island." There was a pause as both women sipped their drinks. It was a comfortable silence.

Charlotte said, "I hear you are getting a dog. Congratulations."

"Yes, I'm really excited about that. She still has some medical issues…a leg that was damaged by a trap had to be amputated but the vet thinks she will adapt pretty easily.

"Well, if you have any questions about Labs, Tom is the one to talk to. He has had a number of them over the years, but Harry is definitely his soul mate."

Isabel laughed. "I have never heard a relationship between a man and a dog described like that."

Charlotte said, "Those two are as close as they can be."

"Does Tom have any family on the island?

Charlotte answered, "No. His wife died of cancer 10 years ago and his son died in a car accident about the same time."

"Oh, that is so sad," murmured Isabel.

"Since neither of us have any family left we've become each other's family. Every Sunday night we have dinner together no matter what else is going on. It's become an important ritual for both of us." She stopped talking abruptly and looked surprised. "I haven't really talked to anyone about that before." She stood up. "Anyway, I'm glad you are getting a dog."

Isabel leaned closer to Charlotte, "That whole thing with Pete...I was scared shitless." she admitted.

"Bravo for you standing up to a bully like Pete. You pushed through it, that takes real courage. Good seeing you, Isabel."

"It's good seeing you, Charlotte."

When she got home she found Dr. Debbie had left a message that Sadie would be well enough to go home in a few days. But before she picked her up, Isabel asked Jason to build an enclosure on one side of the house where Sadie could run and play while being off leash. Jason brought a couple of friends with him and they quickly put up a fenced enclosure.

When she and Jason went to pick up Sadie at the vet's they saw a sign on one of the parking spaces that read "Reserved for Sadie's Mom." Isabel laughed and at the same time was touched by the gesture.

They opened the door to the vet's office as Dr. Debbie came walking out from the back room with a broad smile on her face. "Ready for the big day?"

"Yes, I'm so excited to bring her home with me."

Dr. Debbie said, "That's great to hear. She's doing very well but she will need to take antibiotics for the next week or so. I have an aftercare sheet for you. Now, she may be a little bit off balance initially. She's learning how to walk with three legs and she may occasionally stumble and fall. Don't worry about that, it's par for the course. If she's doing it a lot let me know but judging from how she's been doing here, I don't think she'll have a problem. The important thing is to make sure she keeps her weight down. That's the one thing that would give her a problem having only three legs. If she is overweight it can put a strain on her back. You especially have to be careful with Labs. They have it down to a science as to how to beg for food and look pathetic, like they haven't been fed in months. Don't buy into it. I will tell you one thing. She's a sweet dog. I think you've got a real winner here."

A vet tech brought Sadie from the back. The moment she saw Isabel she started whining and wagging her tail. Isabel leaned down to hug her while Sadie happily covered Isabel's face with kisses.

Debbie added, "She has been chipped and licensed and vaccinated for rabies. In fact, she's up to date on all her vaccinations now. We put a new collar on her and here is a new leash for her too. After much discussion we went with a tie dye pattern."

Isabel laughed, "That's perfect."

"We have a gift for you too. It is a fanny pack filled with treats, a book on dog-training and also a clicker. Whenever she does what you want her to do, say "yes" immediately, click and give her a treat. Click and treat is the best way to train a dog. Always use positive reinforcement. By the way do you have a bed for her?"

"Does she have a bed for her?" echoed Jason in amusement, "She has a bed for every room in the house."

"Well, not every room...but quite a few," admitted Isabel somewhat embarrassed.

The staff crowded around to say goodbye to Sadie. Isabel thanked everyone, hugged Dr. Debbie, and headed out with Sadie to the truck. Isabel wasn't sure how Sadie would behave on leash but she was pleasantly surprised that Sadie was able to do a combination walk/hop step without pulling or balking.

"You know," she said to Jason, "she's walking much better than I expected."

"She's a survivor,"Jason arranged a blanket for Sadie on the truck's back seat and lifted her up onto it.

Isabel settled in the front passenger seat, twisting around so she could see Sadie. The dog looked a little anxious so Isabel stroked her head and murmured "Good dog, it's all right. We are going home now."

Jason got in, patted Sadie on the head, and started the truck, "OK, here we go."

Once they got to Isabel's house, they brought Sadie inside and gave her a tour. They noticed she was uncomfortable going up and down more than a few stairs at a time.

Isabel said, "It looks like she'll be relegated to the first floor for quite a while, maybe for good."

Jason said "I think she'll get used to the steps. It's just brand new for her right now. Let's take her outside to the enclosure and play ball for a little bit with her so she gets a sense of what it's like to have fun. She's had a rough go of it so far."

Isabel opened the new toy basket that had Sadie's name embroidered on the side in bright pink thread and got out a tennis ball and a frisbee. They took her into the enclosure and started playing catch with the ball. Sadie sat and watched for a bit, her head cocked as she tried to figure out what Isabel and Jason were doing.

Isabel rolled the ball directly to her. "Get it, Sadie!" Sadie hesitated and then gingerly picked up the ball. Jason and Isabel cheered her on and she started wagging her tail.

Isabel called "Bring it here, Sadie," and was thrilled when Sadie walked over to her and dropped the ball at her feet. "Oh, good dog, good dog," she exclaimed, ruffling her ears. Isabel threw the ball again, "Go get it, Sadie!" This time Sadie chased after it, grabbed it off the ground and brought it back to Jason.

He laughed. "She knows I'm the better thrower," he teased Isabel.

"Want to bet?"

Jason hurled the ball across the enclosure and Sadie raced after it, grabbing it and bringing it back to Isabel.

She asked Jason, "Do you see her limping at all?"

"No, not at all."

"Neither do I. She's doing really well. It is amazing that she is adjusting so quickly to having only three legs."

They watched her carefully and the moment she showed the slightest sign of fatigue they stopped playing and brought her inside.

Jason left for the night and it was just Isabel and Sadie, alone in the house together. Isabel fed Sadie, walked her around the enclosure before bedtime to do her business, then gave her a dog biscuit as a nighttime snack.

Isabel turned lights on in the kitchen and the living room and got Sadie settled in her living room bed. Then she said, "Goodnight, little one," and started to head upstairs. Halfway up she heard Sadie begin to whine. Isabel sighed, got a blanket and pillow, and headed back downstairs to settle in on the couch for the night.

"OK, just this once. I know it's a new place for you. We'll just have to get used to each other and hopefully you'll be able to make it up the steps at some point. But for now, I'll stay down here with you so I can keep you company."

Isabel lay down on the couch and immediately fell asleep exhausted from the long, emotionally charged day. Halfway through the night, she felt a warm body next to her. She woke up and found that Sadie had joined her on the couch. She laughed, petted her, and fell back asleep, finding her presence comforting.

Early morning and golden sunshine warmed the room. Isabel woke to find Sadie on the pillow next to her.

"Good morning, Sadie." She smiled at the dog who yawned, stretched, and slowly got down off the couch. Isabel followed suit, standing up and doing a few early morning stretches. She reached down and petted Sadie, grabbed a coat and took her out into the enclosure.

"Time to do your business," she told Sadie. She threw the ball for Sadie a number of times before finally heading back inside to make breakfast for both of them. There was a knock on the door and Sadie let out an impressive "woof." Startled Isabel said, "Oh good girl!" and gave her a dog biscuit.

Isabel looked out of the window and was pleasantly surprised to see Tom standing there with Harry at his side. "Come in, come in," Isabel opened the door wide.

Tom was holding a big shopping bag which he presented to Isabel with a flourish. At this point Sadie came trotting into the kitchen yawning. She immediately perked up when she saw Harry. The two dogs did the typical canine getting to know you circle and sniff. Then Sadie ran into the living room, reappearing with a tattered tennis ball which she dropped in front of Harry. The two dogs proceeded to chase each other through the living room, dining room and kitchen while Tom and Isabel watched in amusement. Finally, Harry's age caught up with him and he lay down for a rest in one of Sadie's favorite beds. She lay down next to him.

"Looks like Harry has made a new friend," Tom smiled down at his dog then turned to Isabel, "As a new dog owner I thought there might be some things you need, that you might not know you need. So, I brought you some goodies."

"Oh Tom, that is so thoughtful of you." Isabel was touched by his kindness. She opened the gift bag and began pulling out a variety of treats, toys, and grooming products. She was delighted at the dog brushes as she was newly discovering how much Labs shed. "Thank you so much."

Tom said, "I've got to get back to the store but I want you to know how much it means that you rescued that pup and are giving her a loving home."

"Frankly, I am getting so much more from having her in my life," said Isabel. "She's a treasure."

"It's hard to imagine life without a dog," agreed Tom. He stood up ready to leave and Isabel impulsively hugged him.

After he had gone, Isabel went through Sadie's doggy gift bag and tried out some of the items. "What a nice man," she said to Sadie who seemed more interested if there was any food in her gift bag.

"Breakfast time," Isabel made scrambled eggs for herself and kibble for Sadie.

Jason pulled up in his truck as they were finishing their meal. He knocked and Sadie let out another impressive "woof."

Jason commented to Isabel, "She is going to make a helluva watch dog."

Isabel looked thoughtful, "She definitely will make me feel more secure."

"Are you worried about Pete?"

"Yes, I admit I'm still upset by that whole incident at Dr. Debbie's."

"I don't blame you but the word on the island is he is moving to the mainland for a job."

Isabel felt a rush of relief and a lightness, like a huge weight had just dropped from her shoulders. Impulsively she gave Sadie a hug.

Jason grabbed some tools from the back of his truck. "I'm going to fix the rest of the windows and then the flagstones going down to the dock."

Isabel asked "I have been worried about that dock ever since Captain Charlote mentioned it to me. I'm not sure it's secure enough to withstand a bad storm. It might get pushed into the boat lane and cause an accident. There are also a number of downed trees in the water."

Jason said, "I'll take a look and see what I can do."

While Jason evaluated the dock, Isabel got out the dog training book Dr. Debbie had given her, strapped on her treat bag and called to Sadie. Sadie came trotting in carrying a soggy ball which she dropped at Isabel's feet.

Isabel clicked her clicker and then gave Sadie a treat.

"Sit," she commanded. Sadie sat right by Isabel's feet. Isabel clicked and treated. "Wow, you are good," murmured Isabel reaching down and hugging Sadie who happily wagged with her whole body.

Isabel worked with Sadie on sits, stays and leave-its. She was thrilled with how quickly she learned basic commands in addition to adapting to having three legs. She had tried to get Sadie used to going up and down stairs but anything more than a few steps clearly made Sadie uneasy so Isabel didn't push it. Of course, that also meant that

Isabel was still sleeping on the couch so Sadie wouldn't be by herself at night.

"Time for play," she said as Sadie leaped joyfully around her. "Let's go out to the pen and play ball."

Quite by chance, Isabel and Sadie had started the habit of walking out together to the mailbox each day to collect the mail of which there was little except for bills, and invitations to retirement home dinners. Isabel kept Sadie on a leash so she wouldn't chase after any wild animals they encountered. She was particularly worried about coyotes which she had heard were frequently seen in the area.

About a week after Isabel brought Sadie home, she found a handwritten note in the mailbox. As it was the first non-bill, personalized message she had gotten since moving in, she was excited to open the card.

On the cover was a delicately drawn sketch of the warrior woman. When she opened the card, there was an invitation to dinner from Daniel for the next night for both her and Sadie. She smiled at that and carefully showed Sadie the invite.

"I think we should go, don't you?" Sadie wagged her tail vigorously and gave a short happy bark. "What am I going to wear?" wondered Isabel and then laughed at her stereotypical response.

She wished she had someone, a woman near her own age, to ask for advice as to how people dressed for dinner on the island. She decided to see if Mary the bookstore owner could give her some insight into what to expect.

Isabel settled Sadie in the house and then started on the road to town. She was extra careful and drove well below the speed limit. She ended up pulling off to the side when she realized she was leading a parade of vehicles. She was impressed by the drivers' patience and good humor, many of them waving to her cheerily as they passed. In NYC, she knew they would most likely be waving with one finger.

She finally made it to town and parked near the bookstore. It was quiet when she entered, Mary was at the front desk hunched over a book. Today she was wearing a wizard's cape of deep velvety blue decorated with shimmering silver stars. A matching cap with tassel was perched on her curls. She looked up with a bright smile, "Hello. Isabel, isn't it?"

Isabel nodded, "What a fantastic cape!"

"Thanks, I made it myself.

"You are kidding. That is incredible needlework."

"Thanks. I like my storyteller outfits to look as authentic as possible."

"Well, that one is a real winner."

"Is there something I can help you with?"

Isabel blushed, "Well, this is really kind of off the beaten path but here goes. Daniel the artist has asked me to dinner at his house and I don't really know how to dress for it. I wanted to ask you if you knew him well enough to give me an idea of... do I need to dress casual or should I dress up a bit fancier? What would be your suggestion? If you're OK with me asking that?" Suddenly, it struck Isabel that Mary might be interested in Daniel herself. "Oh God I hope you're not...are you dating him or involved with him. I'm so sorry if I've put my foot in it."

Mary laughed and said "Nope, I"m not involved with him at all. But I can give you some ideas knowing him as I do." She walked over to the kitchenette and put a water kettle on to boil. "I think this conversation calls for a cup of tea and some cookies." She measured out a few teaspoons of loose tea into a well-used teapot and once the water was hot, poured boiling water over them. Isabel watched as Mary then carefully arranged a selection of homemade cookies on a delicate porcelain plate and brought the cookies, teapot, and matching teacups over to a nearby table.

"Oh, how lovely. Thank you," murmured Isabel.

"This all sounds very exciting," Mary sat down in a chair and indicated to Isabel to do the same. "Daniel doesn't invite people over for dinner as far as I know. The fact that he has invited you…"

"And my dog Sadie," interjected Isabel.

Mary looked startled. "Wow, that is even more unusual." She sat there for a moment quietly sipping her tea. "My suggestion for your mode of dress would be casual comfort - jeans and a sweater. Plus, a pair of nice hiking boots in case he wants to take you on a walking tour of the grounds. You don't want to look too much like you're on the prowl. I don't get that sense from you anyway but I think that being authentic and comfortable at the same time would be the best route to go."

"I think that sounds right to me too, thank you. I will be who I am, not trying to be something I'm not."

Mary smiled at her and they clicked their teacups together. "Here's to sisterhood."

Isabel grinned, "You think I could borrow that cape?"
Mary laughed.

CHAPTER 10

Isabel left the bookstore and wandered down the main street doing some light window shopping. She caught sight of a tired-looking woman with mousy brown hair in one of the windows and was shocked when she realized she was looking at her own reflection.

She had been so focused on getting the house in shape and moving Sadie in that she had let herself go a bit. She snorted, thinking, "A bit? I don't call what I'm seeing here a bit." Her naturally curly hair was a mess, shapeless and frizzy. She tried to pat it into some semblance of a shape and suddenly realized she'd been staring into the store's window for quite a while. People inside were starting to notice and stare back at her. She gave a slight smile and an embarrassed shrug and moved on.

As she passed the hardware store on her way back to her car she saw a small hair salon nestled next to it. She peered in, there were several customers inside. A good sign, she thought entering hesitantly, even though the music was new to her and the images on the walls were of celebrities and performers she wasn't familiar with. She paused, feeling out of place and, frankly, old. She turned to leave.

"Hello," a young woman with vibrant green and purple striped hair greeted her. "I'm the owner, Cara."

"Hi, I'm Isabel."

"Welcome, Isabel. What can we do for you today?"

"I'm not sure…"

Isabel looked around the salon and saw that the customers seemed content. Several of them smiled and nodded at her. She took a deep breath. "I'm ready for a change."

"Well, if you are up for it, I'd like to see you in a shorter cut, basically a Pixie cut, and then a different color like a soft blonde. I think what I have in mind would really freshen up your whole look. Are you game?"

Isabel smiled hesitantly, "Yes."

Cara clapped her hands excitedly. "Oh, this is gonna be fun."

Two hours later the women in the salon applauded as Isabel emerged from underneath a hair dryer. Grinning bashfully, she did an awkward pirouette. Her hair was now super short and a beautiful soft blonde. She had never been a blonde before and to her eyes the change was remarkable. Her whole face seemed brighter, more open. In years past she had rarely colored her hair and when she did she used an at home dye kit just to cover the gray. Now she ran her fingers through her hair and loved how silky it felt.

"This is amazing," she exclaimed. "Thank you so much."

"It is a great look for you," said Cara.

Feeling energized and lighter than air, Isabel walked out the door into the sunshine.

Isabel did some training with Sadie and was pleased with how fast Sadie picked up basic commands and responded. She wondered if she should get her certified as a therapy dog. Her personality seemed ideal for that.

When she heard a vehicle pull up she walked outside to see who it was. Jason got out of his truck. "Wow," he exclaimed, "look at your hair! It's fantastic."

Isabel was embarrassed but pleased at the same time.

"I was going to take a look at the dock," he said. "But how about lunch first, I brought some sandwiches."

"Oh, great idea, thanks."

They had an enjoyable lunch together while he updated her on his hilarious efforts to woo a vet tech from Dr. Debbie's practice.

By mid-afternoon, Jason had left, promising to come back the next day or so to work on the dock.

Isabel turned her attention to what she had put off all day – what she was going to wear for the evening. She tried on pretty much every piece of clothing she had in the closet, before deciding upon a sky blue turtleneck sweater, a pair of jeans and a black puffy vest. She pulled on a pair of comfortable hiking boots to complete her outfit.

She brushed Sadie until she gleamed. Then she secured a crate in the back seat of the car for the dog so she would be safe and comfortable during the ride over to Daniel's.

He was waiting for her at the gate to his house, opening it up fully so she could drive through.

"This is Sadie," Isabel said, getting out of the car but keeping the dog safely on leash. As Daniel approached, Sadie surprised Isabel by trembling and pulling back on her leash. But then she thought about the dog's history with Pete and it made sense that she would shy away from men she didn't know. Luckily, Daniel knew dogs and slowly introduced himself to Sadie, letting her choose when and how to approach him. He let her smell his hand and then when she seemed comfortable, stroked her head gently. She leaned onto his leg and gazed up at him.

Isabel smiled, "You have a way with dogs."

Daniel looked at her and said, " I've had a few over the years." He scratched gently behind Sadie's ears. "Would you like a tour of my work while it's still light out?"

"Absolutely."

"By the way I really like your hair…"

"Thank you," Isabel flushed with pleasure.

Daniel led her over to a bush under which there was a group of baby foxes in a den with their mother.

"I just finished this one today."

Isabel got down on her hands and knees to get a better view. There were four baby kits in the den. Curled protectively around them, the mother fox was tenderly nuzzling one.

Isabel was enchanted. She reached out to stroke one of the babies and then stopped herself and asked Daniel, "May I?"

"Absolutely."

Isabel leaned forward and touched the sculpture. It was so lifelike she half expected it to move or make a noise. She glanced over at the mother fox. She could swear the mother fox's eyes were watching her. She almost said something to Daniel but she hesitated, "He'll think I"m nuts," she thought.

"Let me show you one of the first pieces I did after moving here five years ago." Daniel reached down to give her a helping hand.

"Where do you get your inspiration from?" she asked.

"The simple answer is from everywhere. I pick up ideas from television and movies. I watch a lot of nature programs. I try to synthesize all those different elements and bring it into my art."

Isabel nodded, "I love shows about wild animals. My problem is I see the camera focus on a baby animal and I know that somebody is going to end getting eaten and it is probably going to be the baby." She stroked the baby foxes again. "I just wish they would make no-kill documentaries so I can sit and relax and watch the show without getting all tense waiting to see who is next on the dinner menu."

"That's an interesting idea."

He led her to the water's edge and pointed out the sculpture of two great blue herons standing in a quiet pool of water. One was peering into the water hunting for fish while the other was just about to take off, its great wings in the midst of unfolding, ready to catch the wind.

"Oh, how wonderful," exclaimed Isabel.

Daniel smiled at her. "I consider the great blue to be my totem bird."

"What does that mean?

"Simply put, every time I see a great blue I feel it's a gift from the heavens. If I'm feeling down, seeing one lifts my spirits and makes me feel like something positive is on the way."

Isabel looked at him curiously, "Do you often feel down?" The moment she asked the question she wanted to kick herself. Too late she remembered that Daniel had lost his wife to cancer. "I'm so sorry," she stuttered. "I wasn't thinking."

He looked out over the water toward the great blues. "I do miss her terribly…I'd give everything I have for just a few more minutes to talk with her, to be with her."

There was an awkward silence.

Isabel said hesitantly. "Perhaps I should leave."

"No, don't leave. I would like you to stay. It would be nice to have dinner with someone. I usually eat alone."

She turned and faced him, square on. "Why me? We don't know each other. Why invite me over? For that matter why give me that wonderful painting of the Warrior Woman? What is this all about?"

He looked taken aback at her blunt questioning. "I guess…" he stammered, "the fact that you went head to head with Pete and managed to save the dog impressed the heck out of me. You seem quiet, and mild-mannered. Then when Sadie was threatened, you turned into this ferocious lioness protecting your cub."

Isabel was surprised. It had never occurred to her how her confrontation with Pete must have appeared to the outside world.

"I tend to be a very private person," she said.

"I get that," he looked at her and smiled, "Let me show you a couple more pieces of my work and then we can go in to dinner. I'm making something very simple. Salad and spaghetti. I hope that's OK with you."

"That sounds wonderful. Especially since I'm not the one doing the cooking."

"Yeah, it's tough to get the energy up to make a nice, balanced meal when it is just me. I end up eating cereal for dinner far more often than I should."

"Let me guess, Honey Nut Cheerios?" she laughed.

He grinned.

"That's my go-to meal also," she said smiling.

"I'll keep that in mind for next time. Here we are," he said indicating a small tree near the pond. He pointed to one of the branches and Isabel gasped with delight. There was a beautifully articulated hummingbird nest with two babies and a mother bird perched on the edge of the nest feeding them.

Isabel exclaimed, "I've always wanted to see a hummingbird nest but they are so tiny. I've never been able to spot one in the wild." Isabel glanced at Daniel and thought how attractive he was with his green eyes and shock of white hair. He radiated vitality and good humor. His creative energy really appealed to her too. It had been literally years since Isabel had let herself get close enough to anyone to go on a date.

"Let me show you something else." Right near the front steps was a little parade of mice. The father led the way, with a newspaper under his arm and reading glasses perched on his head. The mother mouse followed pushing a pram with twin babies and holding the hand of a little girl. A slightly older boy mouse was running next to them holding a tiny paper airplane.

"These are just enchanting," sighed Isabel. "I can't believe you managed to infuse these sculptures with such incredible detail."

They had dinner under a starlit sky. Daniel had set up a table close by the pond with candles lining the walkway to the dining area. Their soft light was reflected in the crystal wine glasses and porcelain dinnerware. It was a peaceful evening enhanced by a symphony of spring peepers, the deep croaking of a couple of bullfrogs and the soft hooting of a nearby owl.

"What a beautiful night. It is so tranquil here," said Isabel.

"I'm glad you like it. Some of the women I've dated have found it too quiet for their liking."

"After living in New York City, I've had enough noise to last a couple of lifetimes." Isabel reached down and petted Sadie who was stretched out by her feet.

"I was able to block out the noise pretty well," Daniel said. "Except for the ambulances. I find the sound of ambulances really unsettling."

"Sirens always unnerve me," agreed Isabel.

They sat together in a comfortable silence for a while. Then Isabel said "I wanted to ask you, Daniel, if you knew

Catherine Evers at all. I am trying to find out information about her and why she left me the house."

He looked surprised. "I really didn't know her at all. She did stop by one time and asked to see my work. It was a pleasant visit but very short. That was the only time I talked with her at length. Not long after that I heard she was very ill."

"Yes, well, thank you anyway." She stood up. "It's getting late. Thank you so much for a wonderful time."

He smiled at her and said, "I'm really glad you came over. I'll be out of town for a couple of weeks having exhibitions in New York City, LA and then Chicago. But when I get back I would like to see you again."

"I'd like that, too. Good luck on your exhibits." Isabel reached over and gave him a quick peck on the cheek.

CHAPTER 11

A week after her date with Daniel, after he had left the island for his tour, Isabel walked into her kitchen and poured two glasses of fresh, locally pressed apple cider. She handed one to Jason and sipped hers as she leaned against the kitchen counter.

Sadie came trotting in with a tennis ball in her mouth. She dropped it at Isabel's feet, gazing up at her and wagging her tail hopefully. Isabel smiled at her and said, "We'll play ball in a little while, I promise."

Sadie pushed the ball with her nose right up to Isabel's feet and then lay down with a heavy sigh. Isabel glanced down, "Who knew this dog would turn out to be such a drama queen," she laughed. She rested a bare foot on Sadie's silky soft fur and gently massaged the dog's back.

Suddenly they heard a horn. Sadie barked.

"She's here," exclaimed Isabel.

A few days before this, Dr. Mike had called Isabel and asked if he could come and talk to her. When he came out he explained to her that Captain Charlotte had a bad accident. She had been helping a charter guest off her boat when the guest slipped on the gangplank. Charlotte went to grab her and ended up with her leg getting caught between the boat and the dock. It was a serious break requiring steel pins and a big cast to stabilize the leg.

The bad news was she was going to be immobilized for at least the next month. Since she lived alone on a remote part of the island, she needed a place to stay where someone would be available to look after her. Dr. Mike had gotten in touch with a number of people on the island who were more than happy to have her stay with them. The problem was Charlotte. She had her own idea about who she wanted to stay with and after a lot of thought she came up with one name. Isabel.

"Now I know this is a big ask," he said. "Isabel, is there any way you would consider having her stay here with you until she gets back on her feet." He looked at her hopefully but also with what she sensed was an undertone of desperation.

Isabel was taken off guard. "I don't know. I mean I don't know her; she doesn't know me. I am not sure why she would suggest me." She fumbled for the right words. "I had a couple of roommates when I first moved to New York City. They turned out to be nightmare situations that were difficult to get clear of. I swore I'd never have a roommate again. I'm very cautious about who I let into my life. And into my house." She gazed out over her lawn, "After all, I have only been on the island a month."

"That's true, but people like you."

Isabel looked at him surprised, "Really? I barely know anyone here."

"You have made quite an impression already. People have a sense that you fit in, that you're already part of the community. Not just an off-islander who spends a week or two and then is on to the next big thing."

It amazed Isabel that people seemed to like her, that she may have finally found a place that she could call home. She had never had that before, even when she was growing up she hadn't felt like she fit anywhere. Her parents had tried their best but they just weren't really cut out to be parents. They were more focused on each other, their friends, and their social activities. She was kind of an add on...a Plus-One child.

"Let me think about this," she asked, "It is a lot to consider. How much time do I have?"

"Well, she will be coming back to the island in a couple of days. If it doesn't work out it doesn't work out. We'll find someplace else for her to stay. But her only other option right now is to go into a rehab center and I really don't think she would do well in that environment."

"Yes, I can see that," said Isabel.

At this faint glimmer of hope that Isabel might even consider it, he continued, "We would have a nurse here for at least the first week or so, 24 hours a day so you wouldn't have to deal with any of her medical needs Then we would transition to daily nurse coverage. No additional overnights. We would cover all expenses of course."

Isabel said, "I just don't know how we would get along. If we would even get along. I promise you though, I will give it serious consideration."

"That's all I can ask, is for you to think about it," and he swung up into his truck and drove away.

Isabel felt stunned at the request and couldn't decide what to do. Jason came over to do some work on the dock and found Isabel sitting on her porch staring into space. He had to call her name several times to get a response.

"Did you hear about Charlotte," Isabel asked him.

"Yeah."

"Dr. Mike has asked me to have her stay here for a few weeks to heal. I can't decide whether to do it or not."

He looked at her questioningly. "You can always say no."

"I'm afraid if I say "no," people won't..."

"People won't what?"

"They won't like me. There I've said it."

Jason stared at her. "So what?"

"So..." she felt frustrated trying to explain herself to him.

"Look, Isabel, I've known Charlotte all my life and I like and respect her. She is one tough cookie." He sat down on the porch step next to her. "She's had to be to succeed in a male-dominated profession like she has." He picked up a stick and started drawing designs in the dirt. "On the other hand, she was very kind to my mother when she was dying of cancer. She used to bring over funny movies to make my mom laugh and high protein homemade cookies so she would at least get something in her stomach. It meant a lot to both my mom and me that she would be so caring."

Isabel sighed. "I'll think about it."

Now, Jason and Isabel watched as an ambulance backed up to the temporary ramp Isabel had installed since she made the decision to have Charlotte stay with her. Two EMTs and a nurse carefully maneuvered Charlotte out of the vehicle and secured her in a wheelchair her right leg encased in a heavy cast and sticking straight out in front of her. The EMTs pushed her up the ramp as the nurse grabbed a medical bag from the ambulance. Isabel still had misgivings about this arrangement but she was willing to try it. As Charlotte reached the top of the ramp, Isabel walked over to give her a hug. Charlotte stiffened and put a hand up to stop her. Isabel about to welcome her, was caught off guard, and stumbled back a few steps. The nurse looked at her sympathetically as the EMTs pushed the wheelchair into the house.

"It is a difficult situation," the nurse explained. "From what Dr. Mike has told me, Charlotte is a strong independent woman who has run her own business for years.

Now she can't even go to the bathroom by herself. It is a challenging turn of events for anyone but especially for someone like her."

"But she'll recover fully and be able to run her charter business?" asked Isabel.

The nurse shrugged, "We can hope that happens. But frankly we don't know at this point what her full recovery will look like." She picked up her medical bag. "My name is Ellen; I'll be here for the next couple of weeks on a 24-hour basis."

Isabel introduced herself, and asked "What about her emotional well-being?"

"I have the names of a few counselors who have experience with difficult rehabs."

"Why do you call it a difficult rehab?"

Ellen answered, "Sometimes it is hard for a personality like Charlotte's to accept help or even to admit she needs help. Now, I'd like to see her room."

"Oh, of course," Isabel showed the nurse into Charlotte's bedroom as the EMTs prepared to leave.

Charlotte was lying on her back, expressionless, staring at the ceiling.

Isabel felt a lump in her throat as she watched the nurse check Charlotte's vitals. She was so still and there was a bleakness about her.

Isabel walked over to her and said, "I'm glad you are here." Charlotte's expression did not change. She glanced briefly at Isabel but then went back to staring at the ceiling.

After a few moments she sighed, "Thanks, Isabel, for letting me stay here."

"No problem." Isabel turned to Ellen. "Is there anything I can get you?"

"A comfortable chair so I can sit by Charlotte's bed. But first if you could show me to my room so I can freshen up."

"We made up the study for you. It is right next to this room." As Isabel showed Ellen to her room she silently blessed Jason. It was his idea to prepare a room for any visiting nurses. Isabel hadn't even considered the possibility of caregivers needing to stay with them.

As she showed Ellen where everything was, Isabel heard a bark from Charlotte's room.

"Oh no!" She rushed past Ellen. She stopped abruptly in the doorway as she took in the scene before her.

Sadie had dropped her ball on the bed and then sat wiggling with excitement waiting for Charlotte to toss it. Isabel made a move to enter the room when she felt Ellen grab her arm and hold her in place. Charlotte awkwardly reached out and pushed the ball off the bed.

Sadie was thrilled and immediately chased after it. She returned with the ball and again dropped it on the bed. She looked back at Isabel with that happy doggy smile so typical of Labs. She nudged the ball closer to Charlotte and then rested her head on the edge of the bed.

"Nice dog," commented Charlotte.

Ellen murmured in Isabel's ear, "Your dog may be Charlotte's best chance for recovery."

Isabel walked over and picked up the ball. "We'll play again later," she said, petting Sadie's head. The dog lay down next to the bed. Ellen pulled a book out of her bag and sat in an easy chair close by Charlotte.

Isabel walked into the kitchen to prepare a vanilla protein shake for Charlotte's lunch. She had lists and notes taped up all over the place to help her remember Charlotte's medication and meal schedule.

Propped against the blender she found a note from Jason. It read "Good Luck !" with a little sketch of a three-legged dog with its head cocked to one side.

She laughed and thought to herself, "I hope that vet tech realizes what a great guy he is."

After a busy day of transition, it turned out to be a peaceful evening. Charlotte was asleep, with Sadie on the floor next to her bed while Ellen was reading quietly in her chair. Isabel was in the living room watching YouTube videos of how to knit a scarf. She had thought she would enjoy knitting but grew more and more frustrated trying to work with what was rapidly turning into a big lump of yarn. She finally stuffed it into a basket and pushed it under the sofa. "Out of sight, out of mind," she told herself. She switched over to videos of dogs and came across Olive and Mabel, two Labs, and their Scottish sportscaster owner. The videos were hysterically funny and though she kept her laughter low, Ellen heard her and came out to see what was going on. A dog-lover herself she quickly got hooked on the videos and she and Isabel watched them over and over.

Finally, it was time for bed. Everyone settled into their rooms with only the sound of the distant waves and the occasional hooting of an owl breaking the silence.

CHAPTER 12

The next week was a period of adjustment for everyone. Isabel sought ways of entertaining Charlotte so she wouldn't get too bored. She tried board games, books, puzzles, and playing cards. She found that both Charlotte and Ellen were wicked poker players. Worried that she might end up losing the house if they played with dollar bills, she went to the bank and got rolls of dimes. She thought she could handle losing that amount to her in-house card sharks.

Jason came by a couple of times and joined in the poker games. Mary visited and brought some of the latest thrillers and mysteries for Charlotte to read. Dr. Mike stopped in to check on her. Sadie was a constant companion and Isabel had to keep an eye out for the woebegone and grubby toys that the dog would sometimes bury in Charlotte's sheets.

Tom and Harry stopped by with homemade ice cream and they had Sunday night sundaes. Sadie and Harry played until they fell asleep curled together in a dog bed.

Charlotte and Ellen got hooked on a couple of British series especially the baking shows, which they loved. They ended up binge watching them on nights when Charlotte was in pain and unable to sleep. Frequently Isabel would get in her pjs and robe and join them for impromptu movie nights, complete with popcorn.

Isabel was surprised that all the visitors stopping by didn't bother her at all. In fact, she was enjoying it. Which is unusual for her since she had lived so much of her life disconnected from other people.

A week after Charlotte's arrival, Isabel was awakened one morning by a knocking on the front door followed by Sadie's surprisingly gruff bark. She peered out the window but didn't see any vehicles.

She opened the window and called out, "I'll be right there." She grabbed a sweatshirt and sweatpants. Dressing quickly, she raced down the staircase.

Ellen appeared in her doorway yawning and stretching. She walked into Charlotte's room to check on her and reemerged giving Isabel a thumbs up.

Sadie was sitting by the front door, waiting for her. Isabel stroked her silky head and said, "It's okay, Sadie. Good girl."

Isabel swung open the front door and at first didn't see anyone. Then two young girls moved into view peering at her through the screen. They both looked to be about 8-10 years old. Sadie barked again and the older of the two suddenly looked fearful.

"Does your dog bite?" she asked with a quiver in her voice.

"What, Sadie?" Isabel sought to reassure her, "Oh no. She is very gentle."

The younger girl introduced herself. "My name is Annika and this is my big sister, Linnea. We are here to see Coach Charlotte."

"Do you mean Captain Charlotte," asked Isabel.

"No," said Annika firmly. "Coach Charlotte coaches our softball team."

Startled, Isabel said, "Well, she is not feeling well right now…"

"We want to see her," said Annika. "We know she has a broken leg…our grandfather is Dr. Mike and he explained it to us."

"We brought sharpies," added Linnea holding up a handful of brightly colored markers. Isabel looked confused.

"To sign her cast," Linnea explained patiently.

"Oh," said Isabel, "of course. Let me just see if she is open to having company right now."

She peered into Charlotte's bedroom. "Are you up for visitors," she asked the motionless figure on the bed. Charlotte opened her eyes and glanced at Isabel. She shook her head. "Not right now," she said and then closed her eyes again.

Isabel paused and then said, "Okay, I'll tell Annika and Linnea that you are not up to seeing them."

Charlotte opened her eyes. "Wait a minute, I'd like to see them. They're good kids." As she struggled to sit up, Isabel stuffed a couple of pillows behind her back to provide more support.

97

"Do you want me to bring them in," Isabel asked.

Charlotte said, "Yes."

Isabel walked back to the front door and holding Sadie by her collar, opened the door. The girls came inside. Annika striding in confidently, while Linnea entered tentatively, keeping close to the walls, putting distance between herself and the dog.

"I'm going to put Sadie outside," Isabel told the girls. "Ellen, why don't you take them into Charlotte and I'll be back in a minute."

When she came in she found the girls standing shoulder to shoulder by Charlotte's bed, staring at her. Charlotte was staring back at them.

Isabel tried to break the tension by saying brightly to Charlotte. "I understand you coach their softball team?"

Charlotte broke her gaze with the girls and looked at Isabel, "For about two years now. There wasn't any softball program for young girls on the island so I decided to start one."

Isabel remarked "What a great thing to do. I wish I had something like that when I was their age."

Annika said, " We've learned so much from Coach Charlotte."

Linnea chimed in "Yeah, I love being part of a team. It's fun!"

Annika added "Mary from the bookstore is our assistant coach..."

Linnea told Isabel, "She's not very good. She keeps wanting us to read books about baseball."

Charlotte made a noise somewhere between a snort and a cough. Startled, Isabel realized that she was laughing.

Annika moved forward and perched on the bed. "Yeah, that doesn't help us to throw a ball or win a game. Can I sign your cast, Coach?"

"Sure, go ahead."

Isabel said "Maybe Mary could learn. YouTube must have plenty of videos on how to play softball."

Annika turned to her and said, "We are supposed to be training right now for our first game." She took a bright yellow marker and started drawing a sunflower.

"Very nice," said Isabel smiling at her.

Linnea gloomily propped her head on her hands. "We're never going to be ready in time," she said. "We're gonna be big losers. Again."

Annika handed her a blue marker "Less talk, more drawing."

Linnea stuck her tongue out at her younger sister but then started to draw a bird flying across the sky.

Isabel peered over Linnea's shoulder, "Wow, you are both so creative."

"Maybe Isabel could help out," contributed Charlotte "while I'm healing from my broken leg."

"Oh, no," said Isabel. "I have no idea how to play baseball. I don't even know the difference between baseball and softball. Except that one hurts more when you get hit with it."

Watching all of this from the doorway, Ellen said. "I was on the softball team in high school so I can help out a little bit while I'm here."

Isabel said, "But I don't even know how to get started."

Annika said, "We could have the team come over here to watch videos. And Coach Charlotte could coach us from her bed."

Isabel looked at Annika, Linnea, Charlotte, and even Ellen, as their faces turned towards her hopefully. She thought about the quiet home she'd been envisioning for herself. The things she had in mind that she wanted to do like learning how to bake bread and grow vegetables. Trying her hand at sculpting and photography. She had daydreamed of sitting in the morning sun with a wide brimmed straw hat, sipping a cup of tea and peacefully painting a watercolor. It was a nice image but whether she could make it a reality, that was the question. But she thought she'd at least like to try. She sighed. Signing up for this meant giving up on the peace and quiet and solitude she had yearned for when living for years in a noisy, smelly, overcrowded city. It would mean letting a lot of people into her life, especially children with whom frankly she did not have much experience.

She sighed again and visualized herself standing on the edge of a precipice. She took a deep breath and nodded. "Okay I won't coach but I'll help out." And felt herself step off into the unknown.

CHAPTER 13

"Yay!" said Annika and Linnea.

"So, first off, we have to bring Mary in on this," Isabel stated. Charlotte nodded her agreement.

"Why," asked Annika as she drew another sunflower on Charlotte's cast.

"Well Mary has apparently been a part of your coaching team for a while so maybe she has some insights into your training regimen. Plus, I don't want to hurt her feelings by not including her."

The sisters looked at each other. "I guess," said Annika hesitantly. Linnea made a squinty face.

Annika finished her flower and carefully signed her name. "Can we take a selfie with the Coach?"

Isabel looked at Charlotte who nodded.

"Sure," she said.

Isabel heard Sadie bark. "I'll be right back."

"Wait," Linnea stood up.

"I have to bring Sadie in, she's been out there too long. She gets lonely." Isabel spoke directly to Linnea. "I'll keep her on leash, I promise." She saw the young girl starting to look panicky.

"Linnea, I used to be very afraid of dogs too. Years ago, I was attacked by a dog in Central Park and it scared the shi…heck out of me. For most of my life I have avoided dogs. But then I met Sadie. She's a great dog and I love her very much. Let me bring her in on leash and have her just say hi to you. Put your hand out so she can smell it and she will probably give you a lick. If you are uncomfortable let me know and I'll put her in the other room."

Isabel went and got Sadie and brought her back with her and she immediately started wagging her tail. Isabel walked her around to say "hi" to each person. When she got to Linnea, Sadie lay down and rolled over on her back, still wagging her tail, and looking at the youngster from an upside down perspective.

"What do I do?" she asked Isabel.

Isabel responded, "Just give her a little tummy rub and she'll be very happy."

Tentatively, Linnea leaned over, reached out a quivering hand and stroked Sadie's stomach. She looked up at Isabel. "She is so soft," she exclaimed.

Isabel nodded agreement, "She is very soft. Unless she's been rolling around in mud which she is very fond of doing."

Linnea stroked Sadie's stomach a few more times and then straightened up.

Sadie rolled onto her legs and sat up next to her, looking up and wagging her tail. Linnea reached down and gently patted her head. Sadie licked her hand. Linnea giggled.

"Should I let her off leash," asked Isabel.

Linnea looked a little nervous but then nodded her head. Isabel immediately took Sadie off leash. Sadie went over to Charlotte's bedside and lay down.

Jason walked into the room. "It is getting late," Jason said," I need to take the girls home for dinner." He turned to Annika and Linnea, "I'll put your bikes in the back of my truck.

"We have to take a selfie first," protested Annika. Isabel volunteered to be the photographer and took a picture of Annika, Linnea, and Charlotte, with Sadie photobombing at the last minute.

Annika leaned over and kissed Charlotte on the cheek, "I hope you feel better." Her sister did the same from the other side of the bed.

Isabel smiled and then thought to ask, "Jason, did you ever play baseball?"

Shaking his head, he answered. "I'm a Red Sox fan, but I've never played. Soccer was my game in school."

Annika suggested, "I think we can figure out softball strategies and tactics by watching some of the training videos on YouTube."

Surprised, Isabel asked, "Annika, how do you know about strategies and tactics?"

"I watch Shark Tank."

Ellen murmured quietly to Isabel, "I'd invest in that kid in a flash."

Linnea petted Sadie's head one more time and then hurried out as Jason honked his horn.

Isabel stood up and stretched. "I think it's time for me to make dinner. How about spaghetti tonight if that is okay with everyone."

"Sounds good," said Charlotte.

Ellen nodded and asked, "Is there anything I can do to help?"

"No, thanks," said Isabel. She started to walk into the kitchen but then stopped and turned back. "Though actually, there is something you could do. If you could find out how many players are actually on a softball team and then also what positions they play. And what the skill set is for each position. That'd be great."

Ellen responded, "I'm on it."

The next morning Isabel drove into town. She had a laundry list of things to pick up for Ellen at the drugstore but she also wanted to stop in and talk to Mary about the team. She pulled into a parking spot in front of the bookstore. The closed sign was up but she noticed that Mary was inside bustling around. She knocked on the door. Mary looked up and saw her. She smiled, walked over, and unlocked the door.

"I've been thinking about you," said Mary. "How did the date go?"

Isabel was caught off guard by the question and then she laughed. "You know so much has happened since then. It seems like it's been ages since I had dinner with Daniel. I haven't thought about it since."

Mary looked disappointed. "I guess it wasn't that great a date."

"Oh, it was nice and his work is incredible. I enjoyed talking to him and he is certainly good-looking...but I don't know, it felt like something was missing. Maybe I just didn't feel that spark. Hopefully, we'll have another date and see how it goes. But in the meantime, I had some visitors at the house yesterday. Annika and Linnea stopped by to talk to me about the softball team."

Mary said "Oh yes? With Charlotte recovering from a broken leg, I wasn't sure what we were going to do about that."

"The kids, at least these two, are ready to start playing, and they asked me to help out. I wanted to talk to you about that and see if you are still interested in coaching. Frankly, I don't know anything about softball so ...."

Mary said thoughtfully "A couple of the parents have stopped in over the past few days to ask me about the softball season, to see if we're going forward with it. I didn't really know what to tell them. I said I would try to find out what was happening and get back to them. I'm glad to hear there's interest. The kids really seem to enjoy playing. Though we don't have a very good winning record. Especially not compared to the boys' team."

Isabel who had started casually browsing a table featuring the latest book releases looked up, "Really?"

"Our boys' team does really well, they win a lot. Our girls' team on the other hand doesn't get any attention and rarely has enough money for even the most basic of equipment or to cover travel expenses to a game on the mainland."

"That's not right," said Isabel with some asperity.

"I know but that's kind of the way it is here" said Mary. "It's still a macho economic environment primarily based on fishing, charters, and shipping. Our locals feel very strongly about their team sports -- everything shuts down when the Red Sox or Patriots play. Not that they don't love their girls but they really support their boys and their sports."

"That totally sucks," said Isabel.

Mary laughed. "Yes it does actually. You have to realize, though, for some families on the island if their boy does well in sports that may ensure scholarship to a college that they might not be able to afford otherwise. I don't think they believe that their girl participating in sports would have the same opportunities."

"Do you still want to coach?" Isabel asked.

"Well, I think I was more a hindrance to Charlotte than a help," Mary admitted.

"We can learn together." Isabel sounded way more confident than she felt.

"Are you sure?"

"I'm not really sure of anything," admitted Isabel. "Do you have a list of the team members so I can start calling around to set up an introductory meeting? I guess everybody could come out to my house."

"Sounds like a good idea," said Mary. "But do you really want to do this?

"I am used to leading a pretty solitary life. It does kind of scare me to think about getting involved with something like this. I don't have any experience with children."

Mary said, "Well I think you're very plucky for taking it on. But you also have the right to drop out if you don't feel comfortable. After all, you are not getting paid, you're volunteering your time and effort. You have the right to say this is not for you."

Isabel found comfort in Mary's words, something akin to being handed a "get out of jail free" card.

She left Mary's bookshop and stopped by the general store to pick up some construction paper, magic markers, and tape.

"I need to put up some flyers," she said to the girl behind the counter. "Would that be okay?"

"Well, it depends, " the girl said, "What is it for?"

Isabel said, "We're trying to set up a meeting to see who's interested in participating in the girls' softball team."

"OH fantastic!" exclaimed the girl, "My little sister loves softball and she's been hoping the team would start playing again. I'll do anything I can to help promote it." She whipped out her phone "Here let me take your name and number."

"Thanks!" said Isabel.

She started for home feeling that she had actually accomplished something. She had taken the first steps to putting the team back into play.

When she got home she found a tense atmosphere. Ellen was working with Charlotte on her exercises, stretching and pushing against her arm and leg muscles to get her flexible and strong. Ellen was being very patient but Charlotte had enough. She was glaring at Ellen, whose face was bright red. From exertion or frustration, Isabel couldn't tell which. Even the easygoing Sadie had retreated to another room and was stretched out on the living room couch.

"Hi" said Isabel. "How's everything?" Though it was pretty clear to her that things were not going well.

"Why don't you ask her?" Charlotte snarled.

"Ellen," said Isabel, "Could you help me in the kitchen for a few minutes?"

"Sure," said Ellen, following her into the other room..

"What the hell is going on," asked Isabel. "You can cut the tension in there with a knife."

"Yes, I know," said Ellen. "She likes to do things her way in her own time and sometimes we clash over what I think would be good for her and what she wants to do."

"Sadie needs to get some exercise," said Isabel, "Can you throw the ball for her a bit in the dog pen? In the meantime, I'll clean up things here and take care of giving Charlotte a protein drink."

Ellen said, "That sounds good. I could use a break."

Isabel whistled for Sadie. "Just throw the ball back and forth." Sadie came racing in from the other room carrying her Lamb Chop toy which, minus a leg, an arm and part of an ear, looked like it had been through a war.

Isabel said to her, "I'll trade you." Sadie immediately dropped the toy and eagerly took the tennis ball Isabel was offering to her.

Isabel went in to check on Charlotte while Ellen and Sadie went outside to play.

"Do you need anything?"

Charlotte was lying on her back again staring up at the ceiling. As Isabel got closer she saw Charlotte had tears rolling down her cheeks.

She sat on the corner of the bed and said "I can't even begin to imagine how difficult this must be for you. I believe you'll get through this. It may take some time, maybe quite a bit of time but you have the strength, the will and you've got people around you who care about you and are willing to help you get through this."

Charlotte looked at her for a few minutes and then raised her right hand. Isabel leaned forward, curious. Charlotte curled four fingers down, deliberately leaving the center finger erect.

Isabel was startled and then cracked up. "OK," she said "I get it. I guess that was just too much rah rah talk." She left the room, hearing Charlotte laughing behind her.

Isabel went outside to check on Sadie and Ellen. She found them sitting peacefully together on the steps. Sadie was leaning against Ellen. The tennis ball lay at her feet.

"Ellen, would you like something to drink? I have some cold spring water or a beer if you would like that."

Ellen said, "You know a beer would be great right now."

Isabel went into the kitchen and emerged with a couple of beers and a bag of pretzels.

They sat in companionable silence for a while listening to the birds and the sound of the waves breaking onshore. Isabel asked, "Did you always want to be a nurse?"

Ellen took a sip of her beer. "My mother was a nurse. I saw how much difference she made in people's lives; how much she helped them and made them feel better. I wanted to do that, to have that kind of impact." There was a long pause. "She died of COVID two years ago."

Isabel took a deep breath. "Oh, I'm so sorry."

"The worst thing was I was a traveling nurse at the time and was working in an emergency room across the country from my mom and because of all the restrictions and lockdowns, couldn't get back to see her before she was gone. It broke my heart."

"That sounds awful," said Isabel.

"So now I'm trying to decide if I want to go on being a nurse."

"I'm sure having a difficult patient like Charlotte is not particularly helpful in trying to make that kind of decision."

"Actually," Ellen replied, "Charlotte is very much like me in some ways. I can really identify with the difficulty she's having." She stood up, "I have to go check on her," and walked inside.

Isabel wrapped her arms around Sadie and gave her a kiss. "You're such a good girl," she said. Sadie licked her face and thumped her thick plume of a tail on the porch floor.

CHAPTER 14

A week later, Isabel was hurriedly cleaning up the house. She and Mary had created flyers publicizing an organizational meeting for anybody interested in the girls' softball team. Along with Annika and Linnea they had put them up all around town and got a very good response. In addition, Charlotte had made phone calls to previous team members to see if they were interested. Everybody seemed excited about getting the softball team up and running again. Now Mary and Jason were trying to round up some extra chairs for the 20 or so kids and their parents who had signed up for the meeting and would be arriving at Isabel's home shortly. Isabel had looked through all the rooms in the house for extra seating to put in the living room. She even looked in the hoarder's closet. She was delighted to find a couple of armchairs and a bench shoved in there that were useable. Tom offered some folding chairs which Isabel gratefully accepted.

Isabel put out paper, pencils, and pens so people could write down their thoughts. Then she and Ellen got

Charlotte into her wheelchair and bundled her up with a quilt so she could attend the meeting in person. As she was getting Charlotte settled, she heard Jason's truck pull up outside. Isabel smiled as she heard Sadie barking a greeting to Jason. He came in with his arms full of grocery bags. He immediately put them down on the counter and went back out to say hi to Sadie.

Mary came bustling in with a covered dish, dressed in a 1960s Red Sox uniform. "I made some cookies."

Isabel did a double take when she saw Mary then laughed and applauded. "You look fabulous," she said. "Did you make that?"

"Nope. eBay. Here try one of my cookies, it's my own secret recipe."

Isabel took a bite and moaned with pleasure. "Oh my God, what is in these? They are fantastic. You should sell them at the store."

"I've thought about it," said Mary "but chocolate fingerprints and new books don't mix."

At that point Jason came bounding back into the kitchen. "I just love that dog." He grabbed a cookie and took a bite. "Mary, you make the best cookies." He took another bite. "When do you want me to come back and help clean up."

"Actually," Isabel said, "I'd like you to stay, Jason. I have a feeling we might need a bit of testosterone to balance things out."

Jason threw his head back and laughed, and then said, "Oh, you're serious."

She nodded.

"Sure. No problem."

As he spoke, cars, ATVs and golf carts started pulling into Isabel's driveway. Jason grabbed another cookie. "This is definitely a two cookie day," he said.

Isabel, Mary, and Charlotte welcomed everybody and directed them to the living room. Ellen was also on hand to make sure Charlotte didn't get too tired.

The group consisted mostly of mothers and their daughters. It was a happy, noisy crowd and Isabel found to her surprise that she was enjoying herself. She had never been someone who was comfortable being around crowds but for some reason this was different. She especially enjoyed hearing the compliments about the house's fresh look. When Jason walked into the room and saw the crowd, he laughed, looked at Isabel and winked. She grinned back at him. Then went out to the pen and brought Sadie back in with her. The noise in the room rapidly escalated as all the girls wanted to pet her. Linnea called out Sadie's name and the dog walked over and lay down next to her. Linnea hugged her with a broad smile.

Her mother came over to Isabel and introduced herself, "Hi, I"m Pauline and I can't thank you enough for helping Linnea get over her terror of dogs. My husband and I both absolutely adore dogs but have never been able to get one before this. Now we are hoping to add a dog to our family very soon." She walked back and sat down next to Linnea and Annika, reaching over to pet Sadie.

Isabel glanced at her watch, nodded to Mary and Charlotte, and clapped her hands sharply, surprising even herself. "Okay let's get started," she said firmly. The room quieted and everyone turned toward her. "I take it you all want to play ball this season."

"Yes!" said the girls in unison.

Isabel asked Charlotte, "When does the season start officially?

"April 15."

"How often did you practice last season and for how long?"

"Three days a week for about an hour."

"Okay," said Isabel. "First of all, I am going to set up a sign-up sheet. Please print your name, age, address, phone number and position you played in the past or would like to play. Parents, I have a sign-up sheet for you too. Why don't we start tomorrow for an hour? Is there a field we can use?"

"In the past we used the field at the elementary school," explained Annika, "but we need to get permission."

"That shouldn't be a problem," said one of the mothers, "I'm a teacher at the school. I'll talk with the principal and get the okay."

"Excellent," said Isabel. "I think we should put up more flyers in case other children want to join the team. Maybe we could set a goal of signing up 20 players."

"We want them to try out first and see if they are any good," stated one of the mothers. Isabel glanced at her and saw how tight and tense she looked.

"I think," said Isabel, "we should give anyone who wants to play a chance."

"That's nonsense," said the woman tight lipped. "My daughter is very athletic and wants to be on a winning team. Not with a bunch of wannabes."

Isabel was taken aback at the vehemence of the woman. She noticed that the girl sitting on the floor cross-legged next to her had the same tight scornful expression on her face.

"We want this to be a fun experience," Isabel said. "For everyone," she added meaningfully.

"We'll see," said the woman.

There was an uncomfortable silence.

"We also want to have some viewing parties," broke in Charlotte, "to watch some baseball movies and videos to get a better grasp of winning strategies. So, if you have any movies in mind that would be..."

"A League of Their Own," yelled out one girl. And that opened the floodgates. Around the room the girls were calling out the names of movies. Isabel scribbled them down as fast as she could. Even Jason got into the spirit of things and called out, "The Natural," then looked embarrassed.

After about an hour more of discussion as to when and where the next practice would be held, the meeting ended. Everyone started drifting out to their vehicles, hugging one another, and grabbing a cookie or two for the road.

As the last mother and daughter left, Charlotte said to Isabel, "Great job. You are really good at keeping everyone in line and on point."

Isabel collapsed on the couch next to Mary. "What do you think?"

"I think it went well, everyone seemed pretty excited in making this work."

"Except for that one woman. What a pill!" said Isabel.

"That's the mayor's wife, Bobbie, and his daughter, Wendy," commented Mary, rolling her eyes. Charlotte chuckled.

"Oh shit," said Isabel. "Is that going to be a problem?"

Mary said, "No, I don't think so. For one thing our mayor is very good, very ethical. He won't let any backroom issues affect the community."

"Yeah, but this is his daughter we're talking about."

"I believe in him and I trust him," said Mary.

"He's a good guy," agreed Charlotte. "But his wife... what a bitch."

Ellen stood up, putting her hand on Charlotte's shoulder. "Time for bed." Charlotte nodded and slowly rolled her wheelchair into her bedroom, Ellen followed behind her. Mary and Isabel started cleaning up the remains of the meeting.

"Thank you for all your help getting this going. It looks like this might actually come about. I couldn't have done this without you," said Mary. "I know it means a lot to the girls on the island. Ever since we put the flyers up kids have been coming into the bookstore and talking to me about playing. There is a lot of excitement about this."

"We're going to make this happen," said Isabel.

They started rearranging the furniture back to its original positions.

Mary asked Isabel "Where'd you get this rocking chair?"

Isabel said "Oh, from the room upstairs. I call it the hoarders' closet. It has all kinds of furniture and stuff just jammed in there. I was looking for extra chairs and came across some in that room."

Mary looked closely at the rocking chair. She turned it on its side and pointed out to Isabel a name carved in the wood.

"This was crafted by a well-known furniture maker from this region. His furniture is beautifully handmade and considered works of art." Mary stroked the rocking chair appreciatively. "Since he passed away about 50 years ago, his pieces have gone up and up and up in value. You may actually have a gold mine in that room."

Isabel stared at her, "Seriously?"

Mary said, "I'm not kidding. Can I take a look up there sometime?"

Isabel said "Absolutely, I'd love you to take a look and see if there's anything of value. I have a lot of repairs to the house that still need to be made and they are adding up."

CHAPTER 15

The first day of the new softball team practice was windy and cold. Isabel considered cancelling it but then after obsessively watching all the weather forecasts for 24 hours prior decided to go forward with it. She thought canceling it would send the wrong message in terms of the team's commitment.

Isabel called Jason and asked him to pick up Mary, snacks and drinks and bring them to the field.

She decided to leave Sadie with Ellen and Charlotte, packed up a thermos of mint tea, a couple of blankets and set off.

When she pulled in, she saw Mary and Jason were bustling around setting things up. She also noticed Mary was avoiding meeting her gaze. "Something is definitely wrong," she thought.

Pauline walked over to her, looking embarrassed. "I am so sorry Isabel, but Bobbie called everyone who was at the meeting and said you don't know what you're doing and our kids are going to end up being a laughingstock. It was hard to hear and I think some of the parents bought into it. A number of the people that were at the meeting aren't here now."

Isabel responded carefully, not letting her anger show. "Well, she is half right. We don't know what we are doing... yet. But we will and I want to assure you that we will make sure that the girls who participate and play on this team will feel good about themselves whether it is at a practice or a game."

Pauline looked at her searchingly and then nodded. "Okay, I'm willing to give you a chance."

Isabel clapped her hands and started the girls doing stretching exercises. She followed that by having them run around the field 5 times. Then she and Mary assessed the equipment situation – who had gloves, bats, balls, and helmets and who didn't.

"Where did they get the equipment in previous years," Isabel asked Mary.

"Usually from Tom and the hardware store," answered Mary.

"Okay, that is my task for tomorrow."

"Annika," called Isabel, "You offered to create a design for the team tee shirts. Are you still up for that?" Annika nodded excitedly. "Mary, since you have awesome sewing skills can you work with her?"

"You got it," said Mary.

"Okay," called Isabel, "everyone come in!"

The girls gathered round Isabel, Mary, and Jason. Isabel noted which girls were out of breath and flopped down on the ground. She made a mental note to help them get into better shape.

"We've got to come up with a name for our team…"

She hadn't even finished her thought when a little tousled hair girl named Sophie yelled out "Mighty Mice!" Everyone laughed and applauded.

"Annika," asked Isabel," could you draw a picture of a mouse with a helmet, holding a baseball glove and a bat? Oh, and make it a girl mouse."

Annika nodded, "My sister Linnea will help me."

"Okay," Isabel said, "practice tomorrow at 4, after school. Make sure you have your helmets. Nobody plays without a helmet."

Everyone started packing up when a young woman came up to Isabel and asked to speak with her.

"Sure."

"These are my daughters, Cindi and Sandi." Isabel smiled down at the two small girls who were clearly twins. "Girls, why don't you help Ms. Mary pack up."

"Okay, Mom." The girls held hands and went skipping off in search of Mary.

"The thing is…right now we don't have a lot of money for non-essentials. My husband got injured at work and he is out on disability. But the girls really want to play on the team. Is there any way we can get used equipment?"

"Let me see what I can do," said Isabel. "I saw them during practice and they really put their heart into it. We can use that type of enthusiasm on the team."

"Thank you so much."

Jason had overheard the conversation and now he came up to Isabel. "Try talking to Tom. He might be able to help with used equipment." He paused. "There is someone else you might want to talk to…"

Isabel glanced over at him, curious about his hesitation.

"Sam at the marina."

Isabel looked startled. "Oh no. We really got off on the wrong foot."

"I know, I heard. But the thing is, he played with the Red Sox years ago. He could be an incredible resource."

"Hmmm," said Isabel. "I'll think about it."

Isabel sat on the edge of Charlotte's bed and talked about the practice. Ellen was in her chair knitting and Sadie was lying on the floor next to the bed playing with a ball and making it squeak. Charlotte lay in bed her eyes fixed on Isabel as she recounted how each girl had done. Isabel ended her summary by saying she needed to watch some videos teaching kids how to throw and hit a ball.

"Good idea," said Charlotte.

The three women decided to relax and spend a quiet evening watching a rerun of "You've Got Mail." After several late night bowls of ice cream, they all turned in.

The next morning Isabel drove into town, her first stop: Tom's Hardware Store. Tom greeted her warmly. Even Harry came out from behind the counter to say "hi." Isabel reached down and petted him.

"What can I do for you? Need a bigger hammer?" Tom asked with a smile.

"No thank you. I'm wondering if you have used soft ball equipment."

He looked surprised.

"We are getting the girls' softball team up and running," Isabel told him, feeling a glow of accomplishment.

"I thought you had decided against it," he said. "Bobbie, the mayor's wife stopped by today and said that you had given up on the idea, that it just wasn't your cup of tea. She told me to just give all the used equipment away to Goodwill."

Isabel could feel anger starting to boil inside her. She took a couple of deep breaths to calm down.

"Really? Well, she seems a little confused. We are definitely going ahead with the team. We'll get this straightened out," she said. "But for now, do you have any used equipment you could donate?"

"I have some bats and balls and a couple of helmets."

"Whatever you have," said Isabel, "I don't want them playing without helmets."

"Let me put these used ones in a couple of equipment bags for you. I'd also be glad to order some new helmets and whatever other equipment you might need."

Isabel was elated, "Thank you, Tom. That is an amazingly generous offer." She gave him a hug. "This will mean so much to those kids. Oh, and can you recommend a place to get tee shirts made?"

"There is a very talented graphic designer on the island. She should be able to help you."

"Great! One final thing. This has nothing to do with the softball. I have been trying to find out information about Catherine Evers and why she left me the house."

Tom ran his hand through his hair and looked out the front window of the store. " I don't really have much to tell you. She kept to herself. I did hear that there was something about a family member which I guess would probably be you. But I don't know anything about that. She was only here a couple of years before she got sick and went to hospice and then passed away. You might want to try the Historical Society or maybe the town administrator to see if they have any information. Sorry I can't be any more help."

"Thank you anyway," Isabel said. She felt dejected that she couldn't find out more about Catherine Evers.

Isabel gathered the bags from Tom and stowed them in her car. She looked around for a moment and wondered if Bobbie was still in town and if she could possibly catch up with her somewhere. She decided to check out the café which seemed to serve as a meeting place for the community to see if on the off chance, Bobbie was there. Isabel walked in and there was Bobbie. She was sitting with her daughter at a big round table pushed up against the café's front window.

"Of course," thought Isabel, "she wants to see and be seen."

She recognized four of the women sitting with her as mothers of softball team members. They at least had the grace to look embarrassed when Isabel approached the table while Bobbie looked up at her with her customary sneer. Isabel felt like telling her if she kept that up her face was going to freeze like that. The thought made her smile to herself.

"I'm glad I ran into you," she said to Bobbie, "there seems to be some confusion about whether we're going forward with the softball team. I just wanted to reassure you all that we are definitely committed to getting the team up and on its way."

She turned away and then tuned back, adding, "Oh, by the way, I also cleared it up with Tom that we want to go through the used equipment first to make sure none of our team can use it and then we will donate the remainder to Goodwill."

One of the mothers said, "I didn't think you wanted to go forward. At least that is what Bobbie said."

"You are Sophie's mother aren't you?" asked Isabel.

The woman nodded.

"I don't know if you were there when Sophie came up with a great name for the team," Isabel said, "The Mighty Mice."

Sophie's mother blushed with pride. "I wasn't there but I really like that name."

"So do I," said Isabel, "she's very creative. We can definitely use her when we start marketing the team."

"Marketing the team?" Snorted Bobbie. "Just how are you going to market the team?"

"Well," said Isabel, "Off the top of my head, when people come out to watch the games, we can have them buy tickets for refreshments and wearables, and all of that will go to support the team. One of the girls is going to draft up a Mighty Mice logo which will go on everything. We can build a cute brand around that."

Sophie's mother turned and confronted Bobbie. "You said there wasn't going to be a team this year."

Bobbie shrugged and said dismissively, "Let's see if they can actually make it happen."

Isabel interrupted her, "Oh there is no doubt we are going to make it happen. What you all have to decide," she looked directly into each woman's eyes, "is whether you want your girls to be involved in such a positive experience. It's up to you."

She started to leave. That is when she realized that the whole café was absolutely still. Customers and staff alike, were riveted by the drama between Bobbie and herself. She wondered for a moment if she should take a bow. Instead, she gave what she considered the Queen Elizabeth royal wave and left.

She could feel how upset she was as she drove out of town. The sky was a brilliant blue with just a few wispy white clouds drifting across the horizon. She pulled off to a viewing area overlooking the ocean. She practiced deep breathing to calm down and watched a sailboat flying before the wind as it headed around the island. Isabel sat there taking in the view, listening to the soothing sound of the waves on the shore and savoring the fresh sea air. She was struck by how much her life had changed. She had people in her life who were once strangers and now were friends. She had a dog that she loved and she smiled thinking of Sadie. She reflected on her time in New York City and how pale and one-dimensional it seemed now. An empty sort of life she thought, that she had filled with movies, books, and daydreams.

A car pulled up behind her. "Damn," she muttered, irritated that someone had intruded upon this perfect moment.

She glanced in the rear view mirror and realized it was a police car. She saw Dave get out of the car, adjust his gun belt, and hat and walk towards her.

"Everything all right?" he called to her.

"Everything's fine," she replied. "Just enjoying the scenery."

"I heard there was a lively discussion at the cafe that you were part of."

"Lively discussion is right," she laughed. "I was so irritated afterwards I needed to calm down. Luckily, I found this beautiful spot."

He agreed. "It's spectacular, isn't it?"

They both stood quietly, taking in the gorgeous view.

"Do you spend much time on the water?" she asked him.

"I have a small sailboat. I go out whenever I can. But now that I'm chief of police I don't have much spare time."

"I've never been out on a sailboat," Isabel said thoughtfully. Then she stammered, "I didn't mean to sound like I was angling for a sailboat ride."

He smiled at her, "I didn't think you were."

"Let me ask you a serious question. Do you think the softball team is a good idea?"

"Yes, actually I do."

"Did you play sports as a kid?"

"Yes, Jason and I were on the same soccer team. "

There was a buzzing and he pulled out his phone. "I have to get this. I'm glad you're OK."

"Thank you for checking up on me."

He walked back to his squad car, got in and drove off.

CHAPTER 16

Heading home, Isabel stopped at her mailbox and pulled out an armful of mail. One piece in particular caught her eye. It was an envelope with a hand drawn image of a fox in a chef's outfit stirring a pot. "Daniel," she thought smiling. She quickly tore it open and saw he was back from his tour and inviting her to dinner. She felt a surge of excitement.

She went into the house and was surprised to see Sadie lying on the bed with Charlotte while Ellen was in her chair knitting. When Isabel walked in, Sadie immediately looked guilty, wagging her tail apologetically and burying her nose in the comforter.

"So how did Sadie end up on the bed?" Isabel asked, trying to sound stern but failing miserably.

Looking a little guilty herself, Ellen answered, "She just jumped up there and made herself at home. It seems to be helping Charlotte calm down."

Isabel nodded and stroked Sadie's head, "That's fine then, as long as she doesn't upset Charlotte."

"She's a great dog," said Charlotte.

Ellen added, "We were able to get some stretching exercises done without our usual tensions."

"Good."

"So," asked Ellen "how'd your day in town go?"

"Well," said Isabel, "I got some used softball equipment from Tom at the hardware store. He'd been going to give it all away to Goodwill as per instructions from Bobbie the mayor's wife."

"What!" exclaimed Ellen, "What do you mean?

" I found out that the mayor's wife has been trying to sabotage our efforts."

"You're kidding," fumed Ellen, "why would she do that?"

"Actually, that's a good question," said Isabel thoughtfully. "I haven't thought about why she's doing it."

Charlotte spoke up "She doesn't need a reason to try to ruin it for everyone. She is a bitch."

Isabel and Ellen cracked up and after a moment, Charlotte joined in with her raspy hoot.

"Charlotte," said Isabel. "Jason is pushing me to talk to Sam, the marina manager, about his baseball experience." She turned to Ellen and explained. "He played with the Red Sox." She sat on the edge of the bed. "Do you think I should talk to him? Especially given how rude I was to him when I first got here."

Charlotte said, "Absolutely talk to him. He's a good guy."

"OK. I'll do it then." Isabel said. "Anybody want tea?" Ellen said "I could use some. Let me give you a hand." She followed Isabel into the kitchen.

Isabel turned to her and asked. "I saw you nod your head when I asked Charlotte about Sam."

"Asking that question was perfect. Getting her to focus on something other than herself will help her keep her mental and emotional balance in her recovery."

"I'll keep that in mind" said Isabel. As Ellen left the kitchen, Isabel muttered to herself "Who knew getting involved with a girls' softball team would be this full of drama?"

Sadie came wandering out to the kitchen, checking to see if her food bowl had somehow miraculously been refilled. Isabel sat on the floor and Sadie climbed into her lap. Isabel hugged her and kissed her nose. She could feel her stress level dropping as she buried her face in Sadie's soft fur and closed her eyes.

Isabel texted Daniel and they arranged to have dinner in a few days. In the meantime, she was scouring the internet for softball videos. She looked up both good and bad coaching methods, taking copious notes and sharing them with Mary. No matter the weather the girls were good about showing up for practice. Isabel had them doing laps and tossing the ball back and forth as they ran.

But she knew she needed to teach them so much more. Between her and Mary they just weren't experienced enough to know what the next step was. She knew she had to talk to Sam. He was the person who would really be able to help them the most.

Annika and her sister Linnea arrived at practice one day with the Mighty Mice logo prototype. Everyone was excited to see it. Annika held it up covered with a cloth as Linnea made a drum roll sound with her hands. Annika whipped the cloth off to display the image of an adorable little girl mouse in a baseball uniform. There was total silence for a few minutes and Annika's face lost all color as she bit her lip. Suddenly the playfield erupted in cheers and applause. Isabel was stunned at how good the image was and thrilled that it would be on their uniforms. She managed to work her way to the sisters and gave them big hugs.

"Excellent work," she said. Though there were so many people surrounding Annika and Linnea, complimenting them, she thought her words had probably gotten swept away by the group's enthusiasm.

Pauline came up to Isabel. "I wanted to tell you…I can't believe how much more confidence Linnea has, just from the couple of practices she has been to. She used to spend all her time in her room playing computer games while Annika played outside. Because she was considered a geek at school she had a problem with kids bullying her. Now she's out in the sunshine, getting strong, making new friends. She's even going to have a sleepover later this week. I'm over the moon."

Isabel smiled at her, "I'm glad to hear that."

"Listen, I run a catering business and I was thinking of having a bake sale to benefit the team. We could sell cookies and cupcakes at each game."

"Great idea," said Isabel.

Mary came up to her after Pauline left. "What's a great idea?"

"She is going to help us raise money by donating baked goods."

"Oh, her cupcakes are scrumptious," said Mary, "we'll sell out in no time."

"Yeah and I'll probably be our biggest customer...in more ways than one."

She paused for a moment.

"Mary, I'm going to go down and talk with Sam at the marina and see if he can give us some guidance. I understand he was with the Red Sox."

"Yes," said Mary. "He could be a real help to us. I know the boys' team has approached him, and he turned them down. So, I wouldn't get your hopes up but definitely try. You never know."

The next day Isabel drove down to the marina. She could feel herself on edge as she parked. She was aware of how quiet it was. Normally there would be a number of weekend sailors working on their boats. But on this day there were very few in evidence. She didn't see Sam, so she decided to look in the Marina office.

She knocked on the door. "Is anybody there?"

A gruff voice answered, "What do you want?"

"Sam?" she asked, a little nervously.

He suddenly filled the doorway. Startled, Isabel took a step back and felt herself beginning to lose her balance. Frightened that she was about to fall into the water she started waving her arms in a desperate struggle to maintain her balance.

Strong hands reached out grabbed her arms and pulled her away from the edge of the dock. She stumbled forward and felt herself pressed up against his chest. She felt the warmth of his body against hers, the comforting embrace of his arms. His intoxicating scent reminded her of sunshine, sand, and ocean breezes. For a brief moment she let herself lean up against him and felt a shiver of excitement as she felt the tight hardness of his muscles underneath his T-shirt.

Embarrassed, she stepped back and looked up at him. She saw how the sunlight lit up his cheekbones and felt an overpowering urge to stroke his face. She took a deep breath and clasped her hands tightly together. She stammered, "I don't know if you remember me but I am Isabel. We met the day I arrived here."

"I know you," he said roughly.

Isabel's mouth was dry but she was determined to say what she had come to say. "I have always felt bad about the way I treated you when I first got here. When you put out your hand to help me off the boat and I refused to take it. I don't know if you remember that."

"Yes, I definitely remember that." He folded his arms.

She hesitated and then carried on. "Well, when you held out your hand, I guess all I saw was the oil and grease and not the kindness behind the gesture."

He looked at her surprised, "It takes a lot of guts to say that."

"You're not kidding. I feel like I'm going to throw up any moment now."

"I'd appreciate it if you didn't." He looked at her and smiled. His whole face lit up.

Staring back at him she felt like the sun had broken through the clouds.

There was a pause.

"Is that all you came to say?"

Still stunned by how attracted to Sam she was, Isabel tried to regain her focus. "No that's not all. I don't know if you are aware that we are trying to put together a girls' softball team."

He nodded. "I've heard."

"Well, Mary from the bookstore and I have taken on the role of coaches since Charlotte is getting over her broken leg. However, we have no idea what we're doing. We've checked Google and watched videos about softball, but that can only take us so far. We really need some personal on site guidance."

"No." He turned away from her and headed back into his office.

"But wait a minute…just think about all the little girls growing up on this island. Most of them have no chance of becoming part of a sports team. There are so many benefits that kind of comradery can bring. Now and later on in life… teamwork skills that would help them when they are ready to go out into the world."

"No." He said once again with a slight edge of exasperation coloring his words.

"But why?"

Sam slapped his hand down on a railing, making Isabel jump.

"I promised myself that I would never coach softball again. You don't know what the parents are like. It's really difficult to maintain a civil conversation with a father who's screaming at you two inches from your face to put his kid in or else." He picked up a shank of rope and began tying knots.

Isabel hesitated. "You won't be alone. I'll be there. Mary will be there, and probably Jason. So hopefully if anybody gets out of line, between the four of us, we should be able to take them down."

Sam laughed. "I'd like to see that."

Isabel continued, "We could really use a lesson on the basics. If you could come to just one rehearsal…"

He glanced at her, "It's called a practice."

She blushed in embarrassment, "See, we really need your help."

"I'll think about it and get back to you."

Isabel thought if there was one word or phrase, that would turn the tide in her direction. But she couldn't think of anything, and she didn't want to push. She gave him her number and said goodbye.

She thought about her encounter with Sam the whole way home. Remembering how it felt when she was pressed up against him sent shivers up her spine. She was turning into her driveway when her phone rang. She stopped the car and checked it. Sam had texted, "One time only."

Isabel let out a whoop and did a vigorous fist pump in the air. She texted back to Sam, "We meet tomorrow at 4 at Henderson Elementary. Do you want to join us there?"

"Tomorrow."

"Great. See you then."

As Isabel pulled up into her driveway, she saw a couple of cars already parked there. She recognized Jason's truck and Mary's coupe. She realized it didn't bother her at all anymore when people stopped by. She had thought it would be a big problem to have people coming to her house, interrupting whatever she was doing or not doing. But she realized that her need for peace, quiet and alone time just didn't seem as critical as it used to be.

As Isabel walked up the front steps she heard Sadie bark a greeting. From the noise she gathered everybody was in Charlotte's room. When she entered she spotted Sadie on the bed as usual, Charlotte was looking at her tablet. Ellen was knitting. Jason had his feet up on the bed and was reading a magazine. Mary was sewing an elf costume. They were chatting and laughing. When she walked into the room, they all looked at her expectantly.

"Well," asked Jason.

Isabel paused for dramatic effect and then she threw up her hands and shouted, "He's going to do it!"

"Oh my God," exclaimed Mary. "That's amazing."

"Full disclosure, he would only commit to coming to one practice."

Charlotte said, "Hey, we'll take what we can get."

Jason said. "Oh well done, Isabel." He gave her a high five.

Sadie barked a few times, joining in the celebration. Even Charlotte smiled.

Suddenly, Isabel heard a car horn. Startled she was about to go see who it was when Jason zoomed by her, "I've got it," he told her. Curious she followed him into the kitchen where he was paying a pizza delivery man.

"I got three, all different toppings," he grinned at her. "I figured we'd be either celebrating or commiserating." He carried the pizzas back to Charlotte's room. Isabel brought in paper plates, napkins, and cans of soda. The pizza smelled so heavenly; Isabel could feel her stomach beginning to rumble with hunger. She hadn't realized how hungry she was. She had been so nervous about meeting Sam that she hadn't had any breakfast.

Jason opened the boxes and everybody grabbed a piece or two of pizza.

Mary asked Isabel eagerly, "So what happened? Start at the beginning."

Isabel found herself blushing when she thought back to her meeting with Sam. She decided to judiciously share some of what happened.

"Before I do that," said Isabel, "I want to find out what the schedule is. Are all the games on the mainland? How do we get our girls there? How does this whole thing work?"

Mary responded, "Charlotte, do you have the notes from last year? We may already be grandfathered into this year's schedule. Can we take a look?"

Charlotte nodded. "Absolutely. It's all on my laptop which is still at my house. My house keys are over on the dresser there."

"Should we bring your laptop here?" Mary asked Charlotte, who nodded again.

"Let me give you my security code."

"Okay," said Isabel, "so that's what we're going to do. Go to Charlotte's house, get her laptop, bring it here, and see if we can pull up all that information."

"Sounds like a plan," said Charlotte, her hand resting lightly on Sadie's head.

CHAPTER 17

The next day Isabel picked Mary up and they drove to Charlotte's house. Isabel was a little disappointed that Mary had dressed in normal everyday clothes. She told her. "I rather expected you to be wearing a deerstalker hat and carrying a meerschaum pipe."

Mary burst out laughing. "You think Sherlock Holmes should be the order of the day today?"

Isabel grinned at her "I always enjoy seeing what you have decided to wear."

"I've never really explained it fully to anyone before why I dress up.." Mary pulled out a Kleenex and blew her nose.

Isabel glanced over at her. "Are you all right?"

Mary leaned her head against the window looking out at the landscape, "I grew up around here. My father left when I was five and I never really saw him again after that. My mother put herself through school and became a successful real estate agent. She wasn't home much. I spent a lot of time alone in my bedroom, pouring over books. I loved to read, but trying to understand what the words meant, how they fit together, was difficult for me. And then the teachers discovered that I had dyslexia. At that time there were no real programs to help people like me.

"I started dressing up when I was twelve. The whole idea was to escape my life. At first it was very basic, just cheap Halloween costumes I bought with my allowance. But then as I got older. I started learning how to sew. I began making more complicated outfits. Initially the kids at school made fun of me, but then some of them started asking me to make them dresses. I actually had a nice little business going making clothes for women on the island. Then, my mother died in a car accident a few years ago..."

Isabel started to say, "I'm sorry ..."

Mary held up her hand, stopping her. "That's not why I'm telling you this. She left me enough money that I was able to buy the store. I wanted to create a safe, nurturing space where I could let my imagination run riot. Where I could dress up and read stories for the kids who face the same challenges that I did. And for adults like me who never fit in. Who still think about escaping whether through sleeping their lives away or drugs, alcohol, or online." She glanced over at Isabel. "I don't do online. Too many scary people."

Isabel drove in silence for a few miles thinking about the reality of people's lives. "You see people's public facades and you think you know what is going on behind closed doors and it might not be even close to what is actually happening."

"People get very good at maintaining those façades," Mary said as they approached a small cottage perched atop a hill overlooking the water.

"There it is," Mary pointed. They turned into Charlotte's driveway.

Isabel turned to Mary, "Before we go in," Isabel bit her lip. "This is difficult to ask, but have you ever wanted to hurt yourself?"

Mary stared out of the windshield. "Yes. When I was younger. When I realized I was gay."

"Not now?" asked Isabel with a sense of urgency.

"No, not now." Mary opened the car door. She looked at Isabel with a watery smile. "You are the first person I've ever told I was gay."

Isabel debated whether to push it or not and decided not to. As she opened the door to Charlotte's house, she realized it was much like she imagined it would be. Very tidy, very neat. Everything stowed away carefully. They found her laptop in what was clearly a home office, checked around the house to make sure everything was off, locked up and left.

They rode in silence back to the bookstore.

As Mary was getting ready to get out of the car, Isabel reached over and put her hand on her arm, "Have you ever talked to anybody about any of this?"

Mary shook her head. "No, I haven't. We live in such a small community. And it can be pretty conservative. Things get around. I was afraid I'd lose the bookstore if people knew I was gay. I have enough problems with the book burners in the community."

"Do you have a significant other?" Isabel asked.

There was a long pause.

"No," Mary said in such a faint voice it was barely a whisper. "I figured I had to make a choice. Either stay on the island, my home for my whole life and run the bookstore of my dreams or leave. Take a chance that I could find someone to love out there... somewhere." She rubbed her hands over her face. "I was too afraid to try."

Isabel was stunned. "I can understand your concern to keep things private," she said. "But you have the right to be who you are and to have love in your life. I think from what you're saying that it might help you to talk to someone off island, someone on the mainland. I can do some research and find names for you."

Mary looked out the windshield for a long moment. "It might be time. I've been feeling down lately. Stuck. If you could do it in a way that nobody would know, I would be willing to try."

"Would you prefer a woman or a man?" asked Isabel.

"Oh, definitely a woman," answered Mary. She reached over and hugged Isabel, "Thank you."

When they got back to the house, Charlotte was napping so Isabel, Mary and Ellen went through Charlotte's laptop looking for files pertaining to the softball team. After about an hour, they were thinking about giving it up for the day when they came across a file simply titled "playtime."

"I think we've hit the mother lode," said Isabel, jotting down names and numbers of contacts.

"I'll call these people tomorrow and see if we can get a play schedule together."

Mary asked, "Is tomorrow when Sam is coming to practice?"

Isabel answered, "Allegedly."

Charlotte woke up and the women spent the next couple of hours putting together a playbook of team members and positions. They watched a couple of videos demonstrating training techniques for how to throw and catch a ball wearing a baseball glove.

"It will be a while before they get into learning the more advanced strategies and tactics for winning a ball game," said Charlotte. "Right now, we need to focus on the basics. Catching, throwing, batting, fielding. Once we feel like they've got those skills mastered, we can take the game to the next level."

Mary said, "I wonder if they would mind if we taped them at practice. We could look at the videos afterwards and see who needs to work on what skills."

"That's a great idea, Mary," exclaimed Isabel. Mary blushed at the compliment.

"You need to make sure they sign a release form," said Ellen. "So, nothing shows up on social media that you don't want to show up."

"There is no way we can police that stuff," said Charlotte. "Everybody's got a phone."

Mary added with a worried look, "We just always have to be aware that there are phones around us at all times."

"Unless..." Isabel thought through what she was about to suggest. "We have a basket and at the beginning of practice everyone's phone goes into the basket. It will help keep the kids' focus on the game."

Mary interjected, "As coaches, we are exempt, in case of an emergency we've got to have our phones available."

"Agreed."

Isabel looked around the room – Charlotte was nodding off and Sadie was fast asleep on the bed. Ellen was finishing up the scarf she was knitting and Mary was organizing her notes, muttering to herself. Isabel felt a sense of accomplishment that they were actually moving forward with the team. But even more than that, she felt a sense of connection. A sense of belonging that she had never really known before.

That night there was a strong thunderstorm with heavy downpours. Severe weather always made Isabel anxious and she found herself checking the radar updates throughout the night. She counted the minutes till the severe weather warning expired. She made sure her flashlights had fresh batteries and that Charlotte and Ellen had some. Then she drew her curtains to shut out the blinding flashes of lightning and ended up watching reality tv, old movies and listening to music. Anything to shut out the storm.

Near dawn the storm eased and a weary Isabel quietly went downstairs to make a cup of mint tea. A few minutes later, Sadie padded into the kitchen wagging her tail and yawning. She leaned against Isabel who rubbed her back as she waited for her tea. Once it was done steeping Isabel lay down on the couch and wrapped herself in a quilt.

"Come up, Sadie," she invited as the dog gracefully leaped up on the couch and lay down next to her. Isabel hugged her and feeling comforted, she drifted off.

After a few hours, Isabel slowly became aware of someone moving around the kitchen. She stretched, yawned, hugged Sadie, and kissed her on the nose. She got up, peeked in the kitchen, and saw Ellen was making breakfast. She didn't want to disturb her, so she put Sadie on a leash and went outside to walk around the house to see if there was any damage from the storm. Aside from a few downed branches, everything seemed fine. She went inside and found Ellen setting the table.

"Any damage?" asked Ellen.

"No, nothing other than a few broken branches."

The phone rang. It was Mary calling to check in with Isabel.

"We had a bit of flooding in the center of town, but nothing too bad. I sandbagged the front of the store so no water got in. I'm just going to get my assistant to open up and I'll be over at the practice field. Do you think Sam will come?"

"Who knows? Keep your fingers crossed."

Mary and Isabel got to the practice field at the same time and started setting up tables for snacks and refreshments. Team members began drifting in with their parents.

Isabel commented to Mary, "For the first time, I'm seeing some of the fathers show up at the practice, not just the mothers."

Mary looked at her very seriously, "Cupcakes, it's all about the cupcakes."

Isabel cracked up. "You mean Pauline is responsible for all of this?"

Mary responded with a smile, "That would be my guess."

Just then a truck pulled up and Jason and Sam got out. Sam walked over to the team while Jason headed for Isabel and Mary.

"Are you his chaperone," teased Isabel.

"I just thought it would be easier for everyone if I gave him a ride. That way you could be sure he was going to show up."

"Good move, Jason," approved Mary.

The parents had settled in their lawn chairs and were watching intently. Sam clapped his hands to get everyone's attention as he called all the girls around him.

"In case you don't know who I am, I'm Sam Martin. I manage the Mouse Island Marina. But years ago, I had another job. I was with the Red Sox. I played shortstop." There was an excited murmur among both parents and players. "I'm happy to help out. And I'd be glad to answer any questions you might have about baseball."

"Now," he said to the team, "Let's get going. First, I want you to run around the field three times. It's very muddy, so be careful where you place your feet. This is not about speed, it's about building stamina because that's what you're going to need to get through a full game. I'll run with you. And then we'll start doing some exercises to build up your basic skill levels."

Isabel was thrilled when she listened to him talking to the girls and then running around the field with them. It sounded like he was in it for the long haul. She looked over at Mary, who grinned back at her. They gave each other an air high five. Jason, who had wandered over to the cupcake table, came back with a few of the sweet treats on a plate.

He handed one to Isabel and one to Mary, then held up his cupcake, "A toast to our very own field of dreams, to the Mighty Mice team." He bumped his cupcake against theirs.

The practice went well, with Sam taking the team through a number of drills. He had them throw back and forth to each other as he assessed their throwing strength, and control. He took his time showing each girl how to hold and throw the ball properly. He also showed them how to prepare their gloves so they molded to and essentially became an extension of their hand.

He pulled Annika, Linnea, and Sophie out of line and said, "I want everyone to watch how they throw" and he had them throw back and forth to each other. "They're doing this absolutely correctly. This is how I want you all to look when you're throwing. Remember when you are trying to catch a ball to keep the glove in front of you." To the three girls, he said "I want you to mentor the other players. Help them to throw and catch the ball better when I'm not here." Sam handed out diagrams of exercises he wanted them to do, to strengthen their arms, legs, and shoulders and to build core strength. "I want you to do these every day, when you wake up in the morning and when you go to bed at night, just 10 to 15 minutes. "

He turned to the parents, "That's all I want them to do. Between 10 and 15 minutes. When they wake up in the morning, when they go to bed at night, no more. It needs to be slow and steady." He walked to the middle of the field and called all the girls to come into a big circle around him.

"Okay," he said, "Hands in."

The girls put their hands in and chanted along with him "1, 2, 3, Mighty Mice, Mighty Mice, Mighty Mice!"

Everyone clapped and cheered.

Sam started to walk over towards Isabel but was swarmed by parents and got caught up answering questions. Isabel noticed Bobbie hanging on his arm and she was surprised to feel a spark of jealousy. She wished she was comfortable doing something like that. Going up and putting her arm around him. Now, Bobbie was looking up into his face and smiling. Isabel turned away and focused on Mary and Jason.

Jason had his arm around a beautiful young woman in her twenties and was holding the hand of a small girl about six years old.

"Isabel, I want you to meet my sister Caitlin and her daughter Ayeesha." Isabel shook hands with Caitlin.

Ayeesha asked, "Is that your doggy," pointing at Sadie.

"Yes," said Isabel, "Would you like to meet her?"

"Can I?" She looked excitedly up at her mother who nodded. They walked over to meet Sadie.

Jason said in a low voice to Isabel, "She's struggling financially raising her daughter by herself. So, if you hear of any openings…"

"Of course, if I hear of anything," said Isabel.

"I try to help whenever I can," said Jason, "but I'm not making a lot of money either."

Finally, Sam got free of his admirers and walked over to Isabel, Mary and Jason. "How do you think it went?"

Mary, Jason, and Isabel all started talking at once and then began laughing. Sam looked at the three of them.

"I can't tell if that's a good sign or not," he said, smiling. "You know, I was dreading this. But I actually ended up enjoying myself. These kids are great. They're enthusiastic and really committed to playing. Plus, there are a couple of really talented kids on the team. The sisters, Linnea and Annika are terrific. Little Sophie is a total marvel as a pitcher."

Isabel watched his face carefully as she asked, "Did you have any problems with the parents badgering you?"

He hesitated, "Bobbie could be a challenge. She is convinced her daughter is Olympic team material."

"Is she?" worried Isabel.

"She's athletic though not especially talented. But Bobbie is already twisting the knife a bit…"

"What do you mean?" asked Jason.

"Well," answered Sam, running his hand through his thick salt and pepper hair, making it stand up on end. "She casually asked me if I need any repairs done on the marina. Reminding me, of course, that her husband owns the marina and by extension my livelihood."

"Yikes," said Isabel.

Jason muttered, "Welcome to the OK Corral."

"We'll just take it one step at a time," said Isabel. "And hopefully it won't come to anything."

"I hope not," said Sam.

"Well, here's the question of the day," said Isabel. "Are you going to come to the next rehearsal?"

"Only if you promise to stop calling it a rehearsal and call it by its proper name. A practice," Sam said. "Yes, I'll be at the next practice. But when is the first actual game?"

Mary answered. "We have three weeks to get ready."

"Well," said Sam. "Three weeks is three weeks. We'll see what we can do in that time."

"With your help," said Isabel. "At least we have the chance of being on somewhat of a level playing field."

The four of them started packing up everything and getting ready to leave.

Jason asked, "Sam, how about a little one-on-one?"

Sam paused and then said, "You know that sounds good. I could use the exercise."

"You have a ball?"

"I always have one in the car."

They walked over to the schoolyard's basketball hoops and started playing.

Isabel and Mary finished packing up and turned to say goodbye when they saw that the two men had stripped off their shirts.

Isabel muttered, "And that is a sight for sore eyes."

"The glare off those muscles is blinding," Mary agreed.

"Looks like they might be a while, can I give you a ride home?"

"Thanks," said Mary.

"I think I need a shower," said Isabel rolling her eyes at Mary who giggled.

CHAPTER 18

Isabel had taped some of the practice on her phone and was eager to show Charlotte and Ellen.

After she shared it with them, she asked somewhat anxiously, biting her lip. "What do you think?"

Charlotte, "They actually look pretty good."

Ellen nodded. "I think Sam is going to be your biggest asset. He's got them doing the right exercises and learning the correct basics."

Isabel thought for a moment, "Would you talk to the girls about what it's like to play ball in college?"

"Well, I didn't go very far with it. I became focused on biology and pre-med. But I would be glad to share my experience with them."

"Great." Isabel petted Sadie who had entered the room carrying one of her raggedy stuffed toys. "Sadie and I are going to dinner at Daniel's tonight. Do you need anything?"

"We're fine," said Ellen. "Have fun."

As Isabel started to leave the room, Charlotte grabbed her arm. Surprised, Isabel turned back to her.

153

"Sam is a great guy," Charlotte started to say.

"Yes he is," Isabel patted Charlotte's hand, "But I'm having dinner with Daniel." As she said that she wondered why she was having dinner with Daniel when actually it was Sam she was interested in.

Glancing at her watch. She realized she was running late. She quickly jumped in the shower. Then she pulled on a black turtleneck, black jeans and hiking boots and grabbed her brown leather jacket. She took a quick look at herself in the mirror and dusted her face with a powder foundation. She rarely wore makeup but she liked how this foundation made her face look and feel soft and smooth. She smiled thinking how even at sixy-one, putting on makeup made her feel like a grownup.

Isabel suddenly had a flash of memory like a stage curtain pulled aside for an instant. She remembered lying on her mother's bed before school and watching her sitting in front of the mirror carefully applying her Revlon makeup as she got ready for work. It was a daily ritual for her mom – foundation, eyebrow pencil and lipstick. When Isabel started wearing makeup she initially used the same brand and the same technique. It felt like a rite of passage into womanhood.

She took Sadie out for a quick turn about the enclosure to do her business and then got in the SUV. Isabel secured Sadie to the back seat harness and they drove over to Daniel's. He was waiting for them on his porch, sipping a cup of tea. He smiled and waved. Sadie, who had been sleepily gazing out the back window on their drive over, suddenly realized where she was and focused in on Daniel. She perked up and started wagging her tail excitedly. El

Daniel walked down to greet them, giving Isabel a quick welcoming hug and petting Sadie.

"I'm glad to see you, "he said. "I've been looking forward to our dinner all day. I was just sitting on the porch and watching the sun go down and having a fresh glass of homemade lemonade. Would you like a glass?"

"Sounds great," she said, smiling at him.

With Sadie stretched out between them, they sat quietly enjoying the beautiful view stretching down to the ocean. The tall trees, surrounding his house, swayed gently in the breeze.

"This is so peaceful," she said. "You must love it here."

Daniel looked thoughtful. "I do and I don't. I love the peace and quiet, that's for sure. I certainly get a lot of work done here. The wildlife and natural environment spark my creative juices. But... I am almost embarrassed to admit that I sometimes miss the sights and sounds and yes, even some of the smells of the big city

"You're kidding."

"No," he said. "I have terrible insomnia and I used to get up at dawn and walk for miles through the city. The most fantastic smells would waft out of the open doors of bakeries and restaurants as they got revved up for the day. I would get a steaming hot cup of coffee, the first brew of the day, from the local coffee shop, a New York Times from the newsstand on the corner, and donuts still warm from the bakery next to my apartment. There wasn't a better way to start the day."

"Sounds like something out of a movie. All I remember are the trash trucks waking me up at 5:00 in the morning. I never had to set my alarm."

Daniel laughed and stood up. "I'm going to start getting dinner ready."

"Is there anything I can do to help?"

"Sure, you can mash the potatoes."

"I hope you like them with plenty of butter and salt."

"Sounds great," said Daniel, starting to put dinner together. He handed Isabel an apron as she began to mash the potatoes. He commented, "I've been hearing some good things about your softball team. You've really made an impression on people."

Isabel looked at him, startled. "Really?"

"There is quite a lot of back and forth about the team on the island's Facebook page."

Isabel was so shocked she just stared at Daniel.

"You didn't know there was a Facebook page?"

"No, I had no idea."

"You have to be approved to join the group but since you live here now getting approval won't be an issue. You should definitely sign up."

"Can you show me?"

"Now?"

"Yes, now." She felt bad that she sounded so curt but she was really taken aback.

"OK, let me pull my laptop out."

She wondered why Mary or Jason hadn't said anything to her about this.

Daniel brought up the Facebook page. Isabel was startled to see all the pictures of the girls at practice, along with pictures of her, Mary, and Jason. Sam was in there too.

"So much for trying to keep a handle on our social media," she said.

Daniel started to respond when his phone rang. "Excuse me for a moment, I need to take this call." He disappeared into the other room.

Meanwhile, Isabel looked through the Facebook posts to see what people were saying about the team. She saw a number of very familiar names along with plenty of comments. Most of the comments were positive, some not so much. She was not surprised to see Bobbie front and center with the negative comments, casting doubt whether the team would ever even make it to a game.

Isabel could feel herself getting angry as she read some of them. She closed the laptop. She was determined not to get into a pissing contest with Bobbie, for her daughter's sake as well as the team's. But she knew she needed to find a way to diffuse her impact. Her negativity could chip away at the team's confidence.

Daniel came out of the other room scowling.

Isabel asked, "Is there something wrong?"

"Oh, it was just a frustrating phone call. I've got to make a business decision Not sure how I want to handle it." He looked at her and clearly made a conscious decision to lighten up the mood. "But now I need to let that go and just enjoy your company. I'm glad you're here." Daniel looked at her thoughtfully. "You are still upset about the Facebook page, aren't you?"

"I'm sorry," she said "You put together this lovely dinner and I'm being a pill. Thank you for doing this." Isabel impulsively hugged him. She started to pull away but he wrapped his arms around her and kissed her firmly on the mouth. She patted him on the back and moved away.

"Ah, the dreaded pat on the back," he said. "That means I've entered the friend zone."

Embarrassed, Isabel started to change the subject. Then decided she wanted to be more direct with him.

"Sorry, Daniel, I guess I was hoping things would change but I just don't feel that way about you. I want you to know your friendship is important to me and I hope we can continue to be friends but that's all."

"Is there someone else?"

"I don't know. There may be. I don't know at this point."

"OK. Thank you for being honest with me. I am definitely attracted to you but not to the point of trying to make this into something it is not."

"Do you want me to leave," she asked.

"No, I'd like you to stay and have dinner," he said. "I appreciate your friendship, too."

"So, what can I do to help?"

"Basically, it is all done," he said "Really we just have to set the table. Do you prefer inside or outside?"

Isabel said, "It's such a lovely night why don't we eat outside on the deck?"

"Sounds good to me." They set the table together, chatting companionably as they carried out dishes, glasses, silverware, and napkins. Daniel arranged a half-dozen beeswax candles in a circle on the table.

Isabel inhaled their delicate scent as she carefully lit them, "These are wonderful. You have to tell me where you got them."

"There is a couple who live nearby. They raise bees and hand pour their own candles." He turned down the outside lights.

Isabel took her seat with Sadie stretched out on the deck beside her. Daniel brought out a platter with the meatloaf surrounded by mountains of fluffy white mashed potatoes glistening with butter.

"Oh, I almost forgot," he said. Going back inside he emerged with a bowl of freshly picked green beans dotted with sprigs of dill. "From my garden," he explained.

Isabel took one of the green beans and sampled it, "Delicious," she pronounced. "So fresh and tender. I've been trying to get more into eating healthy. If I had this around I would definitely be eating more vegetables."

Daniel encouraged her. "There is nothing like picking your own vegetables for a meal. It gives you such a sense of satisfaction. I can show you how to start a garden if you haven't had one before."

"I did try growing some vegetables on my fire escape at my apartment in Manhattan but they didn't do too well. Not enough sunshine I think." She decided not to tell him she had managed to kill off all her vegetable plants in the matter of a week. Primarily because she forgot to water them.

They chatted and laughed and enjoyed the meal. Finally, it was time to say goodnight.

Daniel turned on the outside lights and walked her to the car.

He stood there waving as she drove down the driveway heading for home.

Isabel said to Sadie. "Well, that was interesting. Now I've got to deal with this Facebook thing." She was dreading having to confront Mary and Jason. She considered them friends and was worried about alienating them. But then she told herself, "I don't have to get into a confrontation with anybody. I just have to ask them why they didn't tell me." She felt herself let go of the tension she had been feeling since she found out about Facebook.

When she got back to the house, she found that Charlotte and Ellen had turned in for the night. She made herself a cup of mint tea and sat on the front steps of the house, Sadie nestled next to her. She gazed up at the stars and listened to the waves breaking on the shore. She felt perfectly content.

CHAPTER 19

The next morning dawned bright and clear. Isabel was in bed enjoying the morning, stretching lazily, and thinking about the day ahead. Suddenly, she heard a loud crash from downstairs. Startled, she sat up in bed. Then she heard Ellen shout her name.

She quickly put on her slippers and robe, calling, "I'm coming," as she hurried down the stairs.

"I'm in Charlotte's room," Ellen sounded stressed.

As Isabel came around the corner, she stopped in shock. Charlotte was on the floor with a bloody cut on her forehead. Her eyes were open, but Isabel was not quite sure how much she was seeing and taking in.

Ellen was on her knees gently cleaning Charlotte's wound. "As far as I can tell she was trying to get up and go to the bathroom by herself and she fell and hit her head. I'm not sure on what... I think it was the bed frame. But she needs to be checked out for a possible concussion."

"I am going to call for an ambulance," said Isabel.

At the word 'ambulance,' Charlotte got agitated, saying, "No…"

"I am sorry," Isabel said to Charlotte. "But that's a nasty cut on your head. You may need stitches."

Ellen nodded agreement. "Isabel, can you bring me a towel to put underneath her neck so she is more comfortable."

"Of course," Isabel grabbed a towel for her and then went out to call the ambulance. But as she walked out, she was thinking maybe she would call Dr. Mike first.

Once she explained the situation to Doctor Mike's nurse, she was put through immediately. Dr. Mike said he'd be there in 10 minutes. He also volunteered to call the ambulance crew and make sure they were on alert if Charlotte needed transport to the mainland.

Isabel draped a light blanket over Charlotte to keep her warm. And then put Sadie into the outside enclosure to keep her secure if people were going to be going in and out of the house.

As she was coming around the front of the house she heard a car horn and saw Dr. Mike pull into the driveway.

She waved at him. He got out of his vehicle and trotted over to her, his medical bag bumping against his leg, his stethoscope dangling around his neck.

She said, "Thank you for coming," and then surprised herself by tearing up.

He put his arm around her and said, "We'll take good care of her." Isabel nodded and showed him into Charlotte's room. He knelt down next to Charlotte and took her hand. She opened her eyes and looked over at him and smiled weakly. "Hello."

He brushed her hair off her forehead. "Hello there, slugger. I need to run a couple of tests to see how you're doing, but you look pretty good, so I'm not anticipating any problems. I just want to check and make sure that you don't have a concussion."

He checked her vitals took out his penlight and carefully noted the responsiveness, size and consistency of her pupils. Then he gently examined her cut.

"Well," he said, "it seems like the only thing I have to do is put a few stitches in and give you some antibiotics and pain killers. Now we'll get you back up in bed and get you relaxed. But I think that's all you're going to need." The three of them carefully helped Charlotte back into bed.

"No concussion?" asked Charlotte

"No concussion," he confirmed.

"That's a relief," said Isabel.

Ellen nodded agreement. Then asked Doctor Mike, "Is there anything we can do to make this room safer for her?"

He took his time checking the room before finally saying to the women. "Just make sure the bed frame is covered with a blanket or pillows or something so that she won't hit the metal if she falls." Then he turned to Charlotte, "And you, young lady, you are going to stay in this bed until other people are around to help you walk. You are not strong enough yet to walk by yourself. You will get hurt and end up going back into rehab. Do you understand me?" He looked at Charlotte sternly.

Clearly embarrassed, she nodded agreement.

After Dr. Mike stitched her up he gave medicine to Ellen, "Be very careful about the use of the painkillers," he warned her. "I'm only giving you a couple of pills. Don't use them if you don't have to. I don't want her to feel woozy and try to stand up and then fall because of that. Charlotte's a tough cookie. I don't think that wound is going to cause her too much discomfort."

He patted Charlotte on the arm affectionately. She smiled at him and then closed her eyes. Dr. Mike walked out with Isabel.

"Thank you," Isabel said.

He looked at her and said, "You know you're the best thing to happen to Charlotte." He leaned on the fender of his vehicle. "Here on the island, everybody knows her, but she lives by herself. Now she has you, Ellen, and Sadie. It's done wonders for her. I can see it in her eyes. She smiles. She laughs. Having you here has helped her recover much faster than I could have hoped for. I think she's going to make a complete recovery." He continued. "I know she can't live here forever and I wouldn't expect her to. But between this and the softball team coming back together, I think it has been immensely helpful for her." He got in his vehicle and drove off.

Isabel turned around and Ellen was standing there. For the moment, Isabel was somewhat taken aback. "Did you hear all of that," she asked Ellen.

"Yes," said Ellen. She paused for a moment. "But the reality is I can't stay here forever either."

Isabel felt like she'd been hit with a brick.

"What do you mean," she stuttered.

"As a traveling nurse I am constantly getting requests for my services. I have already been here longer than normal. I have to start thinking about my next move."

Isabel was stunned. "I guess I just took it for granted that you were going to stay until Charlotte got back on her feet. It feels like you are part of our little group here."

"But I'm not," said Ellen sharply. She took in a long calming beath. "Sorry, that came out wrong." She leaned against the door jamb. "I like it here, I really do. But I don't belong here. It's not my home."

"But could it be?"

Ellen gazed at her and then out over the island. "I need to move on. I'll help you set up the next visiting nurse." She turned and went inside.

Isabel stood there, stunned. It was the last thing she expected to hear. She really liked Ellen. She hadn't even considered that she was being offered other positions and would be wanting to take them. Of course it made sense. After all, Ellen was living in somebody else's house. Living out of a suitcase. With no real long term security. Isabel realized that she had not looked at the situation from Ellen's point of view at all.

Isabel brought Sadie into the house and the dog immediately jumped onto the bed with Charlotte. Charlotte smiled and put her arm around her. Ellen indicated she wanted to talk to Isabel for a moment in the kitchen.

"Just wanted to let you know," Ellen said. "She has her antibiotic on board and I just gave her an Advil so she'll probably sleep for a couple of hours. We'll need to keep a close watch on her, to make sure she doesn't try to stand up again on her own."

Isabel looked concerned. "I have softball practice in a couple of hours."

"That's OK, I can take care of it."

"Are you all right with that?"

"Yes, of course. That's my job." She turned and walked back inside.

Isabel stood there for a while, feeling like a wall had gone up between her and Ellen. She wasn't sure why it had happened or what to do about it.

She shook off the feeling of heaviness that was suddenly weighing her down and got ready to go to practice.

An hour later, Isabel was at the playfield getting things set up for the practice. Refreshments, Gatorade, water, snacks, and of course, cupcakes.

She got the basket out that they had taken to calling the cell phone jail. That was where all the team members would put their phones until after practice.

Isabel was pleased to see that more parents were turning out to watch their daughters play. It was actually becoming a regular event for the people of the island. She felt a sense of pride that she'd helped to make it happen.

She was still upset about the possibility of Ellen leaving but as she greeted the team and their family members she began to feel her spirits lift.

She saw Sam and Jason in an intense discussion by the snack table and headed in their direction. She figured they were probably discussing baseball strategies and tactics. But as she got closer, she realized they were arguing about which was the better cupcake. She started laughing. Both looked at her and grinned.

Isabel scanned the crowd and realized how much she was enjoying it. People were sitting in their chairs, chatting, and sharing photos. The girls were stretching and warming up. At the top of the hour, Sam clapped his hands and called for attention. The team lined up in front of him.

"Excellent!" he said. "Now, I want you to run around the field five times. Take it easy, but I want you to finish no matter how long it takes. Stamina. Remember, that's what we're building, stamina. I'll run with you."

He started off. The team dutifully followed behind him. At one point they were joined by a small Lab puppy who had escaped from his owners and was enjoying romping around the field with the kids. Isabel laughed as Pauline ran onto the field and herded the puppy back to her seat. She gave Pauline a thumbs up. Pauline waved to her and pointed to the puppy with a big smile.

Mary, who had been watching over the cell phone jail walked over to Isabel. "Cupcake?" she asked.

Realizing she hadn't had breakfast or lunch for that matter, Isabel gratefully accepted a chocolate chip cupcake with caramel icing. She took a big bite of the cupcake and sighed with pleasure.

"This is so good." She added, "You're not dressed up today?"

"After our conversation the other day," Mary said. "I thought that maybe I don't need to dress up all the time. Maybe it's time for me to try to be open and vulnerable to people around me, especially with people I trust. Like you, for instance."

Isabel was touched by Mary's comment. She reached over and gave her a hug. Mary stiffened a bit, then relaxed. She looked around to make sure there was nobody within ear shot.

"Have you had any luck finding the name of somebody on the mainland I could talk to?"

Isabel felt guilty that she hadn't done it yet. "No, I really haven't had time. No, that's not right, I should have made the time. I will make the time later today or tomorrow and get that name for you."

Mary and Isabel watched the practice together, clapping and cheering at the efforts of all the team members. Mary leaned over to Isabel, "I'm so impressed with their energy and enthusiasm. It's amazing."

Isabel nodded. "I really feel proud of them."

After a few moments, Isabel muttered to Mary, "Is Bobbie here?"

Mary looked at her curiously. "No, but Wendy is."

Isabel said quietly, "I don't trust Bobbie."

Mary nodded, "I don't blame you. I don't trust her

either actually. Though I don't know what she could do to derail the softball team."

"I saw some of the negative remarks she put on the Island Facebook page. Those comments could make it difficult for us to get local businesses to sponsor us."

"I don't know how much people pay attention to that."

"Speaking of which…," she turned to Mary directly. "Why didn't you tell me about the Facebook page. I had to learn about it from Daniel and then when I looked at it, I was shocked at all the pictures people been posting without me knowing anything about it."

Mary looked ashamed. She glanced down at the ground and back up at Isabel, "I'm so sorry. I should have told you a while ago. I wasn't sure you were really serious about getting involved with the team. And the longer I held off telling you about the Facebook page the harder it got to bring it up. I should tell you that people are also posting about the team on TikTok and Instagram. It's all positive things, very supportive. Bobbie is the only one who's put anything negative up there."

Isabel said, "I guess it just made me feel excluded like I wasn't part of the island community. It hurt."

Mary looked taken aback. "I guess if I look at it from that angle I can understand why it would feel hurtful. I'm so sorry. I didn't think of that. You are an important part of the community now."

"I hope so," said Isabel.

Sam and Jason brought out a large piece of cardboard that had the image of a six foot mouse in a baseball uniform painted on it. There were holes at different spots with numbers underneath them.

Sam called out. "OK, now for something completely different." He smiled, a warm engaging smile. "That was for those of you old enough to be fans of Monty Python's Flying Circus." A number of the watching parents laughed and applauded.

Sam said, "OK, this is to test your focus and your aim. Try to get the ball in the holes that have the highest scores underneath them. Then we are going to add everything up and the person who gets the top score is gonna win our special prize."

Annika called out, "The winner doesn't have to run around the bases for a week?" Everyone laughed at that.

Sam answered, "Well, that wasn't what I had in mind, but that's not a bad idea." He put a basket of softballs on the ground about eight feet back from the target. "Let's see what you can do at this distance." He started to toss a ball to Sophie when Wendy stepped in front of her, nudged her aside and caught the ball one-handed.

"I'll go first," she said.

Sam looked at Isabel. She nodded and stepped forward to make the official call. She said, "Sophie should go first since she's been pitching so well."

Wendy was not happy at that and pulled out her phone to call her mother.

Mary grabbed the cell phone jail basket and walked up to Wendy. "If you remember, you agreed, along with the rest of the team to put your phone in the basket during practice." She held the basket out for Wendy to put her phone in.

Wendy held on to it. "This sucks."

Mary said pleasantly, "When you make an agreement like that and you follow through, you show that you're someone who can be trusted."

Wendy dropped the ball on the ground. "My mother will have something to say about it."

Sam sighed. "I'm sure she will."

Mary held out the basket closer to Wendy who threw her phone into it. There was a sharp crack.

"Somebody will have to pay for that phone," said Isabel gazing directly at Wendy who had the good sense to look away.

"My mom will replace it," she said. "No problem."

"OK," said Sam. "Enough of the dramatics. Everybody line up in a row... Remember the highest score wins."

Sophie asked, "Overhand or underhand?"

"Whichever you're most comfortable with," Sam said, smiling at her. "The focus of this exercise is control."

Sophie stepped up to the line that Sam had drawn in the dirt, took a deep breath, and threw the ball with all her might. It sailed through the hole marked 50. Everyone cheered and clapped, and Sophie jumped up and down in excitement. The team's competitive nature came to the forefront as each one stepped up and tried to do better than the previous girl. Wendy was the last in line and hurled the ball at the hole marked 100. It completely missed the hole and bounced off the cardboard cutout.

Frustrated, she kicked at the dirt pelting her nearby teammates with pebbles and clumps of grass.

Isabel said, "You do that again and you are done for the day."

"Fine with me, I don't care about any stupid old softball team," she said.

"I'm sorry to hear that," Isabel responded. "If you don't want to play softball, that's fine, we have plenty of girls who would like to be on the team. We would miss you because you do bring something to the game. You're a talented player."

Wendy looked stunned. "Thank you," she stammered.

In the meantime, a shiny new Land Rover pulled into the parking lot. Bobbie got out. Immediately Wendy called out to her mother, "They want to kick me off the team, Mom."

Isabel saw Bobbie was building up a head of steam as she strode over to them. Her face was tightly drawn into a scowl and her hands were clenched.

She took a deep breath. She felt Sam take her hand and squeeze it.

At this point, Jason and Mary started herding the rest of the team members away from the increasingly uncomfortable discussion. They led them over to the refreshment table to make sure they were staying hydrated.

As Bobbie stomped over to Isabel, she put her hands up, forestalling a verbal attack. "We did not say that Wendy had to leave the team. She told us that she was not interested in playing softball."

Wendy looked at her mother and said, "They don't like me. They want me to leave. And they took my phone."

Bobbie got in Isabel's face, "You took my daughter's phone? That's her lifeline to me. You have no right..."

Isabel said, "Now wait a minute!"

"You...you don't even have children...what would you know about it," Bobbie snarled.

Isabel felt like she'd been slapped. She was determined not to let Bobbie see how much that cruel comment had affected her. She took a deep breath and said calmly and quietly, "The kids are all watching. And so are the parents. I suggest we deal with this elsewhere. Someplace private."

Bobbie looked around and saw how many parents were staring at them. She put her arm around her daughter and said quietly, "Your teammates are just jealous of you. If you really want to quit that's fine with me. If you want to quit because they're not treating you right that's another issue entirely and one we will have to take up with your father."

Isabel said, "If Wendy wants to play, we'd be glad to accommodate her and provide any extra training she might need."

Bobbie huffed at her, "She doesn't need any extra training, she's already a fantastic athlete."

Sam responded, "Being a fantastic athlete doesn't mean you're a good baseball player. You have to learn how to be a working part of a team."

Isabel added, "If Wendy is willing to try we'd certainly be glad to have her on the team."

Bobbie turned to her daughter, "It's up to you. Do you want to continue playing with these people?"

Wendy hesitated and looked around at everybody. Isabel stepped up next to her and put her arm around her. "What do you want to do?"

"I think I'd like to stay," said Wendy.

Sophie clapped and said enthusiastically, "Good choice!"

Her mother snorted loudly and muttered, "We'll see how this turns out." She stalked back to her car, pulled out her phone, got into the front seat and slammed the door shut.

As the team packed up their gear, the twins approached Isabel and said, "Ms. Isabel, can we ask you a question?"

"Of course you can." Isabel smiled down at the two girls, then looked up and saw their mother hovering anxiously not too far away.

"We looked it up online and then talked to our mom about it."

Isabel was confused, "Did I miss something?"

"We are both having trouble reading in school. I get really nervous and get my words all tangled up whenever I have to read in front of the class. My sister gets so scared she's actually thrown up, and now, the kids make fun of her."

"Oh dear," said Isabel "how can I help?"

The twins looked at each other, Cindi jumped in, "We found this article that reading to a dog has been proven to help students feel more confident about reading in front of people."

Sandi added, "And we were wondering if we could come over and read to Sadie sometime."

Isabel exclaimed, "I think that's an awesome idea. I'd love to have you come over and read to her and I think Sadie would love it too."

The twins smiled at each other and then hugged Isabel. She wrapped her arms around them and thought what adorable kids these were.

Cindi and Sandi saw their mother approaching and ran to her yelling in their excitement, "Mom, Mom, she said it would be OK. She said we could read to Sadie."

Isabel went over to their mom and said, "I think it's a great idea."

"Thank you so much. Kids have been making fun of them and now they don't want to go to school, which they used to love."

"Well, I think when they get more comfortable with Sadie, she might even like to go to school with them as a special guest."

The two girls looked at each other wide eyed with excitement.

Their mother laughed as they grabbed her hands and swung around her in circles.

CHAPTER 20

Isabel was tired at the end of practice. It had been an emotionally draining day, especially given the confrontation with Bobbie. Then the workout had been followed by an hour-long meeting with Mary and Jason to discuss the coming week's schedule. Sam had asked if he could sit in. It was a productive meeting but tiring. She was wiped out and found herself fighting a bad headache. She headed home, looking forward to a quiet evening with Charlotte, Ellen and of course, Sadie. She smiled when she pictured the twins reading to Sadie.

She pulled up to the house and found it quiet as she walked inside and dropped her purse on the kitchen table. She peeked in Charlotte's room. Charlotte was sleeping, Sadie curled up by her side, and Ellen was knitting. She looked up and smiled.

"How did practice go," she asked.

Isabel tousled Sadie's fur as she answered. "It went very well. I think the girls are really coming together as a team and supporting each other instead of just trying to score points."

Ellen said, "That sounds great." She put down her knitting. "Can we talk in the kitchen for a few minutes?"

"Sure."

They walked into the kitchen together with Sadie trailing behind them.

"Would you like a cup of tea?" Isabel asked.

"Actually, mint tea would be great if you have any," said Ellen.

"Coming right up," Isabel turned on the stove and heated up water in the tea kettle. Then she carefully measured out two teaspoons of organic green tea leaves into a tea pot, poured the now hot water over the leaves and set the timer for four minutes. She got out two porcelain teacups, poured honey into a little pitcher shaped like a bee that she had picked up at a yard sale and placed two small spoons next to each cup.

"I feel like I'm at the Queen's tea party at Buckingham Palace," Ellen commented, " You know you've really gotten me hooked on tea."

"Thanks to Mary," said Isabel. "She's the one who taught me how to make tea so that it actually tastes good."

They laughed and walked outside to enjoy their tea on the porch. Once they were settled, Isabel asked Ellen, "So what did you want to talk about?"

Ellen took a sip of her tea, "I've taken another nursing position."

"Oh no," said Isabel. Her heart sank, "That's so fast."

"It starts in two weeks in Milwaukee. I need to leave here in a few days to get myself settled out there."

"I've been dreading this day. Are you sure you don't want to stay any longer?"

Ellen looked at her and smiled sadly. "It's time for me to go. Charlotte's doing very well. She doesn't need a full time nurse anymore. Having a nurse come in for a couple of hours a day to check her out, make sure everything is OK and do physical therapy with her is all she needs at this point."

"It's so hard to see you go. I really enjoyed you being here."

"I feel the same way. You've made me feel at home. But now it's time to take the necessary steps to advance my career. This is a really good opportunity."

Isabel sighed, "Well, if you ever need anything, like a recommendation."

Ellen reached over and clasped Isabel's hands. "Thank you so much. That means a lot." She paused. "I do have a serious question for you."

Isabel was getting distracted by Sadie whining from inside the house. She tried to focus on what Ellen was saying.

Ellen continued, "You know, Mary and I have become good friends over the past few weeks."

Isabel suddenly focused sharply on Ellen.

"I'm going to ask Mary to come out and visit me."

Isabel picked her next words carefully. "I think she would like that. When I've seen the two of you together I get the sense of a strong connection."

Do you really think so?" asked Ellen eagerly.

At this point Sadie gave up on whining and started barking in short staccato bursts. Isabel and Ellen looked at each other and laughed.

"It's her dinnertime and she doesn't want us to forget that. You know she's going to miss you too."

Ellen nodded, "She's a great dog," and headed into the house.

Suddenly a fox screamed into the night, making Isabel jump. "Sounds close by," she muttered to Sadie, making sure she had a firm grip on Sadie's leash as she headed inside.

A few days later, Isabel, Charlotte, Mary, and Sadie drove Ellen down to the ferry landing. There were plenty of tears and hugs as she boarded the ferry and left the island.

CHAPTER 21

Not long after Ellen left, in the middle of the night, Isabel found herself tossing and turning. She finally got up to make some toast and tea. She was puttering around the kitchen when she started hearing rumblings of thunder.

"That must be what woke me up," she thought as she checked her phone for weather reports and saw there was a severe storm warning for the area. Immediately she tensed up. She went to check on Charlotte who was fast asleep. Sadie was in the bed beside her and thumped her tail when Isabel came in. She drew the curtains closed to make sure the lightning wouldn't disturb Charlotte, patted Sadie and went back into the kitchen to finish making her cup of tea. She was pouring it when there was a brilliant flash of lightning and a huge crack of thunder. Isabel was so startled she dropped her cup in the sink and broke it.

"Shit."

Isabel carefully scooped up the pieces as she heard the wind pick up in ferocity and start howling around the house. Then the rain started, coming down in torrents so loud Isabel could barely hear herself think. She went back in to check on Charlotte. Isabel saw that she was wearing noise canceling headphones. No wonder the violent storm wasn't bothering her.

Another flash of lightning momentarily blinded Isabel and she tensed waiting for what she expected to be a deafening crash of thunder. Isabel found herself so anxious she was actually shaking. She tried deep breathing but she wasn't able to focus enough to calm down. She decided to make sure she had available flashlights in every room. She had just finished this task when the lights flickered and went out. Luckily, she had put a headlamp on and went into Charlotte's room to check on her. She was still sleeping and Isabel envied her that peaceful rest.

Sadie, however, was not sleeping peacefully. She was standing up on Charlotte's bed whining quietly and shivering. Isabel gathered her up in a blanket and carried her into the living room. She pulled all the shades tightly closed and curled up with Sadie on the couch.

Isabel checked the radar every few minutes. "It's right over the island now," she murmured into Sadie's ear, getting a warm lick on the face in response. "Here's hoping it will be moving on soon."

Suddenly there was a blinding flash of lightning and Isabel felt a tremendous crash of thunder literally shake the house. A loud siren blared and Isabel held on to Sadie as she checked her phone. She thought it might be a tornado warning but as she scanned through her weather alerts she saw the siren was something different.

She checked on Charlotte who was now awake and looking around in some confusion. "What was that siren?"

Isabel said, "I have no idea, I thought you might know."

"You might want to call the Police Department and see what's going on."

"I don't want to bother them if they're in the middle of something."

"Listen," said Charlotte "in all the years I've lived here I don't remember hearing a siren like that. I don't know what it means and I think we should find out."

Isabel hesitated then called the Mouse Island Police Department. The officer who answered told her there was a big fire on Main Street. He got her name and address and assured her the fire was not anywhere near her residence.

"That's a relief," Isabel told Charlotte, jumping as another crack of thunder startled her. "But I want to make sure Mary's okay." She called and got a busy signal. She sent a text asking Mary if she was all right and to let her know. A few minutes later her phone beeped and she saw a text from Mary that she was okay. She sighed with relief.

The women decided to play a game of Scrabble by flashlight since sleep seemed out of the question with the storm raging overhead. With Ellen gone, it was one of the first times Isabel and Charlotte had spent time alone together and Isabel was relieved that they got along so well.

Finally, a few hours later, the storm let up and moved offshore. The women were exhausted. Isabel said goodnight, stumbled into the living room, lay down on the couch with Sadie and quickly fell asleep.

Early the next morning Isabel's phone rang. The moment Isabel picked it up she knew something was terribly wrong.

Mary was sobbing and almost incoherent. "There was a big fire last night. Tom's house was struck by lightning and destroyed."

"Oh my God." Isabel thought back to how kind Tom had been to her since her arrival on the island. "Is he all right?"

Mary sniffled into the phone. "They have him in a trauma unit on the mainland." She blew her nose. "Apparently Tom made it out of the house but then he realized that Harry was still inside. He heard him bark and he went back in for him. Part of the house collapsed on top of them. The firefighters got them out but they're badly burned." Mary choked back tears, "Nobody knows if either one of them will survive."

"Oh my God, Mary."

Charlotte limped in from her bedroom on her crutches and stared at Isabel. She mouthed, "What's wrong?"

Isabel held up her hand, "Where is Harry?"

"With Dr. Debbie. They don't think he'll make it."

"I am so sorry, Mary," repeated Isabel.

Mary whispered hoarsely, "I have to go now," and disconnected.

Charlotte asked Isabel, "What's going on? I heard you mention Tom and Harry."

Isabel said, "Lightning hit Tom's house last night and set it on fire. Tom went back in to get Harry and they both ended up badly burned."

Charlotte gasped, "Oh no…" her eyes filled with tears. Her voice broke and she stumbled back into her bedroom. Isabel could hear her sobbing as if her heart was broken.

"It probably is," thought Isabel.

A little later, Isabel called Dr. Debbie about Harry. A vet tech answered the phone and placed her on hold. Finally, the vet came to the phone. When she heard who it was she heaved a huge sigh and said, "I guess you want to find out about Harry."

"I hope I'm not bothering you.

"No, you're not bothering me. We've been getting a lot of calls to find out how he is. The answer to that is he's not doing very well. He inhaled a lot of smoke during the fire and has considerable burns over a large percentage of his body. We are worried about infection but he is also in a lot of pain. Add to that, he has rarely if ever been separated from Tom and you can understand how enormously stressed he is."

"Is there a point," asked Isabel trying to tread carefully, "when it becomes too much for him and you need to take other measures to bring him comfort?"

"Are you asking me whether I can put him down or not?" asked the doctor. "Right now, I don't have a signed DNR from Tom. But if it gets too bad for Harry I can and will make that decision and take the consequences of it. I don't want to see Harry in terrible pain either."

"Is there anything I can do to help?"

"Well, I'd rather he was not here at the hospital. It's an added stressor for him. He hears a lot of noise he's not used to. He hears a lot of voices he doesn't know. Doors are slamming, dogs are barking, cats are meowing and we currently have a very large and very vocal parrot here as a patient."

"We can take him. Sadie will be fine with him and might even be a comfort to him."

There was a long pause.

"He needs a calm, nurturing place to rest and heal. But you know he's an old guy and he's very ill. I'm not sure he's going to survive this." The doctor lowered her voice. "You would need to be prepared for that."

"I understand. Tom was very kind to me when I arrived on the island and I would like to help out any way I can. I'll ask Jason to pick Harry up and bring him here, along with whatever medicine he needs and his food."

"That would be really helpful," said Dr. Debbie. "Give me until 5 to get everything ready. I'll include some pain medicine. You can grind that up and mix it with peanut butter."

A few hours later Jason arrived at Isabel's house. She walked out to his truck to see if she could help. She was startled to see that he had been crying. He quickly wiped his face with his sleeve.

"I've known Harry since he was a puppy. When I was a kid, we would go on adventures together around the island. It's really hard to see him right now...he is in such a lot of pain and I just don't know..." his voice trailed off.

Isabel put her arm around Jason and together they walked over to his truck. Harry was lying on a dog bed covered in bandages with a blanket draped lightly over him. Isabel was horrified at how bad he looked. So much of his skin was bright red raw and glistening with antibiotic gel. She wanted to touch him but wasn't sure she could even do that without causing him more pain. She felt helpless.

"How do we get him inside, so we don't hurt him in any way?"

"I borrowed a gurney from the Doc. We can put his bed on that and carry him in."

They carefully and slowly carried him into the house and brought him into the living room. Balanced on her crutches, Charlotte held the door for them, letting out a gasp when she saw the extent of Harry's injuries. They put blankets on the floor to keep him comfy and then started a fire in the fireplace to warm the room. Sadie came over to say hi. Isabel held on to her collar, unsure how she would react to such a severely injured dog .

Sadie very gently approached Harry, nudging his muzzle softly. He whined and Isabel prepared to pull Sadie back. But then Harry shifted, groaning slightly, and reached out to sniff Sadie. Isabel let go of Sadie's collar as Sadie nuzzled him again and laid down next to his bed. Teary eyed, Charlotte sat down heavily on a nearby chair.

Isabel heard a car pull up and she hurried to see who it was before they came in and disturbed Harry. Mary waved to her and came up the steps.

She asked quietly, "How is he?"

Isabel shook her head. Mary came in and knelt by Harry. He opened his eyes but then closed them again and heaved a deep sigh. There was a rattle in his breath they all heard. They looked at each other.

"Not good," said Charlotte.

"Anybody know how Tom is doing?" asked Isabel.

Mary answered, "He's not doing well. Like Harry he inhaled a lot of smoke. He has burns over a third of his body."

Isabel sharply drew in a breath. "He must be in such pain."

"They have him in an induced coma," said Mary.

There was silence as they all looked at Harry. Mary and Jason leaned in close to him and took turns telling him what a good dog he was. Harry stretched out, grunting with pain, and licked Jason's hand.

Jason asked Isabel, "Do you want me to stay here for the night?"

"Thanks for offering but I don't think so." She said, "I'll sleep in here tonight in case...in case he needs anything. And Charlotte is here."

Charlotte leaned forward on her chair, "Anything I can do to help."

A few hours later, Mary and Jason left for the evening. Isabel made some soup for dinner though neither she nor Charlotte had much of an appetite. Both of them sat by Harry's side and talked to him. Sadie was a constant companion, staying by his bed and occasionally nuzzling him with her nose. Finally, Charlotte turned in and Isabel stretched out on the couch.

Around 2 am, the night was absolutely still when all of a sudden a blood-curdling cry split the quiet. Isabel sat bolt upright, confused, half asleep, trying to figure out what was going on.

CHAPTER 22

There was another cry and she realized it was a dog howling. She looked over at Harry's bed and saw he wasn't in it. Startled, she disentangled herself from her blanket and stumbled to her feet.

Charlotte appeared in the doorway wearing her PJ's and robe. She looked exhausted as she said to Isabel, "He's in the kitchen."

Isabel looked at her and saw the tears. "Is he...?"

Her voice cracking, Charlotte said "Not yet but I think soon."

Isabel walked into the kitchen. The first thing she saw was Harry lying stretched out on the floor, Sadie sitting next to him. She looked at Isabel and howled again. Harry's breathing was rapid and shallow. Isabel could hear a crackling with every breath he took.

"Oh no, no, no..." said Isabel as she knelt beside him. She put her hand on his chest. She looked into his eyes and saw the spark of life dimming as they began to glaze over. She turned to Charlotte. "I think he is going. If you want to say "goodbye..."

Charlotte asked, "Can you help me get down next to him?" Isabel brought a chair over and held on to Charlotte's crutches as she slowly eased down onto the floor next to Harry. Charlotte gently stroked his head as tears ran down her cheeks. She told him what a good dog he was and that she loved him. She leaned over to kiss him. As she pulled back she realized he had stopped breathing. She looked at Isabel, who was at Harry's other side.

"He's gone," she said.

Sadie whimpered, a sad, lonely sound.

Isabel and Charlotte gently placed a blanket over Harry.

"I don't know why it feels important that he not be cold even though he's gone," said Isabel.

Charlotte said, in a voice thick with tears, "I want him to be comfortable." They put their arms around each other. Sadie pushed her nose in between the two of them making them both tear up even more.

The phone rang. Isabel and Charlotte looked at each other. Isabel hesitated then took the call. She held the phone up so Charlotte could hear.

It was Dr. Mike. "I want to let you know that Tom died a short while ago."

"Harry died a few minutes ago," Isabel told the doctor.

Dr. Mike took a deep breath, "It doesn't surprise me that they would pass away very close to each other. They were deeply connected. Do you want me to call Dr. Debbie?"

"No, we'll take care of it," said Isabel.

A knock at the door startled both Isabel and Charlotte. A man's voice said, "It's me, Jason."

Isabel got up and unlocked the door.

Jason entered and saw Harry on the floor. Sadie started to trot over to him but Isabel grabbed her by the collar and held her back to give Jason some time with Harry. Jason sank to his knees and put his arms around Harry and held him tight.

"I just had a feeling he was going to go tonight. I thought I'd drive by but wasn't going to bother you if your lights were off." After a while he sat back and gently wrapped Harry in his blanket, laying him back in his bed. Isabel let go of Sadie who went over to Jason and climbed in his lap. Jason wrapped his arms around her and buried his face in her fur.

Isabel reluctantly picked up her phone and called Dr. Debbie's emergency number.

The phone rang for a long time and Isabel was just about to disconnect when the doctor picked up.

"It's Isabel, Dr. Debbie."

"How's our boy?" Dr. Debbie sounded exhausted; her voice raspy.

"I'm sorry to tell you that Harry died about 20 minutes ago. From what I understand, Tom passed away about an hour earlier."

There was a long silence.

"Dr. Debbie? Doctor?"

"I'm here. Just trying to take it all in."

"It's been a rough night."

"I can send someone out first thing in the morning to pick up Harry."

"Then what?"

"Frankly, I don't know. I'll have to talk to some people and see what arrangements have been made for them. I imagine they'll be buried together but I really don't know at this point. I wanted to thank you so much for taking care of Harry…"

"What a minute Doc…" Jason, who had been listening along with Charlotte to Isabel's one sided conversation, broke in.

"It's Jason, Dr. Debbie. I can bring him into the office tomorrow morning.

"Well," said the vet, "that certainly would be a help. This has been such a sad night. Thank you."

They disconnected.

Isabel turned to Jason "Is it all right if I come with you? I don't know if you wanted to be alone with him or if you're OK with me riding in with you."

Jason said "I'm fine with that. Charlotte, do you want to come too?"

"My cast would be difficult to fit in the truck," she said "I'll stay here. What I would like is to have our own memorial here this morning. To share some stories about Tom and Harry."

"Great idea," said Isabel and Jason at the same time.

They heard a car drive up to the house.

"Who could that be?" asked Isabel.

She went to the door and was greatly surprised to see Sam standing there. He looked embarrassed. "Mind if I come in," he asked.

"Of course, come in." Isabel felt flustered.

"I understand you are taking care of Harry," he said.

There was an awkward silence following his question.

"I'm sorry Sam, Harry passed away a short time ago." Isabel hesitated. "We were just going to hold a small memorial for him...sharing some stories about Harry and Tom..." she trailed off.

"Do you mind if I join you?"

"Of course," Charlotte nudged Isabel who seemed momentarily frozen by Sam's presence.

Isabel gave a start. "Let's move into the living room. I'll put some tea on."

Jason gently cradled Harry in his arms and carried him into the other room, setting him into his bed and carefully tucking the blanket around him. Sam passed close behind Isabel as she poured hot water into the teapot.

He murmured in her ear, "Thank you very much for letting me be part of this."

"I'm glad you are here," Isabel blushed.

He looked at her for a moment and then nodded and went into the living room. Charlotte was leaning on her crutches, propped up against the wall, watching this unexpected interaction.

She said to Isabel, "You know, he really is a good guy," and then went into the living room and settled on the couch.

Sadie jumped up on the couch next to Charlotte and leaned against her. Charlotte smiled and put her arm around Sadie.

"You're such a comfort," she said to her. Sadie rubbed her face against Charlotte's, sniffing gently at the tear stains.

Isabel walked in with a tray of teacups and cookies and passed them around.

Jason cleared his throat, "I'll begin…"

CHAPTER 23

Later that morning Jason and Isabel drove Harry to the vet's office. It was a sad moment when they handed Harry over to Dr. Debbie. She thanked them and took Harry into the back room. It was very quiet in the vet's office except for some muted sobs from the staff. Jason glanced over at Isabel arching his eyebrows in an unspoken question. She nodded and they left quietly.

Once they were outside, Isabel asked Jason, "Do you mind if we stop by Mary's for a few minutes I just want to see if she's OK. I haven't been able to reach her by phone."

"Sure, I'll go get a cup of coffee and a croissant at the café and I'll try to find out what the funeral arrangements are."

Isabel nodded.

Jason dropped her off at the bookstore where Isabel saw a large 'sorry we're closed' sign in the window. She peered in the window but the lights were off and she couldn't see inside. She stepped back to look up at Mary's apartment over the store. She thought she saw movement and waved.

She heard the clatter of shoes on the stairs and Mary abruptly opened the door. Isabel was taken aback at how bad Mary looked. Her skin looked ashen, almost grey, her face gaunt, with dark bags under her eyes.

"Have you had anything to eat today?"

Mary shook her head, "No appetite."

Isabel put her arm around Mary and walked her back inside. "Do you have any food…any eggs or bread for toast?"

"I think I have a couple of eggs."

Mary led the way upstairs and Isabel tried to hide her disbelief at the condition of the apartment. Clothes and papers were tossed everywhere, while mugs half-filled with drinks dotted every flat surface.

"Why don't you sit down and I'll make you some breakfast?" she suggested.

Mary nodded listlessly and slumped down on her sofa.

Isabel mixed eggs and milk into a bowl and whisked it briskly. She added butter to a frying pan and turned the heat up. Once the butter started sizzling she swiftly poured the egg mixture in and swirled it around. She looked over at Mary and saw she had her eyes closed. There was a shawl on the floor next to her chair. Isabel reached over and gently draped it around Mary.

While she was waiting for the eggs to cook, she picked up the tissues that were strewn everywhere and tossed them in the trash. Then she gathered up discarded clothing and towels and put them in a hamper she found in the laundry room.

Coming back out to the kitchen, she popped some oatmeal bread in the toaster and looked in the fridge for juice. No juice but there was marmalade. She cleared off the small dining room table and set it for two. Just then the doorbell rang. Peering down the stairs she saw Jason through the window. She jogged down the stairs to let him in.

Jason nodded his head toward the upstairs, "How's she doing?"

Isabel sighed, "She looks absolutely wiped out. I'm making her some eggs right now... oops," she raced back up the stairs to keep the eggs from burning.

Jason saw Mary fast asleep in the chair, "Is there anything I can get at the store... any food or drink or maybe a treat like some Häagen-Dazs?"

Isabel said, "If you could get some prepared meals at the cafe so she doesn't need to cook from scratch."

Jason said, "I'll be back in just a little bit. If you think of something call me."

Isabel followed him to the front door, "You're such a sweet guy." He blushed. She laughed and patted him on the arm.

She put the meal out on the table and opened the shades so that warm sunshine filled the room, gradually washing over Mary and waking her up. She stretched gingerly and then spotted Isabel.

"You must really have needed that nap," said Isabel, smiling at her.

"I guess I did," acknowledged Mary ruefully. "How long was I out for?"

"Just long enough for me to whip up some eggs."

"That sounds great," sighed Mary. "I haven't had the energy to cook since..." she shrugged her shoulders.

"Well, breakfast is ready. Have a seat."

Mary sank into a chair. "This looks wonderful."

Isabel put napkins next to their plates and then sat down herself.

"So how are you doing, Mary?"

Mary pushed her eggs around the plate for a few moments. Then she looked up at Isabel. "I don't handle things like this very well." She smiled ruefully. "I imagine you've guessed that already."

Isabel leaned forward, "Do you want to talk about it?"

Mary sighed and gazed out the window, "After my father left, my mother was busy getting her business off the ground. She used to drop me off at Tom's hardware store and I would sit there behind the counter and do my homework. Tom would talk about what I had learned that day to everyone who came into the store."

She took a bite of her egg. "Sometimes Tom would get a call from my mom and she would ask Tom and his wife to babysit me for the night. His wife was warm and caring. She gave the best hugs." She closed her eyes for a moment. "They made such a fuss over me...I felt cherished. That is the only word for it."

"What happened?"

"She died of cancer about 10 years ago. I didn't think Tom would survive that loss but he did. I wasn't sure

I would…" She sighed heavily. "I just feel like I've lost so much."

There was a banging on Mary's front door.

"That must be Jason," said Isabel getting to her feet and heading down the stairs.

He had his arms full, along with a bakery bag clenched in his teeth.

"Wow, this smells fabulous," she said.

"Sunrise Bakery down by the pier."

"I'll have to try it."

Jason and Isabel spent the rest of the afternoon with Mary. They knew they couldn't erase the pain of Tom's passing, but at least they could let Mary know that she was not alone.

"One thing we have to talk about," said Isabel, "is the softball schedule."

"Without question, we need to delay it," said Mary firmly. Isabel and Jason nodded in agreement.

Isabel said "I'll send out a notice explaining our decision. What do you think? Two weeks off?"

Jason nodded, "I think that is a reasonable amount of time for people to deal with their grief."

"What do you think, Mary," asked Isabel. "Services will be this weekend."

Mary teared up again, but then said in a small voice, "Okay." When they left, after a group hug, Mary looked a little less drained.

A few days later, Sam called Isabel to ask if she wanted to grab some lunch.

"I don't have much of an appetite," she said, "but I need to get something in my stomach to get some energy back. I feel pretty wiped out after everything that's happened. I've only been here a short while and I feel devastated. I can't imagine how those of you who've been here for much longer… how you must feel about this horrible loss."

"It's been a traumatic time for everyone on the island, that's for sure," Sam agreed. "I'll pick you up in half an hour."

As they drove along, Isabel felt refreshed by the spectacular ocean views. She closed her eyes and felt the warmth of the sun on her face. She had not been paying much attention to where they were going but now she saw they were pulling into the marina parking lot. She looked at Sam questioningly.

"The sandwiches from the food truck that parks at the marina at lunchtime are really good. Plus I thought it would be beneficial to get out on the water for a little bit… to try and ease some of this sadness."

Isabel immediately started feeling anxious.

"I've never been sailing before."

"Never?" Sam asked surprised.

"No."

"And yet you chose to come live on an island?"

"Yeah, I guess that doesn't make much sense when you look at it like that." She looked at him and smiled. "Though I did go out on a swan boat in Central Park once. Does that count?"

Sam laughed.

With food bags in hand, He led her down the ramp to where a few larger sailboats were moored. At the very end was a sleek fifty-six foot sailboat gleaming in the sunshine.

"Wow," she said. "Who owns that one, it's a beauty."

"Glad you like it," he said, "that is my boat."

"Really?"

He helped her step on board. "It was my Dad's for many years. Then when he passed away, the marina where she was stored just let her go to pieces. I ended up moving her here to the island and refurbishing her. This is my home now. I live on board."

"Well, she's gorgeous," said Isabel.

"Let me take the groceries down into the galley and we will get underway."

Isabel could feel her anxiety quickly rising at his words. "You are sure it's safe?"

He reached under one of the seats, pulled out a life vest and handed it to her. "I checked the weather and the forecast is for a totally calm day. No bad weather whatsoever. As you can see, the water is totally smooth. But why don't you put this on? We'll only stay out for a little bit. If you feel the slightest ill at ease we'll immediately come back in."

Sam switched the engine on and walked around the boat catching the mooring ropes thrown by a marina worker and tying them off.

He got behind the wheel, engaged the motor and smoothly steered the boat out of the marina. Isabel sat on the cushioned seat near him and watched intently as they headed out to sea. She shivered a bit and he handed her a warm woolen blanket. Gratefully she pulled it tight around her.

Other than the slight chill in the air, it was a beautiful sunny day. Sam pointed out a pod of seals swimming next to them. Isabel was delighted and took out her phone to snap some shots. Sam asked if she was comfortable with him putting up some sails. She hesitated and then said, "Yes."

He raised the mainsail and turned off the engine. The wind caught the sail lifting the boat up and away. Isabel caught her breath as the boat picked up speed, slicing cleanly through the water and heeling slightly to starboard. "It is so quiet," she said to Sam.

He smiled at her, "Yes, that is what I love about sailing. When I'm going with the wind it feels like I'm flying."

"You know it's funny," she said, "being out here on the water, I kind of feel like Tom and Harry are here with us. In spirit."

Sam nodded, "I often feel like my parents are with me when I'm on the boat. I find the thought of their presence here gives me comfort."

She looked at him curiously "Did you ever have Tom and Harry actually on the boat for a sail?"

"Yes I did. Harry loved the water and on nice days when it was warmer and he was younger, he delighted in leaping off the boat and swimming around for a while," Sam's voice trailed off as he glanced over at a nearby boat. "What are they doing?"

A small motorboat with three people on board was drifting with the current. One of the passengers was waving to them and pointing to the shore lined with jagged rocks.

"They look like they have lost power. We need to get them away from those rocks," muttered Sam. He turned to Isabel, "Could you hold the steering wheel for me? Keep it steady?"

Isabel started to protest but stopped when she recognized the urgency of Sam's actions. He moved quickly to drop the main sail then came back to take over the wheel. He started the engine and steered carefully over to the floundering boat.

"My God," said Isabel, "That's Annika, Linnea and Sophie on that boat."

"Take the wheel again and keep it steady while I throw them some rope."

Sam tossed the rope to Annika, who quickly tied it off as Sam put down fenders to protect his boat. He pulled the motorboat closer and helped the girls climb over into his boat. The moment the girl saw Isabel they rushed over and gave her a big group hug.

"I am so glad you saw us there," Linnea explained to Sam. "I don't know what happened. The engine just died. I don't know if there's water in it or what but we didn't have any way of controlling the boat. If you hadn't seen us we could have been drifting for hours."

"Either that," said Sam," or you would have hit those rocks and sunk."

Linnea paled.

"It's so good to see you," said Annika. "We've been missing our softball practices. But since it was so horrible what happened to Tom and Harry…" She teared up.

Linnea came over and hugged her sister murmuring encouraging words in her ear. Annika gulped and nodded, glancing over at Sam. She asked, "Sam, can I use your bathroom?"

"Of course, it's just below to your right."

"Thank you."

A few minutes later, she came back on deck. "I saw the picture of you in your Red Sox uniform, she said to Sam.

Sam smiled at her, "Oh yes?"

"I think that's the game our dad took us to. It was a great game. No wonder you called your boat "The Sure Hitter."

Sam grinned at her and nodded, "It was a great game. Okay, we're coming into the marina now. Make sure you're holding on to something in case we encounter wake. There are signs everywhere telling people to slow down but you know people are people and some of them like to zoom in showing off their big boats…" he shrugged.

They tied the sailboat up at its mooring, secured the little motorboat, put things away and generally cleaned up. Then made sure the girls had a ride home.

Sam said, "Isabel, thank you for helping me."

"Of course. Thank you for my first sailboat ride.

"Do you think you would ever want to learn how to sail."

She hesitated. "I don't know. The ocean scares me. I know that probably sounds silly…"

"Not all. As beautiful as the ocean is you've still got to respect it and understand how powerful it is."

Isabel looked at him surprised. "I thought you would tell me my anxiety was all in my head. That there was nothing to worry about."

"But that would be sugar coating it. The reality is you do have to be careful, take sailing lessons so you know what you are doing and always, always, keep an eye on the weather."

Sam stepped up onto the dock and reached down to help Isabel. As Isabel started to step up she stumbled and fell against him. He put his arms around her and held her tight against him. Suddenly he kissed her softly on the lips. She felt an electric shock go through her. He kissed her again firmer this time with more passion. She wrapped her arms around him and kissed him deeply, savoring the feel of his mouth on hers.

"I can taste the ocean on your lips," she murmured.

He rubbed his face softly against hers. She shivered at how masculine he felt with his 5 o'clock shadow rasping against her skin. She snuggled her face into his neck inhaling his scent - a wonderful combination of soap, shampoo and sunscreen.

Isabel heard a noise behind her and slowly, regretfully disengaged. She couldn't help thinking how much more intense this kiss was than when Daniel had kissed her. She was trembling all over and wanted the kiss to go on forever.

"Do you hear something?" she asked him.

"I believe we have an audience," he murmured into her ear.

As they turned around, Isabel realized that fellow boat owners and marina workers were applauding. She glanced over at Sam and was amused to see that he was blushing.

He drove her back to her house where Sadie was inside barking and jumping up at the screen door, anxious to greet them. As Isabel started to get out of the vehicle Sam put his hand on her arm and pulled her over towards him. He wrapped his arms around her and kissed her tenderly. She kissed him back, snuggling against him, feeling his warmth.

"I really like spending time with you. I'll be in touch."

"I'll look forward to it," she murmured. As she walked towards the house, Isabel thought to herself, "I'll look forward to it? What is this, a job interview? Maybe I should tell him where I plan to be in five years." She turned and waved to him. Suddenly on impulse she blew him a kiss. She saw his face light up as he smiled brightly in her direction. He waved to her as he carefully backed his vehicle down the driveway.

She unlocked the door and Sadie greeted her rapturously. She walked into the living room and found Charlotte painting on an easel in front of the window.

Charlotte glanced around at her. "I hope you don't mind. I was getting kind of bored so I thought I'd try to find something to keep me occupied. I used to paint quite a bit years ago."

"I bought those paints to see if I could make it a hobby of it," Isabel knelt on the floor to play with Sadie. "But there has been so much happening that I haven't had a chance. I'm glad someone is getting use out of them."

She got up and walked over to Charlotte and took a peek at her work. "Wow, you are really good!"

"Do you think so?" Charlotte looked hesitantly at Isabel.

It was the first time Isabel had seen Charlote unsure of herself and it surprised her.

Isabel laughed, "Whenever I've tried to draw a tree it ended up looking like a fat cucumber with thorns. Your trees look like trees. When you are done with that picture I would like to hang it here, in the living room. But only if you sign it."

"That would be great. It would be like your own art gallery." Charlotte started to paint again, then stopped. "By the way, I got a call today from Dr. Mike about a part-time nurse."

"You seem to be getting around pretty well on your crutches. Do you think you still need a nurse?"

"Yes, I would feel safer with a nurse around. She would be here only part of the day."

"Then go ahead and schedule her. Just remember to tell her we have a dog."

"WE have a dog," muttered Charlotte looking down at Sadie and ruffling her fur. Sadie rolled on her back for a belly rub which Charlotte obliged.

"I'm thinking some sort of comfort food would be good for tonight," Isabel said.

Charlotte nodded happily, "I have a great mac and cheese recipe from my mother."

"That sounds good, let's get started. Tell me what I need to do."

At that moment there was a knock on the door. Charlotte and Isabel looked at each other in surprise.

"Were you expecting anyone?" asked Isabel.

"No."

Isabel went to see who it was. When she saw it was Mary she opened the door wide, "Come in, come in."

Mary fidgeted a bit, "I hope it's OK I just stopped by like this."

"But of course, you're always welcome here."

"Thank you. I wanted to run something by you."

Her curiosity piqued; Isabel led Mary into the living room where Charlotte was just cleaning up. Mary hesitated when she saw Charlotte but then shook it off and decided to say what she needed to say no matter who was there.

"You know what I've told you about my background."

"Yes," said Isabel sitting down on the couch. Sadie jumped up next to her and curled into a ball. Sensing this was a serious talk, Charlotte maneuvered herself into a chair and settled in.

Mary took a deep breath. "Ellen has invited me to come out and visit."

"Well, that sounds nice," said Charlotte, looking a little confused.

Isabel looked at Charlotte and then at Mary. There was an awkward moment of silence.

Mary sighed and turned to Charlotte, "I'm gay."

Charlotte nodded, "I thought that was the situation but figured it was none of my business."

Mary looked at her in astonishment.

"I take it you are interested in Ellen?" Charlotte asked.

Mary was still stunned by Charlotte's nonchalant response.

"Yes, yes I am," she said stumbling over the words.

"I like Ellen," said Charlotte. "She's an excellent nurse. She took good care of me."

Isabel nodded in agreement.

"We spent quite a bit of time together and found out we had a lot in common, "Mary said.

Isabel said. "I think you should go. It's time for you to live your own life, to see what is out there beyond this island."

Mary looked at the floor for a moment. "Do you really think I should go?" she asked uncertainly.

"Yes," Isabel and Charlotte chorused in unison.

"There is one problem... the bookstore." Mary took Isabel's hands in hers. "I'd like you to run the store while I'm gone. It would just be for a month."

Isabel sat there shocked. "I love the store but I don't have any experience in retail."

"I wouldn't be leaving for a week or so. I can give you a tutorial in running the store," Mary leaned forward, looking intensely at Isabel.

"I need to think about it. That's a lot of responsibility."

"Of course," Mary stood up.

"Would you like to stay for dinner?"

"Thanks, but I have some errands to run. I have to find someone to stay in my apartment and water my plants."

"You might want to talk to Jason," Charlotte said.

Isabel was surprised, "Really?"

"He's been looking for a place."

"I didn't know that. I think that'd be a great idea for him to take the apartment. Even if it's just temporary. Talk to him," Isabel urged Mary.

"I will. In the meantime, I'll call you in a couple of days to see where you are with things."

Mary said goodbye and left.

Isabel and Charlotte looked at each other.

"Wow, her energy level is off the charts. It's like she has a new lease on life," Charlotte said.

"She looks better than she has for quite a while," Isabel agreed.

It was time to make dinner. Charlotte perched on a chair at the kitchen table and began grating a block of cheddar cheese. Sadie lay on the floor nearby, keeping an eye open for falling pieces of cheese.

After dinner, Isabel and Charlotte played a rousing game of Scrabble, with Isabel winning one game and Charlotte pulling ahead and winning two. Sadie was stretched out at their feet, occasionally twitching and growling softly in her sleep.

"You ever wonder what she dreams about?" asked Charlotte.

"I'm thinking squirrels."

As Isabel put the game away, she asked, "Did you ever think about moving off the island?"

"At one time I seriously considered it. I was very much in love with a man who lived here on the island. He had a charter business too. That's how we met. We were together for five years. But then he decided to follow his dreams and move to L.A. to be a screenwriter. He asked me to go with him but I couldn't do it. I wasn't ready to leave everything I knew on the chance that we might be able to make it work. I was settled here. I knew who I was. I had a successful charter business." She sighed and looked out the window. "Mostly, I was afraid. My parents had a troubled marriage and a worse divorce. They kept dragging each other into court. I never saw them happy and in love. If they couldn't make it work, how could I?"

There was a long silence.

Isabel asked gently, "What happened?"

"He moved to L.A. We talked every day. Two weeks after he got there he was carjacked. He handed over his keys but the bastard shot him anyway. He died there in the street. Alone...." Her voice caught on a half-sob. "It has been eight years but it still hurts like hell."

Isabel put her arms around her. Sadie whined and moved closer.

"I'm so sorry, Charlotte. I had no idea."

"It's all right. I need to talk about what happened. I've kept it closed up inside me for too long. He was a good man and he deserves to be remembered."

"What was his name?" Isabel asked.

"Patrick."

"Tell me about him, if you are okay with doing that."

Charlotte let out a long sigh, "I think I'd like to…but not tonight. I am too tired right now." She struggled to stand up, but Isabel stopped her.

"You know you are such a good artist. Have you ever thought of painting a portrait of him?"

Charlotte turned and stared at Isabel "I think I would like to do that… to recognize his impact on the world because he did have an impact. Maybe it would help me heal a bit too."

CHAPTER 24

The next morning Isabel introduced Charlotte to the hoarder's closet.

"I've been meaning to go through the drawers in here to see if I could find out something about the woman who left me the house."

Charlotte's eyes lit up. "Ohh, a real-life mystery."

"You are definitely more excited about it than I am. Wait till you see the room. It is crammed full of broken down furniture."

Charlotte leaned forward eagerly on her crutches, "So when do we get started?"

Isabel laughed, "I should have guessed how much you would be up for this given all the mysteries by your bedside."

Isabel got into the necessary body slamming position, counted to three and pushed against the door. Taken off guard, Charlotte hooted with laughter as the door gave way.

"Voila," Isabel announced,

"Wow, you weren't kidding," said Charlotte as Isabel carefully cleared a path for her into the room.

The women made their way to the far side of the room where a large dresser leaned crookedly against the wall. They scoured the drawers finding a treasure trove of mildewed clothing and worn-down shoes. Isabel had brought a couple of large garbage bags with her, along with rubber gloves, and they stuffed the contents of the dresser into them.

"Let's try this trunk," Isabel tugged on the latch and it fell apart in her hand.

"Looks like just more clothes," Charlotte's earlier enthusiasm had waned a bit.

"We'll go through this trunk and then have lunch," Isabel suggested.

Charlotte had already started pawing through the clothes. "Look!"

Isabel excitedly peered into the trunk and saw that there were quite a few inches of papers at the bottom of the trunk. "I'm going to put all these papers into a trash bag. We can spread them out on the table and take our time looking through them."

Isabel dragged a couple of the trash bags down the steps. She put the one filled with papers in the living room. She and Charlotte spread all the papers out on the table and began slowly going through them and organizing them into piles.

"It looks like it's mostly utility bills from ten years ago. We should probably shred them. Unfortunately, I don't have a shredder…"

"I have one at my house."

"You up for taking a ride?"

"Oh yes. I'd like to see how my house is doing."

"I think we could all use some fresh air. Let's take Sadie with us."

Isabel, Charlotte, and Sadie piled into Isabel's SUV. The road to Charlotte's house fronted the ocean and they stopped at an overlook to take in the spectacular view. It was a windy day and whitecapped waves were breaking dramatically on the beach.

"Wow, how beautiful," Isabel said.

"Beautiful but wicked cold," Charlotte shivered. "Turn right here."

Isabel slowed down as she drove up the driveway. She could see a small herd of deer ahead browsing on the bushes around Charlotte's house.

"Damn, they are such beautiful creatures. I just wish they wouldn't eat my plants."

Sadie, who had been sleeping in the back seat, suddenly roused, spotted the deer, and started barking wildly. A small fawn near the car gave a startled bleat, leaped in the air, and raced to its mother's side. The mother deer looked over at the car and its passengers and gave what looked remarkably like a disinterested shrug. The whole herd turned and watched as Isabel maneuvered past them and parked in front of Charlotte's house. Slowly, the deer moved away from the house and into the nearby woods.

Isabel helped Charlotte into the house and then went back for Sadie who was excitedly bouncing around in the back of the car leaving nose prints on all the windows. Isabel snapped the leash to the dog's collar and stroked Sadie's head, "Yes, you're coming too." Sadie immediately calmed down and walked quietly next to her.

As they walked through the house, Charlotte motioned, "Can you help me in the kitchen, the window's stuck." The women each grabbed an end of the window sash and with much grunting hoisted it up. Immediately an ocean breeze swept in and freshened the room.

"That's better," Charlotte noted with satisfaction.

"Do you want me to go around and open all the windows?"

"That would be great, and you can let Sadie off-leash."

Sadie immediately raced around the house sniffing out all the new scents. Charlotte made her way into the cozy living room and settled on the couch with a heavy sigh. Isabel watched her with concern.

"How are you doing?"

"This cast is so heavy it takes a lot out of me."

"Well, just sit and relax for a bit."

Charlotte nodded, leaned back against the couch cushions, and closed her eyes. Isabel watched her for a moment or two then quietly left the room. After thoroughly exploring the house, Sadie returned to the living room, gracefully leaped up on the couch next to Charlotte and snuggled in close. Half awake, Charotte smiled faintly and draped her hand over the dog's back.

Isabel came down the stairs carrying a bulky shredder and took it out to the car. She leveraged it into the trunk securing it with two bungee cords. She went around the house closing all the windows, finally ending up in the living room. She said Charlotte's name softly and put her hand on her shoulder. Charlotte opened her eyes, reached for her crutches and slowly stood up with Isabel's help.

"Before we go...Isabel, can you go upstairs to my bedroom and get the photograph that is on my dresser?"

"Is that...?"

"Yes, that is Patrick."

Isabel found the photograph which captured a handsome man in his early fifties standing on a sun drenched beach. His eyes were alight with love and affection as he looked towards the camera.

"Wow, what a nice looking man," thought Isabel. He reminded her of Sam and that thought led to the next... that it was time to give him a call and invite him to dinner or at least lunch. She wrapped the picture carefully in a hand towel and went back downstairs.

As Isabel drove away from Charlotte's house, she glanced in the rearview mirror and saw the herd of deer slowly emerge from the woods and resume their browsing.

When they got back to Isabel's house, an exhausted Charlotte went straight to bed while Isabel made chicken noodle soup for dinner. As that was simmering she started going through the papers they had uncovered. She felt a sense of accomplishment as she fed several bagsful of ancient utility bills into the shredder.

Isabel checked on Charlotte to see if she wanted dinner. But she was fast asleep and Isabel decided not to wake her.

She poured herself a bowl of soup and was going to sit on the porch and eat it with only Sadie for company when she had the idea to text Sam and invite him to join her.

He immediately responded saying he was on his way. Isabel was both excited and nervous about seeing him. She ran upstairs, stripping off her clothes as she raced through her bedroom and into the bathroom. She felt grimy from all the cleaning she and Charlotte had done but she didn't have time for a shower. "What the hell did I just do?" She thought as she washed her face, combed her hair, put on some powder foundation and blush, along with lipstick and mascara. As she was hurriedly pulling on a sweatshirt and a pair of jeans fresh from the dryer, she heard Sam's SUV. She trotted down the stairs just as Sadie started to bark.

"Hush, no bark." Isabel closed the door to Charlotte's room.

Sadie wagged her tail and whined softly. Isabel gave her a quick hug. As she opened the front door she felt her face flush. "Hi Sam, glad you could make it," she stammered.

"Something smells great," he said smiling warmly at her. "Thanks for inviting me."

She handed him a bowl of soup and a homemade roll, cautioning, "Careful, it's hot."

They sat on the porch, sipping their soup, nibbling on the roll, and chatting comfortably. Sam talked about the marina and its erstwhile sailors. One story in particular sent Isabel into gales of laughter. A newbie sailor with no boating experience had just purchased an ultra-expensive yacht when he left his mooring to go for an early morning sail. Unfortunately, he didn't clear the anchor or the mooring lines. As he sailed out of the marina he was blissfully unaware that his anchor had snagged a bunch of smaller boats and he was towing them behind him. A number of the boats had owners aboard who were abruptly awakened to find themselves heading out to sea. Luckily, Sam was up early to do some fishing and spotted what was happening. He immediately got on the radio to alert everybody to what was going on. A worker at the marina jumped into a Boston whaler and headed off the parade of boats. No one was hurt and no boats were damaged. The newbie who caused all this did a lot of damage control by buying everybody drinks at the bar that night and telling the story over and over again till everybody was in hysterics.

"Was anybody upset?" asked Isabel curiously.

Sam laughed. "Sailors love to spin tales and this is a great one for them to dine out on especially if they're part of the story."

They sat quietly for a while enjoying their soup and listening to the bullfrogs, spring peepers and the occasional owl hooting in the distance.

"Was it hard for you to adjust to being here on the island after living in Boston and playing on a professional baseball team? I mean that's a lot of attention, a lot of glitz and glamour... do you miss it?"

"At times. I still watch the games and find it hard not to get emotionally involved in what's happening on the field. But that was another time, another life. I'm pretty happy with where I am now."

"Have you ever been married?"

"Yes. But it turns out she had her eye on someone higher in the organization, someone who was better off than me. She ended up married to a VP in upper management. But then he dropped her for someone younger." Sam looked over at her and smiled ruefully. "What goes around comes around."

"Sometimes, but not always." said Isabel.

"Sounds like there's a story there." He gazed at her. "What about you? Have you ever been married?"

"No. I never really found anybody that I wanted to spend the rest of my life with. Plus, I'm pretty much of an introvert."

"You're kidding. I would never have used that word to describe you."

"Why do you say that?"

"Well, look at the facts. You've only lived here a couple of months and you've gotten yourself involved with rescuing an injured dog, coaching a girls' softball team, helping out a woman who needs a place to stay, and to top it all off, you may be taking over the bookstore while Mary is away. That is a pretty remarkable list of accomplishments."

Isabel scrunched her face up. "I guess. I don't think of myself as being outgoing but I have to say in the few months I've lived here, I have gotten to know more people than in all the years I lived in New York City."

"Well, I'm very glad you decided to move to the island." Sam reached over and gently placed his hands on either side of her face. He brushed his lips across her neck and then firmly kissed her on the lips. She kissed him back wrapping her arms around him tightly. He slid his hands under her sweatshirt and she felt shivers run up and down her spine at the heat of his hands on her naked skin. She pressed against him sensing his growing excitement.

Thwack! The sound of a screen door slamming made Isabel jump.

"Oh, am I disturbing you?" Charlotte grinned at both of them.

Sam moved back, away from Isabel, "How are you feeling, Charlotte?"

"Getting there. Thanks, Sam."

Isabel stood up, "There is chicken noodle soup for dinner if you are hungry."

"That would be great!" Charlotte leaned against the screen door and when Sam wasn't looking mouthed the words, "I'm sorry," to Isabel.

"No worries," Isabel mouthed back and gave a discrete thumbs up.

Off in the distance a fox screamed. Sadie tensed and Sam casually took hold of her harness. Isabel clipped on a lead and led Sadie back into the house.

"Where do you want to eat your soup?" she asked Charlotte.

"The living room would be fine."

Sam stood up and stretched. "I think it's time for me to say goodnight, and head home. It was a great dinner. Thanks, Isabel." He kissed her cheek and sauntered down

221

the porch steps and over to his SUV. He honked as he drove down the driveway.

Isabel let out a long sigh. She glanced over at Charlotte and saw that she was stifling laughter.

"What? What?"

"You should have seen how guilty you looked when I interrupted you." She cracked up.

"We were just kissing…" Isabel was aware her face was now bright red. "Though I have to say he does make me feel like a teenager again."

"Well, you can tell me all about it while I have some soup. Which smells fabulous by the way."

Later that night, Isabel was lying in bed drowsily glancing through YouTube videos of baby foxes when her phone vibrated. She picked it up and then nearly dropped it as she realized the text was from Daniel.

He was back on the island after being away for weeks on an exhibition tour of art galleries across the country. Isabel stared at the text wondering what she should do. She thought she had made it clear to Daniel that she wasn't interested in him romantically though she enjoyed his company. It was Sam whose very presence thrilled her.

She decided to send back a non-committal message. "Glad to hear you're back on the island. I hope the tour went well for you."

He sent back a text with a big question mark. A few minutes later he followed with a text saying "I know it's been a while and I've been out of touch. I'm sorry about that. I'd like to make up for lost time."

Isabel felt a little irritated at his assumption that she had just been waiting for him to come back, like he was expecting to start something up again the moment he got back to the island. "That is not going to happen," she thought.

"Why don't you come over for dinner Friday night, I'm having a couple of people over to say goodbye to Mary before she leaves on a trip."

There was a long pause. "I was kind of hoping for private time with you."

"We'll have time to talk."

"Good. What can I bring?"

"If you want to bring wine or cider that'd be great."

"Will do, see you then."

Isabel disconnected. She snuggled into her quilt and pillows and quickly fell asleep.

The next morning, she was making breakfast and chatting with Charlotte who was sipping her morning tea when the doorbell rang. Sadie barked and started excitedly jumping around.

"What is going on with you, you silly dog?" Isabel glanced out the door and then opened it wide.

"Come in, come in," she said, "It's so good to see you."

The entire girls' softball team walked into the kitchen, followed by a lot of hugging, and barking, which was contributed by Sadie.

"I'm glad to see you girls here. I know how hard it's been. But I think we're ready to get back on schedule."

"That's what we were hoping for," said Sophie. "It has been a rough time on the island. A lot of the grownups seem to have disappeared."

"They didn't really disappear, Sophie," said Linnea with a sharp look at her. "There's just lot of sadness going around."

"I'll tell you what," said Isabel "why don't I make scrambled eggs and toast and we can talk this out."

Just then, Jason drove up. "Come on in," Isabel said, "We're having a party."

She heard another vehicle pull up outside and was startled to see Sam in the doorway. She opened the door for him as another car pulled in. Mary got out of the car and waved to her.

The kitchen was now overflowing with unexpected guests. Sadie was thrilled, working her way through the crowd, getting hug after hug.

Isabel had to raise her voice to be heard over the excited hubbub. "Why don't we go into the living room where there's actually room to sit."

Jason came over and hugged her. "I haven't seen you for so long. I've been on a construction job on the mainland. Good money but I missed the island and everybody here."

Sam said, "Glad to see you, Jason," patting his back as he helped Charlotte into the living room. Sadie followed them and the decibel level increased exponentially.

Isabel went to the doorway, "Does anyone want something to eat?"

The girls immediately put their hands up. They looked around and started giggling.

"I'll make some eggs and toast."

Mary and Sam followed her into the kitchen, "Can we help?"

"Yes, that would be great. If you could break the eggs and mix them. And Sam if you could get the paper cups out of that cabinet there and pour some orange juice. We don't have a lot so if you could limit how much…"

"Got it," said Sam.

Mary cornered Isabel. "We need to talk about the store."

"Yes we do. I'm sorry I have been procrastinating on this."

Mary smiled sympathetically at her, "I know, it's a big decision."

"Yes, it is," Isabel was relieved that Mary understood. "But you are right, we do have to talk this through."

She put a big pan of scrambled eggs on the kitchen table along with a platter of buttered toast and cups of orange juice. Then she called the girls in and handed them paper plates, napkins, and utensils. Returning to the living room, the girls found places to sit either on chairs, cushions or on the floor. Isabel banished Sadie to the kitchen after she spotted her sneaking a piece of toast off Annika's plate.

Isabel stood in the midst of the team and caught up with what they were doing. She hadn't realized how much she missed being around them and their positive energy. She loved hearing their laughter as they good-naturedly teased each other.

"A penny for your thoughts." Isabel looked around and saw that Sam had come to stand beside her.

"I was just thinking how much I'm enjoying having everyone here."

He put his arm around her waist and muttered in her ear, "Now, that doesn't sound like something an introvert would say." She laughed.

Sophie asked, "When can we start playing softball again? We've been practicing."

"What?" Isabel was startled.

Annika answered, "We decided that we wanted to be ready so we've been practicing on our own pretty much every day."

Isabel said, "You guys are awesome."

She turned to Sam. "Have you been keeping busy, too?"

He said, "I work with our local school system, teaching a sailing course for kids who have gotten into trouble at school. Detentions, a lot of missed days, getting into fights- that kind of thing. I give them jobs to do on the boat and if they complete them satisfactorily they get first-hand experience steering the boat. Fact it's been such a successful program that they've offered me a full time position to teach it as a combination safety and discipline program. The students learn geography, astronomy, math, physics, biology, and logic. I even have them sketch the boat. I really like working with them. In fact, I'm considering taking the offer."

She gazed at him for a long moment.

"What?"

"You are just so unexpected." Isabel's face softened as she looked at him.

He leaned over and kissed her. Immediately there was a long "oooh" from the watching girls. Isabel blushed and buried her face in Sam's soft flannel shirt.

Jason cleared his throat loudly. "If I could have your attention, please..."

There was giggling along with loud shushing noises.

He said, "I've talked to the softball league people on the mainland and they said that given the circumstances that we could still participate in some of the games. However, we wouldn't be eligible for the award level. But it would be a great experience and I think we'd have a lot of fun. Is anybody up for doing that?"

The girls all put their hands up, "Yes!"

Isabel smiled and said, "OK I'm up for that too. How about you, Charlotte?"

"Yes, I'm definitely up for it. I may not be able to get around too well but I'm getting my cast off soon and I should be able to get some mobility back."

Jason and Sam looked at each other. "Yeah, we're both in. Definitely!"

Mary hesitated and then said, "Well I am going to be leaving the island for a month pretty soon so I won't be able to go along with the team. But I'll certainly try to follow you on Facebook and Instagram."

There was a shocked silence following this announcement.

"What? You're leaving?" asked Sophie her voice trembling.

"I'm so sorry," Mary said. "I really didn't think there would be this much of a reaction about me going away for a month."

"Of course, people are going to react," said Charlotte. "You're a fixture on the island."

"But why?" Sophie sniffled.

Mary shifted around so she could see Sophie. "I just want to try something different."

Linnea pouted, "Why can't you do that here, on the island?"

Mary looked exasperated.

"Okay, that's enough," said Charlotte.

"What about the store," whispered Sophie.

There were murmurs from the girls.

"I've asked Isabel to watch the store for me," said Mary. "She's still making up her mind. Know that if it's her or someone else I'll make sure it's in good hands before I leave. Whoever takes over the store, I need you to be helpful and to show them how we do story time."

"Will Sadie be allowed in the store." Linnea had her arms around the dog.

"Of course," said Mary.

That information seemed to soothe some of the team's anxiety.

"Okay, let's clean up," Jason started picking up discarded plates and cups. The girls joined him in making quick work of the task.

Isabel was in the kitchen scraping off the plates and washing dishes. Sam was next to her drying. When his phone rang he pulled it out glanced at it and then did a double take.

"I need to take this."

"Is everything all right," asked Isabel.

Sam said, "I'm not sure. This is just totally unexpected. I've got to go." Distracted he kissed her cheek and hurried out of the kitchen.

Isabel gazed after him, feeling disturbed but not sure why.

"What's up," asked Charlotte hobbling into the kitchen on her crutches.

"I've made-up my mind about the bookstore," answered Isabel. She turned to Mary who had just entered the kitchen with Jason close behind her. "I want to run the bookstore. I love the kids and I love books so I think this will work out well."

"Oh excellent!" Mary happily clapped her hands.

"You'll have to show me the software programs that you use to keep the financial books. I want you to introduce me to your vendors. Also, if you have any teachers who would work with me to choose what books would work with their curriculums that would be great." She turned to Jason. "What was the name of that teacher you introduced me to when I first got here?"

"Oh, that was Mrs. Canty. She'd be great. She'd have lots of ideas for you."

Mary smiled at Isabel, "Wow, you're raring to go. That's excellent." Mary hugged Isabel. "And Jason will be right upstairs. He's agreed to sublet my apartment. He'll be available if you need any help."

Jason nodded and grinning at Isabel, said, "Yeah, anything you need, just grab a broom and pound on the ceiling."

Isabel laughed. "I'll keep that in mind."

Mary and Jason said their goodbyes and headed out the door.

Charlotte sat down at the kitchen table with a thump and leaned her crutches against the wall. "Sounds like things are going well," she said. "I did see Sam dash out of here. What was that about?"

Isabel joined Charlotte at the table. "I don't know. He got a phone call and basically ran out the door."

Charlotte looked closely at Isabel. "You're both adults. If you have a concern ask him about it." She ran her fingers through her hair, "That's what always makes me nuts about romantic movies. So often the whole premise is based on a stupid misunderstanding. If the couple would just talk it out…" She laughed, "I guess that would make for a boring movie though."

"You know I am really getting excited about the store. I think it'll be fun."

"I can see how energized you are by this." Charlotte paused. "You know I'm supposed to get my cast off within the next week and then go to an air cast and crutches and then eventually be free of all of this." She took a deep breath. "I'm really hoping that I can stay here for a little longer. I don't know if you're comfortable with that."

Isabel said, "Well, I'm going to be busy with the bookstore but I've really enjoyed having you here and you are welcome to stay as long as you want."

"I'd like to try to find the answer to the mystery of who left you this house. While I'm continuing to heal, I'll have the time to go through that room upstairs."

"That would be great if you wouldn't mind doing that."

"I'd love to do that. Not only will I feel like I'm solving a mystery but also kind of paying back for all you've done for me. Taking me in, supporting me. You've done so much to help me recover… I don't know if I can ever thank you enough." Sadie rested her head on Charlotte's knee and gazed up at her with a forlorn look.

Charlotte and Isabel cracked up. Isabel said, "Only a Lab can look like that pathetic."

Charlotte said, "I don't know. I've known a couple of men who could give her a run for her money in terms of looking pathetic."

The two women laughed even harder. Isabel leaned over and kissed the top of Sadie's head.

Charlotte sipped her tea, "I want to talk to you about something. I have a friend who's been running my charter business while I've been on the DL. He offered to buy it off of me."

Isabel was shocked "What sell your boat? Are you seriously considering that?"

Charlotte looked down at the table, "You know in the time I've been off I'm begun thinking that maybe the charter business is a younger woman's game or a younger man's game but it may be too much for me now. I just don't feel like I can do it physically anymore."

Isabel said "Oh, come on, Charlotte, you're the strongest person I know and that includes both men and women. Once you get the cast off and you're doing physical therapy on a regular basis, you'll get stronger and I think you'll feel more ready to take on the world again. Maybe you're feeling down right now because after all you're still wearing a heavy cast and using crutches. That has got to be exhausting."

Charlotte continued, "Look, I'm fifty-eight and I really have to think long and hard about how I am going to take care of myself as I get older. He's offering me a lot of money for my business. It's in good financial shape. I've learned how to use social media to get people interested in coming out and taking a boat ride so that's really expanded the business. Plus, I monetize everything, every souvenir, every sailor's hat, every tube of sunscreen. I have a whole bunch of branded supplies on the boat that I sell to people who come out with me who are not experienced enough or prepared enough to know what to take on a boat ride," she sighed deeply. "I think his offer is something I really need to consider."

Isabel listened quietly as Charlotte talked her way through this life-changing decision.

Suddenly, Isabel asked, "What about Tom's store?"

Charlotte looked at her in astonishment. "What do you mean?"

"Since Tom died that general store has been empty. We need to have a viable general store on the island. With your background, you would be a great resource for all the DIYers who live on the island. I think it'd be a good option for you to think about."

Charlotte stared at her, "Well that's actually a really good idea. I never even thought of that." She pulled out her phone, "I'm going to call a realtor friend of mine and see what the cost of the general store might be. An approximation...if it's even a possibility."

"I think you'd be really good at it," repeated Isabel, "you have such a mechanical bent of mind anyway with all the things you had to do on the boat. And people like you and trust you."

"Wow, thank you for those encouraging words. In fact, I was thinking about asking you if I could pick up some hours at the bookstore."

Isabel shrugged, "I don't know how much money is coming into the bookstore. I need to look at the books and see what the reality is."

Charlotte said, "You don't really think that Mary would do anything..."

"No, no, no," stammered Isabel. "That's not what I meant. But I do think the bookstore serves a fairly narrow niche and I'm not sure if that's an effective use of its resources. I think it could be more open to other areas of the community, to make it more of a social hub with reading groups and writer's clubs and special events. While at the same time continuing to host children's programs."

"Wow," murmured Charlotte, "You really are ready to take on the world."

Isabel blushed. "I've always worked for someone else and my bosses were all men. This is the first time I feel like I am taking ownership of my future."

Charlotte grinned at her, "Should you be waving a flag?"

"Maybe."

Charlotte's phone rang, she grabbed it, excused herself and disappeared into her bedroom.

Isabel took Sadie into the dog enclosure and played catch with her.

After a while, Charlotte came out on the porch and called "Isabel!"

Pleasantly out of breath, Isabel and Sadie walked back into the house. Isabel poured Sadie a nice cold bowl of water and then poured a glass for herself. "What's up?"

"I talked to my realtor and she put me in contact with the executor of his will. She wants to talk to me. Do you mind if she comes over in about half an hour?"

"No problem. Do you want me to be here?"

"Actually, I'd really like you to be here. Just to have another person present when she says what she has to say to me."

"Why, what do you think she is going to say to you?"

"I don't know. But once lawyers and money come up in a conversation, I get very nervous."

"I can understand that. I'll be glad to be here and be your wing man."

Charlotte snorted. "That's not the phrase I would use to describe you."

Isabel asked "Why what is a wing man? I thought it was a good thing."

"A wing man is a guy who goes out with a friend and makes sure that he doesn't end up with someone he doesn't want to end up with or gets in a fight or god forbid an accident."

"Oh," said Isabel, "I guess that's not me."

CHAPTER 25

A short time later the executor, Gail, drove into the driveway and parked. It turned out she was Sophie's mom so all three women immediately relaxed as they chatted about the softball team and what they could look forward to in the coming weeks. Isabel poured tall glasses of iced tea for everyone as they settled in the living room.

Gail was delighted to hear that the girls were going to start playing again. She told the women that before Sophie had started playing softball she had been very timid and withdrawn. Getting involved in the team had made a world of difference. Sophie now had actual friends that she would go and do things with instead of just holing up in her bedroom watching video after video.

There was a pause in the conversation and it was time to get down to business.

"I'm not sure why the realtor told me I needed to talk to you," said Charlotte.

"You don't know why? Nobody has mentioned anything to you?" Gail was curious.

"No," said Charlotte looking confused.

"I didn't know whether Tom had mentioned anything to anybody," said Gail. "He had a lot of friends including people he grew up and went to school with. I thought maybe he had gone to them to talk things out. I guess not. It's a small island," she said looking at Isabel. "Things do tend to get around."

"I got that," said Isabel.

Gail cleared her throat and took a long drink of iced tea.

"I believe you and Tom were very close?"

"Yes," said Charlotte. "We had dinner together every Sunday night."

"Once his wife died he didn't have any immediate relatives left. However, he told me that he considered you family."

Charlotte teared up as she looked at Gail. "I felt that way about him too. We often talked about how important we were to each other. I know he was uneasy about growing older on his own."

Gail looked through the pile of papers in front of her and then folded her hands on top of it. "Well, he continues to care for you even after passing away." She took a deep breath. "He left you the general store and his existing property. All the taxes have been paid, it's yours free and clear. He wanted you to be able to do whatever you wanted to do with this considerable gift. If you want to run the store that's certainly an option. If you want to sell it, that's an option too."

There was a dead silence following Gail's explanation. Isabel looked over at her friend trying to gauge what was going on inside her head. Charlotte looked absolutely blown away. Stunned she opened her mouth to try to say something but no words came out.

Finally, she looked at Gail intently, "Tell me if I have this straight. He left me everything including his store, all that property and all those taxes are paid up?"

"Yes. Tom and I had a long discussion about this and he really wanted you to have it free and clear so you could do whatever you wanted to do with your life. He loved you very much, in his words 'like a daughter.'"

Charlotte bent over the table and began sobbing loudly. Gail discreetly moved the legal papers out of the way.

Isabel put her arm around her friend, "Gail, do you mind waiting outside for a few minutes to give Charlotte some breathing room."

"Of course. I'll be outside in my car making calls." As she walked past Charlotte she reached out and gently gave her shoulder a gentle squeeze.

The two women waited until they heard the kitchen door close. Isabel reached over and grabbed a box of tissues and handed them to Charlotte. With her foot she pushed a small wicker wastebasket closer to Charlotte. "How are you doing?"

Charlotte wiped her eyes and blew her nose. "It is just such a shock." She dropped a handful of used tissues into the wastebasket.

Isabel walked into the bathroom and wet a washcloth with cold water and brought it back out for Charlotte to press against her face.

"Here," she said, "this will make you feel a little bit better."

Charlotte looked at her, "Nothing is going to make me feel better right now."

Isabel felt like kicking herself. "True enough."

Charlotte said "First, losing Tom…"

There was a soft clicking sound of toenails as Sadie came into the room to sit beside Charlotte. She put her head on Charlotte's leg and gazed up at her.

"She knows something is wrong," said Isabel.

"What a good girl," Charlotte wrapped her arms around the dog, and buried her face in her silky fur.

"Do you want me to tell Gail to come back at another time?"

" I don't know, maybe I should get this over with now."

"You don't need to do anything you don't want to do. You're fine just sitting here and doing nothing but feeling what you're feeling."

"You're right, I don't have to do anything like you said. But just sit here and do nothing. Thank you."

"You are very welcome. Now, how about a nice cup of tea?"

Charlotte snorted with laughter, "That's your answer for everything…a nice cup of tea."

Isabel smiled at her, "Somewhere I must have British ancestors. Because I do find tea a comfort."

"And the Brits do love their dogs so that's you, too."

There was a knock on the door.

They looked at each other.

"I'll tell her that we'll set up a time in a few days to drop by her office."

"Sounds good," said Charlotte.

The next day, Isabel returned home after running errands in town. She went upstairs to change. Before leaving the house she had asked Charlotte if she would look through the hoarder's closet to see if there were any papers there.

Now, Charlotte called up the steps after her. "By the way, I found a small filing cabinet with a combination lock on it. With your permission, I want to break it open and see what's there."

"That's exciting. I want to be part of it. Just give me a few minutes I'll be right down."

Sadie was at the bottom of the steps. She was whining a bit.

Isabel leaned over the banister to talk to her, "I'll be down in a few minutes. Be a good girl and lie down."

Sadie grumbled a bit walked in a tight circle several times and lay down with a heavy sigh.

When Isabel entered the room she found Charlotte holding a screwdriver and pliers. Charlotte grinned at her.

"Ready to see if we have the answer to the mystery here?"

Isabel nodded. She found her mouth was dry all of a sudden.

She cleared her throat, "I don't know why I'm so nervous."

Charlotte looked at her thoughtfully "Would you rather do this by yourself?"

"No, actually I'm glad you're here."

"Okay then, let's see if we can force it open."

Between the two of them they were able to pry the lock apart.

Isabel laughed, "Turned out to be a lot easier than I thought it was going to be."

"So, let's see what's in here." They opened the case and found a handful of papers and a sealed manila envelope.

Charlotte reached in and handed it to Isabel "You should open it…"

Isabel said, "No, I think maybe you should."

They stared at each other for a moment.

Isabel handed the envelope to Charlotte, "Please…"

"Okay," said Charlotte. She carefully tore open the envelope, took a deep breath and peered inside.

For a long moment she just stared…

"OK, what's in there? What are you seeing? You're killing me here."

Charlotte looked at her and said slowly, "It's a birth certificate."

CHAPTER 26

Charlotte handed the envelope to Isabel who hesitated and then reached over and took it with shaking hands. She cautiously pulled out the birth certificate and stared at the tiny footprint on the certificate.

Isabel raised her hand and tenderly pressed it against the footprint.

Then, she read the names on the certificate.

"Oh my God, that's me. That is my name on there."

She read further.

"But wait… those are not my parents' names."

She looked up at Charlotte in confusion.

"What the hell is going on?" Her voice became increasingly agitated.

Charlotte poked around in the case. "There is another envelope in here addressed To Whom it May Concern." She handed it over to Isabel who started looking through it.

"There is all kinds of information in here, about the house, about everything."

"Wait a minute," Charlotte had found another sealed envelope. "This one has your name on it."

Stunned, Isabel slit it open. She started to read the letter out loud.

"Dear Isabel, I know this is going to be a shock to you….."

"You've got that right,…" she murmured.

"My name is Catherine Evers. I am writing this letter to you because I want you to know the truth.

"I am your biological mother. I had you when I was 16 years old. Your father and I met at school and we fell in love. Then I found out I was pregnant. My parents threatened to have him arrested since I was underage. To protect him, his parents moved away and I never saw him again. My father was a prominent city council member in our town and my parents didn't want the stigma associated with a teen pregnancy. My parents told me if I didn't give the baby up they would cut all ties with me."

As she read those words, Isabel started to tear up. She continued reading.

"I was so young. I was an only child with no relatives other than my parents. I had no idea what to do. I was very frightened so I bent to pressure and gave you up. My parents set up the adoption and made sure that it was a binding private arrangement. Because I was underage I had no real say in the process. My parents had arranged it so I'd never see you at all but a kind nurse snuck you in and put you in my arms after you were born. I was able to hold you for a short while and in that time I fell totally in love with you and realized I had made the biggest mistake of my life. Nothing was worth losing you. When the nurse came in and took you away from me, I felt like my heart had been ripped out.

"I finished high school then ran away from home as soon as I was able. I hitchhiked across the country and ended up in Boston. I lived in a homeless shelter for a while, first as a resident, then as a volunteer, then as an employee. That job enabled me to go to college where I earned a PhD in social work. I ended up becoming a college professor teaching classes on strategies for dealing with homelessness. I even wrote a book about it.

"A few years ago, I retired and moved permanently to Mouse Island. I was generally content but every day I thought of you. I hoped and prayed that you were doing well.

"Over the years, closed file adoptions have become more accessible so, I decided to try to find you. I didn't want to cause any problems in your life by making a sudden appearance but I did want to see how you were doing.

"Unfortunately, around that time, I was diagnosed with terminal cancer. I found out I had very little time left. So, I hired a team of investigators to track you down and found out you were living in New York City. I was excited to get that news even though I knew I was getting close to the end of my life. I hoped that we would be able to meet but the cancer proved to be too much. I didn't have the strength to make the trip to New York. I ended up in the hospice which is where I am right now.

"It feels like the end is very near now and I regret that I didn't have the courage or strength to reach out to you when I still could.

"I wanted to write this letter to explain who I am and why I am leaving you the Evers House. It's a place for you to live and be happy for the rest of your life, which is what I wish for you.

" I want you to know that I never stopped thinking of you and loving you every day. In my mind and heart, I have always been your mother,

"Love, Catherine.

With tears in her eyes, Isabel looked up at Charlotte who was also crying.

"I never got the chance to meet her." She wiped her eyes and blew her nose on a tissue Charlotte handed to her.

Charlotte said, "There's a photo album in here."

"Oh, let's see." They had been so immersed in the emotional impact of what they had discovered they hadn't noticed the time going by. The sun had set and it was now dark outside.

Suddenly the doorbell rang, startling them.

Isabel said, "I'll go down and see who it is. You just take it easy. Rest that leg." She clattered down the steps and went to the front door. She turned the light on and saw Sam was standing outside. She felt her face flush and her heart beat a bit faster at the sight of him.

So much had happened in such a short amount of time. Physically and emotionally, she felt wrung out. She wasn't sure she was ready to deal with Sam right now. At the same time, she didn't want him to leave. She felt confused and torn in different directions.

She hesitated for a moment then opened the door for him. He looked at her questioningly. "What's going on?" He said, "For a moment there, I wasn't sure you were going to let me in."

Sadie came up to him and rubbed her head against his leg. He reached down and scratched her back.

"I'm sorry," she said, "It's been an emotional day. I found out or rather Charlotte and I found out who the woman was who left me the house and why. I'd like to tell you about it but not right now because I just am totally wiped out."

She leaned against him. "I didn't mean to make you feel like you were not wanted. It is just..." To her embarrassment she started to cry. Sam made a soft soothing sound, put his arms around her and held her tightly.

"I'm so sorry. Whatever, whenever you want to tell me, it's fine. Is there anything I can do for you right now?"

"No, thank you," she said. "I really appreciate you stopping by, but I just think I need some time to work through this stuff."

Sam nodded, "I can understand that." He gently kissed her cheek. "If you need anything just call. Even if you just want to talk." He hugged her and headed out the door.

Isabel closed it behind him, wiped her eyes and went back up the stairs.

CHAPTER 27

She helped Charlotte make her way down to the living room. Sadie, who had been waiting impatiently for everybody to come downstairs, started jumping around in circles tossing a tennis ball in the air.

Isabel grabbed the ball from her and rolled it across the floor, "I have some leftover chicken pot pie. Is that OK for dinner?" Sadie dropped her ball in front of Isabel who grabbed it and rolled it across the floor again. Sadie chased after it, catching up with it, plopped down and started chewing on it.

"That sounds great," Charlotte answered distractedly. She was sitting on the couch busily collecting the papers and photos from the file.

Isabel came over and looked at what she was doing. "You're amazing," she said. "You are so good at putting this stuff together. Thank you."

"I've always been a good organizer. I find it easier to work if everything is in its place and I know where everything is. It has certainly helped in my business."

"Well, I can definitely learn from you," said Isabel. "That's why you'd be so good at running the hardware store. You'd track down the best inventory, at the most cost effective prices and display them for the maximum impact."

"You know the more I think about it," Charlotte said, thoughtfully, "the more I think I could really make a success of it. Anyway, enough about me." She picked up some pictures and showed them to Isabel. "I've pulled these together, starting from, I think, an early shot of Catherine as a baby."

Isabel leaned closer to Charlotte and peered intently at the photos. "I have to reframe it in my mind that this is my mother, my biological mother. Not the woman who raised me."

"This next group of photos are from, I believe, her teenage, years. You can tell she was very unhappy during that time. Her eyes look haunted, rimmed with dark circles."

Isabel nodded, "Yes, I can see that."

"Later on, there are photos of her when she was in college, she doesn't look as sad, she looks more professional. I imagine this is from when she worked at the college. Next is from a book signing. Finally, there are some images from when she was here on the island. She definitely looks more content, more relaxed. The last picture is when she was in a hospital bed, probably in hospice. I'm not sure who took it but she doesn't look very good. It must have not been long before she died. I don't know if you want to see that image or not."

Isabel said, "I want to see all of them. If she went through it, I could definitely stand to look at the images."

Charlotte nodded, "That makes sense."

"You know, if she had a book on homelessness we should be able to Google it."

"Oh, of course," Charlotte smacked the side of her head lightly. "I can't believe I didn't think of that before this."

They both settled before Charlotte's laptop and put in Catherine Evers' name. Within seconds, her bio appeared on the screen, then the cover of her book, a list of reviews and awards and a link to buy the book on Amazon.

"Wow," murmured Isabel.

"Go to YouTube," urged Charlotte. "There has got to be videos of interviews she did..." She reached over Isabel and started to input the information.

"No! Wait!" Isabel spoke sharply.

Charlotte was startled and quickly jerked her hands back.

There was a painful moment of silence, then Isabel apologized. "I feel overwhelmed right now and though I definitely want to see videos of her, it feels like it is just too much. I am still trying to absorb that the woman I thought was my mother for all these years was not my biological mother."

"I am so sorry," Charlotte also apologized. "I can't begin to imagine what you are going through. I kind of got caught up in the search for information and lost sight of what the emotional impact would be on you."

Sadie trotted over to Isabel and rested her head on her knee. Isabel leaned over and buried her face in the dog's fur. Sadie whined softly and snuggled closer.

"I think it's time to take a break and have some dinner," suggested Charlotte.

Isabel was quiet for a few moments and then said, "I am glad you are here. Your support and companionship mean so much to me. I can't imagine going through this without you."

"You know," said Charlotte, "I never had a sister but living with you has given me a feel for what it would be like. I really missed out."

"I never had a sister either." Isabel paused and then said, "Just a minute, let me put the soup on." She went into the kitchen and started heating the soup.

When she came back she said to Charlotte, "What do you say that we agree to be each other's sister, each other's family. That would mean a lot to me."

Charlotte stared at her, "That's a wonderful idea. I would love knowing that I'm not alone in the world, that I have someone I can count on, who has my back."

"It's a commitment to be each other's family, no matter what comes down the pike. What do you think?"

"Definitely yes."

At that, Isabel leaned over and held up her right hand, "Pinky swear," she said half-laughing, half-serious.

Charlotte grinned, "Pinky swear," and hooked her little finger around Isabel's.

"Now, we're supposed to spit."

"I think we can forgo that."

In the following days, Isabel spent a lot of time reading her biological mother's letter over and over. She cried a lot and wished with all her heart that she could meet Catherine.

She had Mary track down and order Catherine's book which was out of print. She watched a YouTube video of an interview with Catherine about her book.

She researched the homeless shelter where Catherine had lived and worked. Unfortunately, it had closed years previously and she couldn't access the paperwork.

She joined Ancestry and looked up Catherine's parents. For some reason there was no mention of Catherine in the family tree. She found out Evers was a middle name that Catherine had decided to use instead of her parents' last name. When she ran away from home, her parents disowned her. They scrubbed her very existence off the family rolls.

Catherine had been deeply hurt by her family and in the end she chose to be alone. Isabel recognized how much their lives had followed similar paths... up to a point. Catherine's generous gift had opened the door for her to find a community she cared about, and where people cared about her. If she had not moved to the island she would have continued living a solitary life, alone and isolated.

CHAPTER 28

A week later, Isabel had the going away party for Mary. It was a warm, starry night so Isabel and Charlotte put some chairs along the porch. After helping out, Charlotte collapsed with a clatter on a nearby chair, with her crutches by her side and her cast stretched out in front of her.

"That's it. I'm beat."

Isabel nodded. "Just sit there and take it easy. We pretty much have it all set up."

"I wanted to ask you while we were still alone," said Charlotte. "Are you more interested in Daniel or Sam? I thought Sam was the front runner but now I'm not sure."

Isabel grinned at her. "Who do you think I'd be more interested in?"

"Well, Sam."

"Bingo."

"That's a relief."

"Why?"

"I kind of have a crush on Daniel."

"Really..." muttered Isabel, feeling a sense of relief and at the same time happy for her friend.

"Don't you dare say anything to him," pleaded Charlotte.

"Of course, not..."

"Pinky swear?"

"Pinky swear."

They locked pinkies and then burst out laughing.

"Sounds like the party has already started." Sam peered through the screen door. "What can I do to help?"

"You could get some more ice. I don't think I have enough, especially since it is a warm night."

"Will do," he said. "I'll run to the store and get a couple of bags. "

"He's certainly very helpful," said Charlotte rolling her eyes at Isabel after he left.

"He's a nice guy," smiled Isabel.

"Just nice?"

Isabel blushed. "Do you want to help me decorate the house?

"Sure."

By the time the guests arrived the house was party ready with pussy willows, native grasses and ferns in vases scattered around the house.

"Too bad it's not time yet for the wildflowers to fully be in season," said Charlotte.

"I really like this natural look," Isabel gazed around her house feeling a sense of pride and ownership.

People started arriving and soon the living room was full of excited chatter and laughter. Sam set up an informal drinks table while Isabel kept busy filling and refilling platefuls of snacks. Sadie wound her way through the crowd happy to be petted but also hopeful for any snacks coming her way. Isabel kept an eye on her to make sure she wasn't scarfing down anything that would upset her stomach.

They partied late into the night sharing stories and memories along with ice cream and cake.

Daniel arrived late with two young women in their twenties in tow. Isabel was a little surprised but then shrugged it off, after all she wasn't interested in Daniel but...suddenly she remembered who was. She spun around looking for Charlotte. She spotted her in a corner having an intense conversation with Dr. Mike. She made a beeline for the pair. Charlotte glanced up at her as she approached.

"Daniel is here," she muttered into Charlotte's ear.

"Oh good," Charlotte took a sip of her drink and looked around the room. Daniel was by the drinks table chatting with Sam. Charlotte started to walk towards him when the two young women he had come with appeared by his side. He put his arm around one while the other leaned against him. Isabel glanced over at Charlotte and saw her stop, pivot, and slip out the kitchen door. Isabel followed her and found her on the porch swing. She joined her there. They sat in silence for a while looking out over the sea grasses to the ocean beyond. They swung back and forth, not talking, just sitting quietly. Laughter and conversation drifted out from the living room.

Isabel smiled as she listened, happy that people seemed to be enjoying themselves. This party was her first in many years. She had a painful experience in her twenties when she had invited coworkers over for her first big adult party, decorated her apartment lavishly and put out lots of snacks and drinks. She had been so excited waiting for people to arrive. But then the clock ticked by and no one came, no one called. She ended up sitting alone on the floor, sifting through the snacks for any chocolate she could find, and crying. She left that job soon after.

Tonight's get together went a long way toward healing the bad taste left in her mouth from that long ago humiliating experience.

She nudged Charlotte, "Do you want me to find out who they are?"

Charlotte gave her a long look. "What good would that do? What are they, in their early 20s? Add them together and they are still younger than me. I can't compete with that."

"What a schmuck." Isabel said ruefully. "I'm sorry I invited him."

Sam came out onto the porch with Sadie, carrying a cold bottle of beer. He leaned against a pillar and took a long sip. "What are you guys doing out here?"

Isabel said "Oh, just talking. We'll be in a minute." The moon was full and bright and Isabel, Charlotte and Sam sat for a while basking in its glow as it sailed across the night sky. Sadie was leaning against Isabel. "I don't think I'll ever get tired of this view."

Sam said "It's beautiful all right. I would like to photograph it if you don't mind."

"That would be great," said Isabel.

"I'd come over around dawn when the light is just right."

"Anytime," said Isabel.

Struggling to get to her feet, Charlotte said "If someone could help me get up off this swing I'd like to go back inside."

"Of course," said Isabel taking one of Charlotte's arms and steadying her. Sam took her other arm and grabbed her crutches. Together they slowly walked back inside. Sadie followed close behind.

The moment Isabel walked in, Daniel made a beeline for her. He gave her a quick hug. She stepped back and then found herself looking at the two young women standing next to him.

"I want you to meet my nieces," he said. "I hope it's okay that I brought them with me. They just arrived on the island today and I didn't want to leave them alone on their first night here. This is Nikki and Sammi."

Isabel felt a weight drop off her shoulders as she greeted the two girls. She took them over to meet Charlotte and saw her friend's face relax as she explained who they were.

She walked around the room making sure everyone had something to eat or drink and then veered out into the kitchen. Sam was filling snack bowls and had a pile of dishes soaking in the sink.

"What are you doing!"

"Just helping out," he said.

"You should be in there enjoying yourself and talking to people."

Sam rinsed off a plate, dried it and neatly placed it in the nearby dish rack. "To tell you the truth, I enjoy talking with people but I'm not a party person. That's not my thing."

He washed a mug, "I just like being out here, having Sadie with me, looking out the window and doing the dishes. I find it very peaceful, soothing."

"I know what you mean," said Isabel "I feel the same way. She laughed, "Well anytime you want to come over and do the dishes you're welcome to do that."

"Do you mean that?" There was a long pause.

She looked directly into his eyes. "Yes. I really enjoy your company."

"I enjoy your company too."

Isabel felt a flutter in her chest, it almost felt like her heart skipped a beat or two. "I'd like that," she said breathlessly.

They walked towards one another and were just reaching out...when Daniel walked into the kitchen with his nieces in tow. "Oh, excuse me." He turned to back up and leave the room but his nieces were blocking his way. There was an awkward moment when he looked like he was going to try to push his way through but then he turned back and said, "We've had a wonderful time but we are all kind of bushed from our trip to LA so we're going to head out if you don't mind."

He strode over to Isabel. "Thank you so much for inviting me to your party. It has really helped me feel connected to the island again. I missed being here. I don't feel very creative when I'm on the road." He seemed to realize that he was babbling and stopped abruptly. He gave Isabel a hug, shook Sam's hand and headed out the kitchen door followed by his nieces.

Isabel felt a little embarrassed but also disappointed that her moment with Sam had been interrupted. She felt bad about Daniel but seeing him just now confirmed for her that she didn't have feelings for him other than that of a friend.

Charlotte appeared in the kitchen doorway and said, "I think Sadie needs to go out."

Isabel said, "Thanks, I'll put her in the pen for a little bit."

Sam folded the dish towel and draped it over the edge of the sink. "I'll go out and play with her, throw the ball around, give her a chance to exercise."

"That would be great, thank you. I have a feeling the party is starting to wind down anyway."

Charlotte said, " Dr. Mike is getting his ukulele out of his car. That is usually the death nell for any party."

Isabel cracked up, Sam started laughing and Charlotte joined in. The three of them were soon laughing so hard that Isabel had to wipe the tears from her eyes. Slowly she regained her composure. As they started quieting down, they heard the sound of a ukulele being tuned up in the next room. They burst out laughing again.

After a few moments, Charlotte went back into the living room. Sam took Sadie out to the pen and Isabel finished cleaning up. She found herself humming a little tune as she dried the glasses and silverware.

CHAPTER 29

It was two days after the party and Isabel was still worn out. She lay stretched out on the couch, half-asleep, with a book propped in front of her. She thought about checking on Charlotte but then she heard loud snores coming from her bedroom. Isabel smiled, she was not the only one taking a few days to recover from the party. Charlotte was definitely enjoying a midday nap. Sadie came in and dropped a decrepit and very moist tennis ball on her lap.

"Yuck!" Isabel gently tossed the ball across the room. "Not right now, kiddo. I'll take you out to play in a little bit," she said giving Sadie a kiss on the nose.

Her phone rang. Mary was on the line.

"Do you want to come over? We can have lunch and go over some of the historical books we have."

"That sounds perfect," said Isabel. "Can I bring Sadie?"

"Of course. Do you think she would ever wear a costume?"

Isabel snorted with laughter, "I'll have to ask her." She disconnected and looked down at Sadie, "Are you ready to play dress up?" Sadie wagged her tail and gave her a soft 'woof.'

"I'll take that as a yes."

Settled in one of the bookstore's cozy reading nooks, Mary and Isabel poured over the store's historic ledger. Isabel turned the pages carefully as they were brittle and crackled like they would disintegrate at the slightest breath.

"I got this from the previous owner," Mary said. "I know it's difficult to read. I have a feeling she used a quill pen." She sighed, "I'm not sure how helpful it is.... Though as a matter of pure curiosity, it is fascinating to look at the books that were popular at different times in the life of the bookstore, to see what people were reading 25 or 50 years ago."

Isabel blushed, "I cannot tell you how excited I am to have this opportunity."

Mary laughed, "Opportunity," she exclaimed. "You sound like you're in a job interview."

Isabel grinned, "Yeah, it does sound a little bit like where do you want to be in 5 years?

"Thank God, I didn't have to go through that type of interview. I bought this store from an elderly woman who was more than ready to retire. She pretty much just threw the keys at me and the ledger and then she was gone."

"Do you have any computer software to help keep track of your sales and customers?"

Mary bit her lip. "I bought QuickBooks a while back, but trying to learn how to use it gave me a headache. I ended up going back to writing everything down in a ledger." She reached under the counter and pulled out a thick volume with the current year printed on the front.

Isabel asked, "Do you mind if I use a computer instead? It will be so much easier to track things."

"Whatever is easiest for you. Do you think you'd be comfortable running the store next week?"

Isabel was startled. "I guess so," she said nervously.

"Remember, you can text or email me at any time."

"How are you feeling about your visit," asked Isabel curiously.

"Betwixt and between," laughed Mary. "It will be the first time I've had a girlfriend. The first time I've been introduced as someone's girlfriend. I'm excited and stressed at the same time. I am so used to hiding who I really am from everybody. I'm not sure how to behave. What if I don't like this new me?"

Isabel leaned over and put her hand on Mary's arm, "Just be who you are. You are a kind, creative, caring, and intelligent woman....beautiful inside and out. I am so happy to have you as a friend. When I moved to the island, I had no idea what to expect. I was in my 60s and still didn't have a good idea of who I was as a person. I spent most of my life closed down and shut off from people, only interacting on the most superficial level. Moving here has transformed me. It's helped me to open up, to let people in. To trust. Which I never did before…"

"It's all about trust isn't it?" said Mary in a slightly teary voice.

Isabel nodded and said, "It's not only about trusting other people, but about trusting yourself too, and that can be a hard thing to learn."

Mary leaned over and hugged her, "I know it's only a month, but I'll miss you."

Isabel murmured, "I'll miss you too.

Just then, they heard Jason come home, heading for his upstairs apartment, his boots thundering on the wooden stairs. Mary and Isabel grinned at one another.

"Just how big are his feet?" Mused Isabel.

"Elephant-sized."

"More like an entire elephant herd."

"He's a good guy," said Mary. "Anything you need he'll be there for you. He has your back."

"Well so do I," Isabel nodded. " I have your back too. Always remember that. You have me as your back up." She stood up and stretched. "Now where did that dog of mine go?" She glanced down one of the rows and stepped quickly back to Mary's side. "You have to see this." Very quietly the two women peered into the children's books section. Sadie was curled up next to a little girl who was reading to her from a colorful picture book and then carefully showing her the pictures. Sadie looked at each image and then looked at the little girl and softly gave her a lick on the cheek. The little girl giggled and hugged Sadie.

The child's mother was standing off to one side, taping this on her phone, at the same time she had tears running down her cheeks. She looked at Mary and Isabel, "This is just wonderful. She's been having difficulties reading. I didn't know you had a pet therapy program."

Mary and Isabel looked at each other, "We do now," said Mary.

"I definitely want to sign my daughter up."

"We are just getting that program underway. Stop back in a week and we'll have more information for you."

Isabel put Sadie's leash on her and got ready to leave, promising to open the bookstore the next Monday.

When she arrived home she discovered Charlotte finishing a watercolor of the view from the living room.

"Oh, that's wonderful!" Isabel admired the painting. "Make sure you sign it."

"I doubt anyone would buy one of my paintings," said Charlotte.

"I don't think you realize how good you are. You have a real gift. Don't sell yourself short. In fact, if you would do some paintings of scenes from around the island I'll put them up in the bookstore."

"That would be absolutely awesome."

Both Isabel and Charlotte decided to call it an early night and turned in. Isabel found herself walking up the steps to her bedroom with a broad smile on her face. She perched on the big window seat in her bedroom. Isabel gazed at the moon rising over the ocean, painting the waves with streaks of silver. She thought about all that she had learned. It was clear to her now why she had never felt very connected with her adoptive parents. They'd been caring and took good care of her. But she had never really felt like she belonged, like she was a part of the family. There were times when they would be sitting in the kitchen talking to each other in low tones, laughing and leaning against each other and she felt like she was intruding. Ironically when she was a teenager she had even wondered if she was adopted, she had felt so out of touch at times.

She was in her thirties when her adoptive mother got cancer and died. Isabel had taken a leave of absence and was intending to move home for a while to take care of her father who was very depressed. Before she could do that she was notified that he had passed away. It was the first time she thought it was possible for someone to literally die of a broken heart.

She got into bed, snuggled into her comforter, and pulled her pillows around her.

"I love this place. "Thank you, Catherine." She hesitated and then corrected herself, "Thanks, Mom," she said.

CHAPTER 30

Isabel woke up early the next morning, went downstairs and released Sadie into the enclosure. She leaned against the fence and drank a cup of tea as the sun came up and Sadie raced around. They played for a while with the ball and then she called Sadie to come. As they walked towards the front door Jason drove up in his truck. When he saw them he started honking his horn.

"Good morning, Jason," called Isabel. He got out of the truck and raced over to her, grabbed her around the waist and twirled her in a circle.

"What's going on?" she asked, laughing.

He let her go, grabbed Sadie's front paws, and danced with her.

"I got into medical school!" he shouted up into the sky.

She grabbed his arm, "That's fantastic!" They both did a crazy wild celebratory dance. All of a sudden Charlotte came out on the porch, and stood there hands on hips, "What's up?"

Jason raced over to her and grabbed her carefully not to knock her over and hugged her fiercely. "I got into medical school."

"Oh, Jason," Charlotte burst into tears. "That's wonderful."

"Then why are you crying," he said sternly. "You never cry."

"I do now, it's a new hobby of mine." said Charlotte. "I'm so happy for you, I think you'll make a fantastic doctor."

"Come inside and tell us all about it," said Isabel.

He said "I can't, I have to go see Dr. Mike. I already called him first thing this morning. I woke him up, he let out a big whoop at the news and that woke up his wife. Apparently scared her half to death." He grinned, "He's talking about maybe setting me up as an intern following him around until it's time for me go to school in the fall."

"What a great idea," said Isabel.

Jason kissed both of the women on their cheeks. "Gotta go!" He ran back to his truck, hurled himself into the front seat, honked and waved and tore out of the driveway.

The two women looked at each other.

"That's great news," said Isabel.

Charlotte sighed. "There's no guarantee he'll come back here after he gets his degree."

"I know we've been through a lot of changes recently."

"People leaving, people dying," said Charlotte.

Isabel helped Charlotte back into the house and got her seated at the kitchen table. "I'm not going anywhere." Isabel poured Charlotte a cup of tea.

Isabel's phone vibrated. "It's the girls!," she said to Charlotte. She answered the phone and was delighted to hear the team was at the practice field and ready to play.

"I'll be there in an hour," she glanced over at Charlotte. "Do you want to come with me?"

"It's still hard for me to get around, I may just sit in the car and watch."

"I am going to take Sadie with us. It will be good for her to get out and meet people. She needs a little socializing."

Within the next half hour, they were both ready to go. They piled into Isabel's car, secured Sadie in the back seat, and set off for the school athletic field. When they pulled in they found there were a large number of cars already parked by the field.

Isabel said "Look how many people are here. I see Mary and Jason over by the donut table. No surprise there. And there is Sam, talking with Dr. Mike."

She waved at Sam, feeling that familiar rush of excited emotion upon seeing him. He looked over and saw her and his face lit up. He trotted over to Isabel and gave her a warm hug. He murmured in her ear, "I am so glad to see you." He gave her a soft kiss on her cheek and she blushed.

Sadie was still in the car, wagging her tail furiously and whining. Isabel reached in, attached the leash to her collar and brought her out.

She turned to Charlotte, "Why don't you sit by the snack table and just relax? You haven't been out in the fresh air recently."

Charlotte hesitated and then smiled, "Okay. I'll be in charge of the cupcakes."

Dr. Mike and Sam supported Charlotte and helped her walk across the field to the table. Isabel was delighted to see her friend laughing, her eyes shining and her blonde hair glowing in the bright sunshine.

"She's something," said Sam as he came back to stand by her.

Isabel felt a fleeting stab of jealousy and then let it go. "It's been a long time since I've seen her laughing like that. It's good to see."

At that moment, the team came rushing up to Isabel, Sam, and Sadie and surrounded them with hugs, all talking at once. Isabel cracked up trying to listen to who was saying what. She felt a lightness of spirit as she listened to the girls.

"There is Charlotte," said Sophie and the girls rushed over to say hi to her.

Sam called, "Let's get going. Everybody come in. Form a tight circle around me. We'll do a couple things today. It's gonna be a long practice day. First we're going to jog around the field five times, do some stretching, and practice throwing and hitting. Then we'll have a practice game where we split up into two teams and battle it out. Make sure you are drinking plenty of water and stay hydrated."

The team was excited and chattering but when Sam gave an earsplitting whistle they all turned to him and quickly focused on what he had to say. Isabel walked over to Charlotte and sat down.

"He's a true leader," said Charlotte nodding at Sam "He knows how to get people working together as a team."

Jason meandered by picking up a cupcake. " That's probably why Kevin Grant from the Boston farm team is here."

"Who is here?"

"He's a scout with the Boston Red Sox farm team. Apparently his niece lives here on the island and happened to mention to him that a former professional baseball player was coaching the girls' softball team. It's not that our softball team is any great shakes but Sam has a good reputation. He used to help other players, giving them pointers informally. I think I read somewhere that they have been trying to get him back in the fold for a while now." Jason walked away whistling, tossing his cupcake in the air, and catching it one-handed behind his back.

Isabel was stunned. "Who is Kevin Grant?"

Charlotte glanced at her. "You heard Jason. Someone with the Boston baseball team organization." The two women looked at each other and then out at the play field as the team raced to assume their positions.

"Do you think Sam might leave the island to go back to professional baseball?" Isabel asked anxiously. She felt a heaviness in her chest.

Charlotte looked at her friend with concern, "I don't know."

Isabel said "I really like him. I'd hate to see him go. "

After the practice was over everybody pitched in, cleaned up the field and put litter away into the trash bins. Jason and Isabel helped Charlotte get into the car with Sadie.

Sam walked up to Isabel, "I was hoping we could have dinner tonight."

"Not tonight, Sam. I am really tired. I think I'm just going to go home and rest."

"Can we talk for a moment?"

"I don't think there is anything to talk about."

He looked at her with a confused expression in his eyes. "What's going on? Is something wrong?"

Isabel turned to face him. "I understand that somebody from the Boston farm team was talking to you today at practice."

"Yes, that was Kevin, we used to be teammates."

"Are you planning on leaving the island?"

He looked at her in astonishment, "That's what this is all about? Isabel, all I know is he wants to talk to me for some reason. I don't know why."

"Really?"

"Really. As soon as I know what he wants I'll let you know." He gave her a hug and walked back over to a group of players and parents.

Isabel got in the car and started the engine. She glanced over at Charlotte, "That makes me nervous. How can I compete with professional baseball?"

Charlotte sighed, "You are not competing with anybody. You are who you are. As far as Sam goes, you don't know enough about the situation to make any kind of decision. So just let it go for now."

Isabel said, "I'm glad you're here with me."

"It's like that scene in Moonstruck," said Charlotte, "When Cher tells Cage, "Snap out of it!"

"Loved that scene and that movie. Why don't we rent it tonight?" Isabel put the car in gear and slowly drove off the field. Just then, Dr. Mike waved them down. Isabel pulled up to him and lowered the window. He leaned in and scratched Sadie's head. "How are you doing, Charlotte?"

"Much better, thanks, Dr. Mike."

"Ready for me to take a look at your leg and see if you're OK to take the cast off?"

"What, now?"

"My office is right around the corner I can take a look and see if we can take it off and replace it with an air cast. Much more comfortable for you."

Charlotte eagerly turned to Isabel. "Do you mind if we do that? It'd be so great to have this cast off."

"Of course," said Isabel "We'll follow you, Doctor Mike."

"Good," he patted Sadie on the head and jumped in his truck to head over to his clinic.

Two hours later Charlotte was freed from her heavy cast and wearing a lightweight air cast instead. She told Isabel she felt like dancing.

At that, the doctor turned to her said sternly, "Do not dance. At all. I don't care how good the music is you do not dance. Not until we get the air cast off for good."

"I want you to wear it all day every day until nighttime when you can take it off in bed. But your leg looks and feels good. You've healed nicely. You just want to be careful now the next couple of weeks until you're fully recovered to take it easy. Make sure you don't take any chances. You're going to need physical therapy to build up muscle. I'll give you the number of a therapist." He patted her on the shoulder, "Good job," he said. He reached in his pocket and with a flourish handed her a lollipop. Charlotte beamed at him.

―――

It was finally time for Mary to go visit Ellen. Isabel, Charlotte, and Sadie drove her to the ferry terminal to the mainland and waved goodbyes as she sailed out of sight.

CHAPTER 31

On Monday Isabel opened the bookstore for the first time on her own. She put a big picture of Sadie holding a welcome sign in her mouth on a sandwich board inside the front door. Next to it she put a table that had carafes of hot cocoa on it, along with coffee, tea, and hot water. Isabel also had a basket of muffins that she had warmed up in the microwave. She put that out along with some napkins.

Then she hung up some posters that she'd gotten from various publishers that highlighted the top 10 new titles that had just come out.

Finally, she stood back, examined her handiwork and was very pleased with how everything looked. She turned on the lights, got the gas stove going and put on some soft music. She pulled Sadie's bed next to the front counter where she could keep a closer eye on her.

Isabel was a little worried that no-one would stop in. To her delight people started lining up at the front door once she turned the lights on and put the open sign out.

She was pleased with the different age groups who wandered through the store. A number of them immediately took advantage of the large fluffy cushions she had found in the back storage room. They settled in and got cozy as they browsed through a selection of books.

Of course, Sadie drew a crowd with people of all ages coming over to say hi to her and to pet her. Isabel was relieved with how Sadie was behaving. Not bothering anybody, and willing to give a kiss on the cheek when asked. She pretty much stayed by her bed near the front desk.

By the end of the day Isabel had sold a number of books, much more than expected. But she was exhausted. She realized she was definitely going to have to bring at least one person on board to spell her during the day and help with inventory and packaging. She went online and found a cartoon image of a woman carrying a huge pile of about 30 books which towered over her head. Isabel inserted the word 'Help!' underneath the image, created a flyer and posted it on the front door.

Not long after that, she heard a knock on the window and looked up. Jason was standing there waving at her with the flyer in his hand. She gestured for him to come in.

He smiled at her. "The store looks fantastic." He indicated the flyer. "Are you looking for part time help? If you are, I have the perfect person for you."

"Who?" asked Isabel.

"My sister . You've met her. She's looking for part time work, starting immediately. She is totally reliable, loves books and loves kids. This is the perfect job for her."

"She sounds great," said Isabel. "When can she come in and talk to me?"

Jason grinned, "She is actually standing outside the store right now."

Isabel said "That's fantastic. if you could watch the front desk I can interview her."

Jason leaned closer to Isabel and said in a low voice, "She really needs the money. She's raising a child on her own. I try to help as much as I can but I don't have a lot of money either. If she could get some extra cash with this job, especially doing a job that she would enjoy, it'd be a great help."

Within a few minutes of meeting and talking to Jason's sister Caitlin, Isabel knew she had struck gold. Caitlin was exactly the type of employee that every employer dreams of and hopes to find someday. Isabel hired her on the spot.

A day later, Sam stopped by the bookstore to ask Isabel to lunch. Since it was a beautiful day, Sam suggested they take their sandwiches, find a park bench, and sit by the water.

Once they were settled, Sam said, "I wanted to talk to you about the job offer I got from the Boston farm team." Immediately Isabel felt her stomach twist and turn.

"They've offered me a position as a coach. I would make quite a lot of money and I'd travel with them around the country.

"Where would you live?"

"I'd be based in Boston."

Isabel sighed. "How often do you think you'd make it out to the island?"

"It depends on how the team is doing. I'd try to make it out here as often as possible but I don't know what my schedule will be like."

Isabel promptly lost her appetite. "It sounds like something that is important to you."

"I have to admit, I love the whole experience of a baseball game. The feel of it, being on the field on a hot summer day, the smell of the grass, hearing the crack of a ball on a bat, the cheers of the stadium crowd."

He turned and took her hands in his. "But I also care about you. A great deal. In fact, the only thing that makes me hesitate about accepting this offer is you." He looked intensely into her eyes, "I don't mean to put a guilt trip on you. I just want you to know how I feel."

Isabel asked hesitantly, "Do you really think we can still make this work?"

"I want to try." Sam ran his hand through his hair, "I don't want to let go of you."

She leaned against him, "I feel the same about you." She reached up and kissed his neck. He groaned with pleasure. "It'd be really difficult if you left the island. I would miss you so much.

"You could always come visit."

Isabel said, "I would definitely want to do that, but the reality is I have a lot of responsibilities in my life right now…my house, my friends, my dog, the girls' softball team, and now the bookstore." She felt herself tearing up. "If you were gone, how long would you be gone for?"

He looked at her and reached out and held her hand. "I'd be gone for quite a while. Especially in the beginning when the team and I are getting used to each other.

"Is this what you really want?"

"I can only go by how I felt when they talked to me about it the other day. I could really feel myself getting excited about the possibility of working with an organization I respect and where I think I could make a difference."

He murmured in her ear, "I was worried to talk to you about this because I was afraid that you would want to end the relationship."

She shifted around and looked at him directly, shaking her head, "You mean too much to me."

He kissed her gently and pulled her close in a tight embrace. She wrapped her arms around him and they kissed again, a deep passionate kiss this time.

Sam's phone vibrated loudly. "Damn it, I'm so sorry, but I need to take this." He scrambled to his feet and walked to the water's edge.

Isabel sat quietly thinking about what they had both said and realizing that she might end up doing a lot of waiting in the future if he took this job.

Sam came back to her side.

"They need me sooner than expected. "I've got to go." He walked her back to the bookstore. There he grabbed her by the shoulders and gave her a searing kiss. She wrapped her arms around him, and they kissed again.

He broke away. "I'll be in touch." He hugged her and Isabel stood there, watching as he walked away. She felt herself getting emotional and went inside the bookstore as tears trickled down her face. She waved to Caitlin who was helping a customer and went directly back to her office. Sadie was on the floor in her dog bed. Isabel sank down on the floor next to her and put her arms around her. She buried her face in her dog's warm soft fur and felt comforted.

There was a knock on her door and Charlotte asked if she could come in.

Isabel sat up and blew her nose. "Yes."

"What's up, what has happened?"

"They offered him a job as a coach for the Red Sox farm team. He would have to move to Boston and then travel around the country working with the team."

She paused and blew her nose noisily. Charlotte handed over a box of tissues.

"I am so sorry," said Charlotte. "Believe me, I know how hard it is to have a long distance relationship. But it's got to be easier with today's technology. I mean you can do Facetime and Zoom."

"Well, I'm willing to take it one step at a time and see what happens."

"Sounds like a plan." said Charlotte.

"Are you OK with me talking about a long distance relationship? I mean with Patrick and everything," asked Isabel.

"I'll probably always have that ache inside when I think of him and what could have been. I don't believe that loss ever goes away fully. But I don't want that to stop you from talking to me about what you're dealing with."

At that moment Isabel's phone rang She answered and when she heard who it was she mouthed the words ,"It's Sam," to Charlotte.

Charlotte put her hand up and pointed at the door. Isabel nodded and Charlotte left quietly.

"Hi. It's me. I just wanted to apologize for rushing out of there so fast."

"I appreciate you calling."

"I was wondering if you wanted to meet me in New York City next week. We have a big game scheduled there and I'm hoping we could spend the weekend together. I'd have a hotel room for you so no pressure there."

"That sounds great, Sam." She heard raised voices in the background. "Is everything all right?"

"Just a high energy discussion," he laughed. "Gotta go. Talk to you soon."

"Are you going to see Sam anytime soon?" asked Charlotte as they had dinner later that evening..

"He asked me down to New York City in a week. He's going to put me up in a hotel and we'll go to a game."

"Well, that sounds like fun."

"Can you watch Sadie?"

"Oh absolutely. We'll watch doggy movies together."

CHAPTER 32

A week later, Isabel boarded a small commuter airplane to take down to New York City. She wasn't a great flyer so she was nervous about the plane. It looked awfully small to her, kind of like a Volkswagen Bug compared to a 747. She kept her eyes closed for most of the trip and used deep breathing techniques whenever she felt especially anxious. There were a couple of pockets of turbulence but overall the flight was not too bad.

Sam was waiting for her at the airport and she was thrilled to see him. He looked gorgeous to her. He was dressed a little more formally than normal wearing a sports coat, shirt and tie and khaki pants. She was tempted to run to him and throw her arms around her but decided to be more restrained than that.

He was on the phone when she first saw him but then he turned around and saw her and immediately put the phone in a pocket. They walked quickly towards each other and embraced. He kissed her softly on the lips and she felt a tingle go through her. Sam nuzzled her neck and said, "It is so good to see you. You look wonderful."

"It's good to see you, too," she said,

He grinned at her.

"Let's get out of here," he said.

As they exited the airport terminal, Isabel spotted a luxurious car parked in the valet section. She nudged Sam. "Wow, look at that. What a gorgeous car."

As they approached the vehicle a man dressed in a formal chauffer's uniform stepped out of the vehicle and opened the passenger door with a sweeping gesture.

Isabel stopped, abruptly confused. Sam took her arm and said with a smile, "This is Charley. I borrowed him and the car for the day.

"It's a Bently," the driver said with pride, polishing an invisible speck of dust off the fender with his sleeve. "Where would you like to go?"

Sam said, "Do you want to go to the ballpark first or do you want to go to the hotel where you can freshen up."

Isabel said, "I think I'd like to freshen up first if you don't mind."

She just had an overnight bag with her and when she saw the car and how luxurious it was she was embarrassed that she had not brought a fancier set of clothes with her. She had packed clothes for going to a baseball game not an evening at the Met.

She turned to Sam and said, "I'm embarrassed to admit this but I don't have any swag."

He looked at her and raised an eyebrow. "Swag? You don't have any swag?"

"Yes, you know the stuff they give out at award shows and sports events. I don't have anything that says Boston Red Sox on it."

"That's OK. I've got a bag in your room that has a whole bunch of swag in it."

"You are saying you swagged me?"

"Yes, I swagged you. There is a bag of swag on your bed."

At that, they both got the giggles and were falling all over the backseat of the car like two little kids.

They checked into the hotel and Sam brought her up to her room which had a gorgeous view looking over the city. They stood and looked at the view for a while but then slowly turned and started kissing. Isabel couldn't remember ever being so excited kissing someone. He started kissing and nibbling on her neck. She closed her eyes and shivered.

His phone buzzed, he read the text and apologized. "I've got to go."

They kissed again and he reminded her to be ready at the front desk at 6 p.m.

He headed out the door but then as soon as the door closed there was a knock. Laughing she opened it and he stood there smiling.

"Don't forget the swag." She cracked up. He gave her a peck on the cheek and then he was gone.

Isabel reached into the bag of swag Sam had left on her bed. She was delighted to find a sweatshirt, T-shirt, sweatpants, baseball cap and warm-up jacket, all emblazoned with the Red Sox iconic logo.

She changed into her new gear and headed down to the reception desk. Her driver was waiting.

At the ballpark, she was dropped off at the VIP section which allowed access to the corporate suites. She was directed to the proper suite and when she opened the door she gasped. The field was brilliantly lit and highly visible from the rows of captain's chairs lining the front of the suite. A waiter stopped and asked if he could get her something to drink.

"A seltzer, please."

"There are plenty of snacks," he pointed out. "Help yourself."

"Thank you."

At that moment, a young girl in her early twenties came up to Isabel and said, "Hi I'm Lola, Sam's intern. He wanted me to tell you that during the game he'll be down in the dugout and not be able to be with you."

"Oh, okay," said Isabel, feeling let down that she wouldn't be able to share the experience with Sam.

Lola looked at her sympathetically. "There is a meeting after the game. You can either choose to stay here and wait till he gets done or have the car return you to the hotel. Which is what I would suggest and then he can meet you there."

"I choose door number two," said Isabel, smiling at Lola.

"I'm sorry, I don't understand. What is door number two?"

"Never mind," said Isabel.

She enjoyed watching the game, which unfortunately the Red Sox lost, and meeting and talking with fellow spectators in the suite. When the game ended she realized how tired she was. and decided to get the car back to the hotel. Once in her room, she ordered a pot of herbal tea and enjoyed watching a Hallmark movie.

She was starting to drift off when her phone rang. Sam was downstairs asking if he could come up.

"Of course," she said. The moment she disconnected she raced around the room cleaning things up, throwing clothes in closets and drawers and making sure she was wearing her Red Sox swag nightgown and sleep socks.

There was a knock on the door, she flung it open and there was Sam. He looked exhausted but she was so glad to see him she put her arms around him and gave him a big kiss. He was so tired he staggered.

She took his arm. "Come on and lie down for a bit," she said. He walked over to the bed and sank down on it.

"Why don't you lie down and close your eyes. Just rest. You don't have to do anything. Relax. I know you had a long night."

"That meeting after the game was a grind." He undid his tie and kicked off his shoes. "I'm just going to close my eyes for a bit."

"That's fine," said Isabel. "I've got a book to read. It's the advantage of managing a bookstore."

She laughed and looked over at Sam. He was already fast asleep so she got up and put a comforter over him to keep him warm. She went back to her reading chair and as she picked up her book she glanced out the window and saw a beautiful moon lighting up the cityscape. She sat watching it for a while and then went back to her book.

Next morning Isabel woke up next to Sam. She had gotten into bed after reading for a while. She found it very comforting to sleep next to him. She hadn't slept with someone for many years... other than Sadie of course. She laughed to herself.

Sam yawned and stretched. He rolled over and put his arms around her. "Good morning," he said giving her a warm smile followed up by a soft kiss. She kissed him back. He ran his hands slowly down her arms and snuggled his face against her neck.

Sam and Isabel put their arms around each other and kissed long and deep. He moved so he was on top of her. It felt wonderful and exciting to feel him pushing against her.

They were both getting more aroused by the moment.

Suddenly the phone rang and there was a knock at the door.

"I'll get the phone," said Sam.

"I'll get the door," said Isabel. She pulled on her bathrobe and opened the door to an enormous food service tray pushed by a smiling waiter.

"Good morning," he said.

"Good morning," Isabel said, "We didn't order any of this."

"This is courtesy of the Red Sox. There is a variety of food here, eggs, bacon, pastries, fresh fruit, tea, coffee, and juice. If you need anything else, please let me know and I'll bring it right up. There is also a New York Times on the tray. Have a good morning." He closed the door behind him.

Isabel started lifting tray covers. "My God, there's enough food here to feed an army or should I say a baseball team."

She pushed the breakfast tray over to the window. She turned to Sam who was just disconnecting his phone call and had an unhappy expression on his face.

"What's up?"

"I'm sorry I just found out I have a meeting this afternoon. We'll only have a few hours together before I have to get ready to leave. But for now my time is yours. What would you like to do?"

"It's a beautiful day, how about a walk in Central Park?"

"That sounds great," he said. "But first a little music." He pulled out his iPhone and plugged in his playlist.

"Shall we dance?" he asked putting his arms around her and sweeping her into a graceful twirl.

"Oh, you're good," she said laughing.

He drew her close and began gently kissing her face, her neck, her lips.

She quivered with excitement and kissed him back. They danced for a while longer and then sank onto the bed and spent the next few hours cuddling and making love.

CHAPTER 33

"So, what happened next?" asked Charlotte.

"Well, we never made it to Central Park," Isabel laughed. "That's all right I've seen Central Park before. But it was wonderful, Charlotte. I really think I'm falling in love with him. Now I'm at the airport waiting for the fog to clear so I can catch a plane for home."

"When are you going to see him again?"

"That's up in the air right now but hopefully soon. He said he's going to try to make it out to the island within the next couple of weeks. We talked about taking a boat ride and having dinner out on the water on the sailboat."

"Sounds lovely."

"Yes it does. I'm looking forward to it. So, what's happening with you and Daniel?"

"He's invited me over to dinner next week," said Charlotte.

'Well, that's encouraging. I'll keep my fingers crossed for you so that it goes well. Oh, they just called my flight. Gotta go. I'll see you later tonight."

Two weeks later, Isabel and Charlotte were getting ready to head to a Mighty Mice baseball game. The team had not won many games since the team resumed playing after Tom's death but they'd been playing with a lot of heart and Isabel was proud of them. Charlotte had taken over coaching responsibilities once Sam had taken the job with the farm team.

Suddenly there was a knock on the kitchen door. Sadie started barking her head off.

"What is going on, Sadie?" Coming into the kitchen, Isabel shushed the excited dog. She glanced out the window and flung the door open.

"Sam!" She said excitedly and wrapping her arms around him gave him a big kiss. "How are you? Come in, come in."

He handed her a paper bag. "NYC bagels," he said smiling.

"Ooh goody." She opened the bag and took a deep breath. "H&H?"

"Where else?"

"Did I hear someone mention bagels?" Charlotte asked as she entered the kitchen.

"Yes, we have our own personal supply chain now." Isabel laughed.

"Hi Sam, it's good to see you," Charlotte gave him a hug. "Are you coming to the game?"

"I'll be able to come for part of the game."

Isabel clapped her hands together, "The girls will be so happy to see you."

"I've been watching on social media how they've been doing and I'm impressed. They need to hone their skill set but their spirit and enthusiasm is excellent."

Isabel found herself just gazing at Sam, trying to imprint his face in her memory. She glanced at Charlotte and saw her indicate her watch. She nodded. It was time to go.

"The opposing team is coming to us," she said to Sam. "We have to get going so that everything is set up for them."

"I'll ride with you," said Sam.

Just as Isabel expected, the team went crazy celebrating when they saw Sam. They were all talking at once, hugging him and shouting questions at him. Isabel and Charlotte finally calmed everyone down and got them doing stretches and warm-ups.

Sam was smiling and laughing as he greeted the players and their parents.

"It's great to see everybody," he said to Isabel. "I didn't realize how much I missed this atmosphere, these people. To see everybody. I can't tell you how good this feels."

"You could have this feeling all the time," said Isabel seriously.

"You mean if I were to give up the baseball farm job and move back here?"

She looked at him and said quietly, "I miss you."

"I miss you too. I find myself thinking about you all the time. Wondering how you are. What you're doing. If you are thinking about me."

Isabel smiled briefly, "I have to confess I scour all the footage from the games hoping to see you. Even just a brief glimpse."

Sam laughed, "I cannot tell you how good that makes me feel! I was afraid you'd forget about me."

Shocked, she said "Never."

Then she looked ashamed, "I'm sorry I put that out there. I don't want to lay a guilt trip on you. If you're getting what you want out of the experience that's great. I want you to be happy."

He leaned over and kissed her, "Thank you for saying that."

The umpire called out, "All right, let's get this game underway."

Whether it was because of Sam's presence, or the beautiful weather or the team's energy, or all three, the Mighty Mice won the game handily. Annika and Linnea both hit home runs while Sophie pitched five perfect innings. Sam sat through the whole game, next to Isabel, cheering and clapping. Isabel felt full to the brim with happiness. As a reward, the team was treated to pizzas and milkshakes at a local diner. Sam was able to stay for a slice of pizza but then had to leave. Isabel walked out with him and they hugged each other goodbye.

As he walked away, Charlotte came out of the diner and put her arm around her friend. Isabel looked at her with tears in her eyes.

"It is so hard when he leaves."

Charlotte said, "I know. I know. But you should see how he looks at you and how you look at him. There's really something there. Somehow you are going to make this work."

CHAPTER 34

A week later, Isabel was sitting at the kitchen table with Charlotte and Sadie. She was getting ready to go pick up Mary at the ferry landing on her return to the island.

Sipping her tea, Charlotte asked, "Isabel, did you enjoy working at the bookstore? Did you get anything out of it?"

"Yes, I really got a lot of it. I loved working with the kids and helping them find just the right book to read. I wanted them to experience how a book can transport them to different worlds without having to charge something or download an app."

"The kids really seem to enjoy reading to Sadie."

"They loved it. She loved it. It was a win win situation all the way around. I'm really hoping I can continue with that program even when Mary comes back."

Isabel glanced at the clock. "Oops, speaking of Mary, I got to go. Do you want to come with me to pick her up?"

"Yes."

Isabel helped Charlotte get into the front seat of her SUV and secured Sadie in the backseat.

As they drove towards the ferry landing, Charlotte asked, "Is Sam going to make it to the game next week?"

"I'm not sure."

"The kids were really hoping he would come to see them play. I think they look at him as a good luck charm."

As they pulled into the ferry parking lot Isabel spotted Bobbie and her daughter Wendy waiting in line for the ferry.

Charlotte said, "I wonder what they are doing here."

Wendy turned and spotted Isabel and Charlotte and came running over to them. Bobbie stayed where she was and scowled at them.

"Pleasant as always," muttered Charlotte.

"Shush," said Isabel, stifling a laugh.

Wendy hugged Isabel. "I am so glad I got a chance to see you and to say goodbye. My Mom and I decided it would be best if I go off-island to school. My Mom will rent an apartment by the school and I'll live there and study and play ball. I am so excited."

Isabel smiled at her. "Wendy, you'll do well whatever sport you decide to play."

Just then the ferry came into view.

"Wendy," called Bobbie.

Wendy hugged Charlotte and Sadie and raced over to her mother.

"God help the softball coaches down there," they both laughed at that.

"OK, time to change the subject," said Isabel. "How is the restoring of the hardware store going?"

"It's going really well. Jason and Daniel have been tremendously helpful. I think we're going to be in decent shape for the opening in a couple of weeks."

"That's excellent news, if there's anything I can do to help…"

"Actually, there is something you can do. I'd like to have a table with a bunch of books on home repairs by the front door so people can browse through them as they enter. I am also going to offer some art classes. Daniel is going to teach them. So, any books on metal artwork would be appreciated."

"What a great idea," said Isabel. "I want to sign up for one of those art classes myself."

"There's been a lot of interest," said Charlotte, nodding. "You know it's funny I thought it'd be more men interested in it. But women seem to be just as interested in creating and using heavy duty tools to create art."

"Have you decided on a name for your store?"

"Yes." Charotte smiled at her. "Charlotte's Hardware Store."

"Perfect!"

"Ohh there's Mary," said Isabel. They rushed towards each other hugging and laughing and talking all at once. It had only been a month but it felt like much longer for the three close friends.

Two weeks later the whole island celebrated the opening of the Charlotte's Hardware Store. There was food, games, balloons, and toys on site. Plus, lots of giveaways.

"It looks like everyone on the island is here," Charlotte handed a bright red balloon to a little girl. Mary handed a coloring book to another youngster.

Jason said, "I haven't seen Isabel. Is she even on the island?"

"I'm surprised she didn't let me know what her plans were for today." Charlotte frowned slightly, a worry line creasing her forehead.

Daniel put his arm around her, "I'm sure she will show up at some point."

Mary nudged Jason and nodded to Charlotte and Daniel who were now holding hands.

"Who are you talking about?"

Charlotte spun around, "There you are!"

Isabel stood there smiling.

"Is Sam coming?"

"I honestly don't know. He said he would try. I hope so."

Charlotte felt something pressing against her leg. She reached down to see what it was and felt a wet nose nuzzling her.

"What the…" She looked down and saw a yellow lab puppy sitting there looking up at her wagging its tail frantically.

"Oh, you are gorgeous, where did you come from? Whose dog are you? Are you lost?" She leaned down and scooped the puppy up into her arms.

"There's a collar," Isabel pointed out. Charlotte looked at the bright blue collar and saw it had her name on it along with her phone number.

"Oh my God, did you get me a dog?"

Isabel smiled, "Well, you sold your cottage and bought a house in town and now you've got your own brick and mortar business so I felt like you needed your own dog! Congratulations on your grand opening!"

While still holding the puppy, Charlotte hugged Isabel. "Now Sadie has a playmate."

Dr. Debbie walked over to say 'hello' to the puppy. "Bring him by for a well puppy visit and we'll make sure he's up to date on all his shots. He's a cutie," she said kissing him on the nose.

Charlotte asked, "Where did he come from?"

Isabel said, "He was rescued from a puppy mill."

"I see there is a new addition to the family…" a familiar voice broke into the conversation.

"Sam!" Isabel grabbed his arm and pulled him close. "I didn't know you were going to make it today."

"I couldn't miss this party," he said holding her close.

Still carrying her puppy, Charlotte came over for a hug, "Hi Sam. It's good to see you."

He grinned and said, "And who is this little one?" He took the puppy and cradled him in his arms.

Watching him, Isabel felt a rush of love. Sam was asking Charlotte what she was going to call the puppy when he glanced over and caught the intensity of Isabel's look.

He handed the puppy back to Charlotte and took a step towards her just as a man in a pilot's uniform walked up to him.

"Are you going to be able to stay for the game," Isabel asked.

"No," said Sam. "I'm so sorry about that game this afternoon. I've got to get to Toronto for a game this evening. But you are doing great. I've been watching you online. Your enthusiasm is off the charts. Sophie's a phenomenal pitcher, Annika is wonderful at first base and Linnea hits the ball like nobody's business."

"Sorry to interrupt you, Sam.," said the pilot ."We need to go soon if we're going to catch that flight to Toronto."

Sam kissed Isabel, "I am sorry I can't stay. I was hoping to get some time with you. At least I got a chance to see you and give you a hug and a kiss. Hopefully, I'll be able to come home soon and spend some time on the island."

He started to walk away with the pilot but then turned back. "It just occurred to me, do you want to come with us? We'd have you back here tomorrow. We could spend time together. Toronto is a beautiful city."

"Sorry I can't. I have to help Charlotte at the hardware store tomorrow. I am going to be working with her part time. Tomorrow's going to be our first big day of business."

Sam said, "I wish I had thought of this sooner. I could have set this up so we could spend time together. I miss you."

"I miss you too. Maybe next time."

Sam and Isabel held each other for a long time and then said their goodbyes.

Isabel watched him walk away and then pulled her attention back from him and looked at Charlotte.

"Do you have a name for that little guy yet?"

"Yes, I'm going to name him Patrick."

"Perfect." Isabel turned and looked after Sam as he walked away. He turned and looked back at her. They gazed at each other for a long moment. Then he was pulled away by the pilot.

The next day Charlotte breezed into the hardware store carrying Patrick. "I can't believe I found a decent house in town that's close to the hardware store and has a fenced in yard." She paused. "And that I was able to sell my own house so easily. That cottage is way too far out for me now. I really like being around people. Who knew?"

Isabel laughed delightedly and hugged Charlotte. "Who knew?" she echoed.

Patrick spotted Sadie and began climbing all over her.

"Manners, little man," Charlotte said. The puppy gazed up at her adoringly and plopped down on his well- rounded rump.

"Good boy!" Charlotte handed him a small treat. Sadie nudged her hand and Charlotte gave her a small treat too.

"I am so delighted I'm going to be working here with you," said Isabel, "this is going to be so much fun."

Charlotte nodded and then she said, "Well first things first. Let's have a cup of tea and then get started inventorying stuff."

"Aye, aye, Captain." said Isabel. She paused for a moment and then asked, "Are you sure you want to move out? I'm going to miss you terribly, not having you at the house. I enjoy your company so much."

"I know. I feel the same way," said Charlotte, "but it's time for me to live independently again now that I can walk better. Plus, I've got so much going on at the hardware store it's better to live closer."

"And there's Daniel of course," Isabel said.

"I really am enjoying spending time with him. We seem to have the same perspective on a lot of things."

"That's good," said Isabel, "I'm so glad for you." She glanced down at Sadie lying next to Patrick.

Charlotte nibbled on a scone, "So how goes it with Sam?"

"We talk and Facetime all the time but his schedule is crazy. When he is free, I'm not. When I am free, he's not. I really miss him."

"Well, it's supposed to be a full moon tomorrow night. Perfect for a boat ride. I have a good offer for my charter boat that I am probably going to take. This could be your last chance to go for a ride."

"You know that sounds really nice. I think I'd like to do that."

"Meet me at Mouse Island Marina at about 5:00 p.m."

"Should we take the dogs?"

"I don't have a PFD for Patrick yet. Do you have one for Sadie?"

"No, so okay they won't go with us this time.

The next night, Isabel met up with Charlotte at the marina. She had brought a picnic basket filled with wine, cheese, French bread, and grapes.

"Just some nibbles," she said as she handed it to Charlotte.

"Are you thinking Gilligan's Island?" And with that Charlotte handed Isabel a picnic basket in exchange. Isabel laughed as she opened it and saw many of the same things in Charlotte's basket.

The marina workers untied Charlotte's boat and she carefully backed the boat around and started to head out into open water.

"We're not going out into the ocean?" asked Isabel nervously.

"Nope we're just going to go around the island keeping to calm waters."

Isabel poured two glasses of wine, handing one to Charlotte. "How is the hardware store doing?"

"We have more business than we know what to do with. People are constantly popping in to pick something up. Best of all I love the fact that so many longtime customers are sharing stories about Tom and Harry. I think I'm going to paint a portrait of Tom and Harry and hang it in the store. It makes me feel like I'm continuing their legacy."

"That's a wonderful idea," said Isabel. "How is Patrick?"

"That is the amazing thing, he is totally at home in the store. He loves to greet people when they come in the door. I feel like he's channeling Harry."

They both were silent for a while enjoying the beauty of the setting sun on the water.

"How is your relationship with Daniel going?"

"I really enjoy his company, "said Charlotte. "Also, he's teaching me how to do metal work and I'm loving it!"

"That's a perfect fit for you given your mechanical aptitude."

"I think I'm learning how to be more creative."

They came around the end of the island and Isabel said, "I can't wait to see my house from the water with its new paint job and landscaping."

She stood by the bow and gazed at the shore. "There's the house. It looks so much better than when I first saw it."

"It is hard to believe it has been almost five months since I moved here." She looked at Charlotte and smiled. "You must have thought I was nuts that first ride out here. Moving to a place I had never been before to a house I had never seen before."

Charlotte said, "I have to say I didn't think you would be staying very long. Yet you've made a place for yourself. People like and respect you."

"I've learned so much about myself and made some very dear friends since I moved here."

Charlotte nodded and spun the wheel, bringing them into the marina. She slowed down to a crawl and carefully maneuvered the boat through crowded fishing boats, yachts, and day sailors until she reached her mooring.

She called out, "Can somebody give me a hand?"

There was no response so Charlotte called out again. Still no reaction.

"Damn, where are they?"

Meanwhile, Isabel was looking towards where Sam had at one time moored his sailboat.

She gave a deep sigh and started to turn to Charlotte when a familiar voice said, "Welcome to Mouse Island."

Startled she looked up and there on the dock next to the boat was Sam. Just like when she first met him he was wearing his Mouse Island Marina cap tugged down low over his salt and pepper hair. His blue eyes gleamed with affection, his dimples flashing, as with a warm smile he leaned down and stretched his hand out to her. She gave him a dazzling smile in return and put her hand in his. He pulled her up onto the dock into his arms, holding her tight and passionately kissing her.

"Welcome home, Isabel," he murmured softly. She reached up and stroked his face.

"Home," she said, "what a wonderful word." She wrapped her arms around him and luxuriated in his warmth.

A little later, they said goodbye to Charlotte who hugged Isabel fiercely and whispered, "have fun" in her ear. They settled in Sam's sailboat and headed for a quiet cove that was one of his favorite spots. He dropped the anchor and the boat swung peacefully at the end of the chain. Overhead a multitude of stars sparkled like diamonds on black velvet.

Sam noticed Isabel shiver and he pulled out a soft fleece blanket and draped it around her shoulders. She was about to thank him when she heard what sounded like a high-pitched wail. At first she couldn't determine where it was coming from. It was an unusual sound.

"What is that," she asked Sam anxiously. Then she realized it was coming from underneath the boat.

"It's a mamma whale singing to its baby. They've just migrated up from Florida."

"Oh, that is amazing," Isabel murmured. "How magical to hear that."

"She's probably telling him all the best spots for take-out." Sam grinned at her. She laughed.

They sat there for a while, hand in hand, listening to the song of the mother whale.

"That's a hopeful message," said Isabel. "For our future and what it holds."

Sam cleared his throat. He turned and faced her. "I have been through a lot of changes recently," he explained. "It took me a while but I finally realized that I didn't want to be on the road constantly going from one city to the next every day and not having a home or someone to come home to. Remember I told you about the offer from the schoolboard to teach that sailing class that combines math, discipline, and science. Well, I accepted their offer last night to teach it. I am moving back to Mouse Island."

"That's fabulous, Sam! I'm so happy."

"Isabel, I want to come home to you. I want to spend my life with you. I love you."

Isabel looked at him with tears rolling down her cheeks. "I love you too, Sam. Whatever adventures lie in front of us, I can't wait to share them with you."

He gently kissed Isabel as a shooting star suddenly streaked across the night sky. They both gazed upward watching it. "Did you make a wish?" he smiling at her.

Isabel placed her hand gently on his cheek. "I have everything I could ever wish for right here in front of me."

THE END

MORE INFORMATION

PARKINSON'S DISEASE

Parkinson's Foundation

The Parkinson's Foundation makes life better for people with Parkinson's disease by improving care and advancing research towards a cure. Everything they do they build on the energy, experience and passion of their global Parkinson's community.

Website: parkinson.org
Email: contact@parkinson.org
Phone: helpline 1-800-4PD info (473-4636)

Michael J. Fox Foundation

The Michael J. Fox foundation exists for one reason to accelerate the next generation of Parkinson's disease treatments. In practice that means identifying and funding projects most vital to patients: spearheading solutions around seemingly intractable challenges, coordinating and streamlining the efforts of multiple teams. It means leveraging the core values of optimism, resourcefulness, collaboration, accountability and persistence and problem solving.

Website: michaeljfoxfoundation.org
Email: info@michaeljfox.org
Phone: 1-212-509-0995

SERVICE DOGS

Adele and Everything After

This powerful documentary captures the remarkable relationship between a woman with an untreatable heart condition and the service dog that transforms her life.

Website: adeleandeverythingafter.com

Canine Companions for Independence

Canine Companions for Independence is leading the service dog industry so their clients and their dogs have greater independence. They provide service dogs to adults, children and veterans with disabilities. Since their founding in 1975, their dogs and all follow up services are provided at no cost to their clients.

Website: canine.org

PET THERAPY

PAWS for People Pet Therapy

PAWS (PET Therapy for People) PAWS is a nonprofit organization committed to providing therapeutic visits to any person in the community who would benefit from interaction with a well-trained loving pet. What makes PAWS stand above other pet therapy services is the emphasis they place on providing individualized therapeutic experiences for every person they visit. Their strict standards and training and their testing ensure every therapy team is capable of meeting the various needs of their diverse clientele. PAWS is most active throughout Delaware and also serves areas in southern Pennsylvania, and southern New Jersey.

Website: pawsforpeople.org
Email: info@pawsforpeople.org
Phone: 302-351-5622

IF YOU ENJOYED READING THIS STORY, PLEASE LEAVE A REVIEW ON AMAZON. THANK YOU.

andreejannette-writer.com